# The Byrds of Shywater

"... it is given to love to reveal the frailties of the heart."

# The Byrds of Shywater

Paul Joseph Lederer

**FIVE STAR**
*A part of Gale, Cengage Learning*

GALE
CENGAGE Learning

Farmington Hills, Mich • San Francisco • New York • Waterville, Maine
Meriden, Conn • Mason, Ohio • Chicago

**LIBRARY OF CONGRESS CATALOGING-IN-PUBLICATION DATA**

Names: Lederer, Paul Joseph, author.
Title: The Byrds of Shywater / Paul Joseph Lederer.
Description: First edition. | Waterville, Maine : Five Star Publishing, a part of Cengage Learning, Inc. [2016]
Identifiers: LCCN 2015047688 (print) | LCCN 2016000367 (ebook) | ISBN 9781432832162 (hardcover) | ISBN 1432832166 (hardcover) | ISBN 9781432832087 (ebook) | ISBN 1432832085 (ebook)
Subjects: LCSH: Trappers—Fiction. | Families—Wyoming—Fiction. | Frontier and pioneer life—Wyoming—Fiction. | BISAC: FICTION / Historical. | FICTION / Westerns. | GSAFD: Western stories.
Classification: LCC PS3559.R6 B97 2016 (print) | LCC PS3559.R6 (ebook) | DDC 813/.54—dc23
LC record available at http://lccn.loc.gov/2015047688

First Edition. First Printing: June 2016
Find us on Facebook– https://www.facebook.com/FiveStarCengage
Visit our website– http://www.gale.cengage.com/fivestar/
Contact Five Star™ Publishing at FiveStar@cengage.com

Printed in the United States of America
1 2 3 4 5 6 7 20 19 18 17 16

# The Byrds of Shywater

★ ★ ★ ★ ★

# Part One

★ ★ ★ ★ ★

# Chapter One

## Rendezvous

The time of the savages had just begun. Jonathan Byrd felt as if he had fallen into some chaotic, bewildering wonderland. That is, he was only now entering his twentieth year of life and this was his first Rendezvous. They had arrived at the French camp near Granger, Wyoming, with pine-thick mountains rising around them—peaceful, beckoning; but here in the valley where thousands had gathered to trade, the rush of people, the sound and throb of it was as disconcerting as any metropolis at holiday.

Jonathan had met no more than two dozen people in his entire life before joining his partner and friend, Calvin Gunnert, at this year's Rendezvous. "It's time for you to travel there with me," the old mountain man had told Jonathan. "I won't always be around to do the trading for us, you know." That was the way they had previously handled matters. Both had worked equally hard the year around collecting pelts: beaver, sable, wolf, marten, and fox, setting their snares in the harsh weather in the deep mountains and icy streams in forest and meadow. When spring arrived, however, Jonathan had always been willing to let Calvin take the load of furs out by himself. Calvin Gunnert liked to talk to people, to deal with the traders, to drink. Jonathan Byrd longed for none of that. He provided himself with all the company he required. Calvin always returned with unlikely, bloody, and ridiculous stories, enough to last them through another summer and winter, and so Jonathan never felt deprived by avoiding the gatherings.

Now the din of the trading camp seemed savage and offensive to Jonathan, used to the silent solitude of the high mountains. From the camps of the Indians across the river came the constant discordant sounds of drums, shrieking bone whistles, bells, and chanting, unnerving and foreign to the ear. There were hundreds, perhaps thousands, of Indian lodges here, in separate encampments. The Blackfoot people lived by themselves, similarly the Crow, Nez Perce, and Flatheads. The few Cheyenne who had made their way to the trading festival had their retreat half a mile away among the trees.

On top of the racket they made was the uproar contributed by a hundred or so French-Canadian men; that many American mountain men and adventurers, including the agents of the fur company; whisky and arms dealers; and even a few exploring travelers, some from as far away as Europe.

These all kept mainly to themselves as well, until the whisky was broken out. After that, the camp was alive with shouting, attempts at music and dancing, fights, and much sporting of both the athletic sort and the type practiced by the men who knelt on their blankets throwing dice—some losing the proceeds from an entire year's work on a single roll.

Jonathan was not equipped by nature to be a part of this barbaric tapestry.

Whooping loudly, a dozen Indian boys blowing on bone whistles would rush among the white men, leaping and taunting in a game that might have been preparation for war. Here and there an older tribesman wearing many feathers in his hair would stand observing impassively, shooing the children away should they prove too troublesome to the fur traders.

"Well, what do you think of it?" Calvin Gunnert asked his young partner.

"I think of it as a crime against the wilderness," Jonathan

muttered. Gunnert laughed.

"I suppose it is in a way. Myself, I don't mind seeing all these folks around, but I believe I like 'em better when they're kind of spread out across the mountains as we're more used to. But then," Gunnert said, removing his fur hat to wipe the perspiration from his broad brow, "there wouldn't be any sense in us being up here in the first place if it weren't for Rendezvous. We need to sell our furs, not just take them.

"Besides, it was a long, bitter Rocky Mountain winter and all of us could use a little distraction, a little fun before we return to our day-to-day labors."

A fistfight between two burly Frenchmen had broken out not fifty feet from them. Both of the fighters staggered into a parked two-wheel cart loaded with furs.

"There's two already having fun," Jonathan observed.

"That? Oh, let it go," Gunnert said, waving a dismissive hand. "You'll see a dozen such before the day's over. It's only after the trade whisky's broken out that it gets dangerous. Men kind of lose control of their mouths. Knives and guns begin to appear in abundance."

A shirtless Indian boy about ten years old darted toward them with a whistle in his lips, veering away at the last possible moment before he would have crashed into Jonathan's legs.

"What are we going to do now?" Jonathan asked. He had to shout above the tumult to be heard.

"Set up our camp first thing; then I'll go off and find a representative of the American Fur Company and find out when they're going to open for business."

"I thought you always dealt with the Rocky Mountain Fur Company," Jonathan said as they started their cart forward.

"I always did before. They got shut out of the Rendezvous this year. Some sort of business politics." Calvin shrugged and pointed toward a fairly sheltered, available camp site among the pines, and turned the horses that way. "Someone got this upstart, Astor, riled. That's all I know of it, and I can't see that we need to know any more as long as they treat us right.

"Jonathan, you keep a close eye on our goods while I'm gone, will you? You might also want to check over that list of supplies we've been needing."

"I'll watch, all right!" Jonathan said. There was no way they were going to lose a year's work to anyone.

Leaving Jonathan Byrd to his work setting up a rough camp, Calvin Gunnert sauntered off, lifting a hand here and there to men he knew or had met before.

Jonathan set about unhitching Calvin's stocky bay from the cart, picketing his own gray horse beside it on a patch of grass among the pines, in sight of the camp he was roughly making. He fashioned a fire ring out of found stones and fixed it for a night-fire with dry sticks laid over a bed of brown pine needles.

Then, a little tired, he settled in to sit beside the fur cart, wary of possible thieves. The nearest that menace came to taking form was a wandering white dog Jonathan found bouncing up and down on the far side of the cart, trying to snag a fur from their stores. At a warning shout from Jonathan, the dog skulked away, tail tucked between its legs.

"Thought you'd got one of those fur thieves," someone said, and Jonathan Byrd lifted his eyes to see a slightly built, buckskin-clad man with long, shaggy blond hair watching him.

"Just a dog," Jonathan answered, sniffing at the unusual odor wafting through the air.

"My name's Reggie Foote," the stranger said, approaching. "Most people just call me 'Stinky.' I was looking for Calvin Gunnert—I thought I saw him over here a while ago."

"He's taking a little tour of the camp," Jonathan said. "He'll not be gone long."

"I could tell that," the man said, coming nearer. "You've still got a full load of furs, so he hasn't been paid. It's when they get paid and buy their whisky that men kind of lose track of time."

"Is that what Calvin does?"

"Him and just about every other man here," Stinky said.

"Well," Jonathan said, "it's not my business what Calvin does. He always comes back with my share of the proceeds."

"He's your partner, is he?" Stinky asked, leaning against the cart, arms folded.

"For some time," Jonathan said. He was now more than aware of the odor drifting from Reggie Foote's body. It was not the to-be-expected salt sweat smell of a man long at work and with little in the way of facilities for cleaning up. Foote—Stinky—smelled of feet that had never seen the outside of their boots, of rotting teeth, armpits clotted with the crust of the years, of dying flesh and buffalo wallows. Jonathan edged away; his eyes were beginning to water with the scent of the unwashed man.

"I got some coffee boiling at my camp," Stinky offered, "if you could use a cup."

"I told Calvin I'd wait here until he got back," Jonathan said, thankful he had an easy excuse for refusing the offer.

"All right," Stinky said amiably. "Look me up if you feel like having someone to talk to."

"I'll do that," Jonathan promised, although he would be happy enough if he never again shared the man's company. Didn't Stinky know that? Apparently he plain did not care.

After Stinky had been gone an hour or so, the heavy plodding of Calvin Gunnert's approach brought Jonathan out of his sunset reveries. Carrying his musket, eyes bright, but not intoxicated, the big man squatted down next to the cold fire ring and told Jonathan, "I talked to the fur company representative. They're going to send a buyer over right now. I thought it best to get our trading done as soon as possible. The prices might drop after they near their quota. Besides, there is a rumor that there's a fur thief lurking."

"Sounds smart to me," Jonathan agreed. "Then we wouldn't have to be guarding the cart." He said nothing to Calvin concerning his suspicion that the fur thief was only a wandering white dog with a liking for fresh hides. "I met Stinky, by the way."

"That kid!" Calvin laughed. "He's still around, is he? I thought he'd have been shot or at least exiled by now."

"Then I'm not the only one who finds his smell a little offensive?"

"We are legion!" Calvin laughed. "I judge him to be a fairly good kid, but not a man in the mountains can stand to be around him for more than a split minute."

"Must be a lonely life," Jonathan observed. "Hasn't anyone ever told him?"

"Hasn't everyone?" Calvin said. "The trouble is that he can't smell himself. They say he had his nose fractured when he was only a boy and never regained that particular sense. He lived with the Crow Indians for almost two years, you know—after his father and mother caught the cholera. They tell me that as the Indian judged Stinky to be of a man's age, they threw him out of the tribe because of that very thing. That could be just a tale. I don't know . . . but here comes our fur buyer."

The man the fur company had sent was a smallish, wildly mustached man named Stuyvesant. He moved to the cart without having been invited and quickly sorted and stacked their furs, sometimes "tsking" under his breath as he found a damaged or imperfect pelt, which he placed to one side. Behind him had come two silent, solemn faced half-breeds who moved behind him, ordering the furs by type, which were then placed onto a smaller, hand-drawn cart.

Calvin and Stuyvesant went to one side of the clearing while Jonathan watched the half-breeds at their work. When Calvin returned with the fur company man, both were smiling, Stuyvesant as if it were an unaccustomed, painful part of his job to look cheerful. The two men shook hands, and Stuyvesant motioned his men away in the direction of the fur traders' store where the furs would be sorted one final time, baled, and carried aboard one of the two riverboats waiting at the shore, heavily guarded.

"Better than last year," Calvin Gunnert told Jonathan in a low voice, weighing his purse in his hand. "What about helping me spend some of it?"

"Not now," Jonathan said, "although I wouldn't mind seeing what they've brought to trade in their stores."

The operation of the fur company seemed weighted in favor of the traders to him. They bought the furs men had worked many arduous months collecting, paid them, and then took most of the money back from their sale of goods, selling the furs at much higher prices downriver in St. Louis or St. Jo. However, Jonathan realized he did not have any idea how much capital it took for these people to organize, finance, and arrange a Rendezvous, and he supposed it worked out as fairly as possible for all concerned.

Besides, what was the use of trapping without a market for their goods? Let this man, Astor, whoever he was, get as rich as Croesus. So long as he and Calvin, men like them, were treated fairly, what did it matter?

Stinky had arrived again, looking a little disheartened—an outcast who did not know why he was so marked—and, growing bored, Calvin and Jonathan walked along with him to Stinky's camp. Stinky's partner was a half-breed Crow called Dave—his real name, Stinky explained, troubled the white man's tongue.

"But he's a good man. He's *Awaxaawaxammilaxpaake,* like the people I was raised with."

"What the hell does that mean?" Calvin asked touchily. *"Awaxa . . ."* Calvin nearly growled his question. Perhaps nearness to Stinky was drawing his temper tight.

"It just means he's of the Mountain Crow people," Stinky explained. "I understand it's difficult for *Baashciile* to pronounce. That's why I just call him Dave in front of others. Their language sounds difficult to the unfamiliar ear, but so would manymenmaymockourmountainmanners give them fits. It's all what your ears are attuned to."

"What's that second word you dropped?" Jonathan wondered.

"What? *Baashciile?* That's just the word they always used for Frenchmen—it means yellow eyes—most still use it for anyone white."

Calvin was tired of his lessons. "What we come by for was to ask if you'd watch our horses while we take an evening stroll," he said, turning briefly away from Stinky's not-so-delicate scent.

"Sure," Stinky agreed. "I'll tell you what. I'll have Dave take care of them so I can walk around with you." Probably Stinky was just jumping at the chance to attach himself to other men, but they could hardly refuse him after they had asked him for the favor.

The two horses were left in the charge of the silent Dave while the other three men made their way slowly across the massed camp in the hour before sundown. Before they had gone far, they came upon two men in a wrestling match. One of them was a young Indian brave stripped to the waist. His opponent was a burly French-Canadian mountain man who had at least a hundred pounds on his adversary.

"Must be a challenge match," Stinky, who knew the Indian ways, commented. A group of blanketed Indians—Flatheads, Jonathan guessed they were—stood watching their young champion with stoic faces. As Jonathan, Calvin, and Stinky came up on the scene, they saw the young Indian leap at the big man's legs, trying to scissor them with his feet.

"That's a good move if you've got a knife in your hands to finish your enemy," Calvin commented, "but it's kind of futile here. If he takes big Louis to the ground, he'll really find himself in trouble. The Frenchman has the size to break him in half."

Jonathan found the wrestling match uninteresting and started walking away, followed by Calvin and Stinky. "There's a man with not much chance of success," Stinky said, nodding his head toward a gaunt white man dressed all in black who was holding forth to a crowd consisting of three young naked Indian boys and one Frenchman with a jug in his hands and a dazed look in his eyes.

"What's he trying to do?" Jonathan asked in puzzlement.

"Salvage the heathen souls for the Lord," Stinky said. "I've seen him around before. His name's Caleb Blaylock—*Reverend* Blaylock. He's got a little tent city down south a ways. He comes up here every year to tell the Indians to clothe themselves, to tell the trappers to put aside their liquor. You can tell how much luck he has had with that style of preaching."

"Why does he continue?" Jonathan asked.

"It's a job. Or a noble task, some would say. He's only a little foolish, not all bad, it seems to me," Calvin Gunnert said. "From time to time he takes a little Indian orphan back to his tent town when nobody else will have him."

"Sounds like his heart is in the right place," Jonathan commented. They passed another camp of Crow Indians where the men were dancing in a tight circle while the fire flared up and the drums and whistles encouraged them on. Next they entered a sparsely wooded area where two Frenchmen and twice that number of Flatheads had apparently gathered for a contest. This one involved throwing axes at a target tree. A hefty mountain man went first and split the cottonwood tree they had designated as their target. Laughing, the fur-clad mountaineer retrieved his axe and they all searched for another suitable target.

Emerging into another circular camp set on a long, almost barren flat, they came upon the stubborn Crow Indian. He was tall, twenty, wearing a red blanket across his shoulders. His hair was fixed into a sort of pompadour with two braids flowing, over which he wore a split horn headdress. He was obviously a man of some standing among his people. As they started past the Indian, he stepped quite deliberately in front of Jonathan, blocking his way.

"What's this?" Jonathan asked Stinky. "Tell him I don't want any trouble."

Stinky and the man, who was another Mountain Crow, had a short conversation during which the Indian glowered mockingly at Jonathan.

"What's his trouble?" Jonathan asked when the men were finished talking.

"It's a challenge," Stinky said. "He wants to race you."

"Race me?" Jonathan glanced again at the Indian, who had strolled back to join his companions, casting haughty looks in Jonathan's direction. "Why does he want to do that? Do you know who he is?"

"I know him," Stinky said. "His name is Fire Sky, and he thinks he's the pride of his entire nation.

"He challenged you because he wants to prove to his friends there that he's as good as he brags about being," Calvin said. Now a few of the other mountain men had begun to gather around Jonathan.

"He wanted to race me earlier," one of them said. "He's challenged three or four whites. You've got to race him, kid," the trapper said. "For the rest of us."

Jonathan hesitated. He didn't care about the pride of the group. He looked across the clearing at Fire Sky. "He does think a lot of himself, doesn't he? How long is the race? I don't think I could win in a short sprint, he's got long legs."

"It's a course of about two miles," Stinky said, sensing Jonathan's firm decision wavering. "At least that's what it was last year."

Jonathan, who frequently ran distances in the mountains over rough terrain, considered it. He was still young, true, but the Crow Indian seemed formidable, certain of his strength and swiftness.

"Come on, kid," another mountain man urged.

"What else are you going to do this evening?" Calvin Gunnert prodded.

"I'll give it a shot," Jonathan said, taking a deep breath. "What have I got to lose?"

"Thatta boy," one of the fur-clad trappers said, slapping Jonathan on the shoulder. "Show him what we're made of!"

Someone passed the word to the Crow contingent, and Fire Sky began slowly, carefully, removing the head adornment he wore, shedding blanket and breeches. Beneath these was an astonishingly well-built young man with long, tapered muscles and a sleek form. He continued to smile taunts toward Jonathan.

"I don't know, Calvin," Jonathan said. "The man looks like a runner."

"So do you, my boy. Let's get those clothes off you—can't run a race in furs. Do you want to wear my moccasins?"

"I suppose so, it might improve my chances," Jonathan answered, removing his fur-wrapped boots and slipping into Calvin's lighter moccasins, which he had worn to the Rendezvous only because he knew they would not be working there. "Any advice for me?"

"Just keep on his shoulder," Calvin said. "He knows the course, you don't. Save a burst of speed for the last sprint."

It wasn't much as far as advice went, but Jonathan nodded

and went forward now to meet the haughty Fire Sky, who was standing at a roughly sketched starting line, still smirking and waving to his friends.

"I'm starting not to like you," Jonathan muttered. In response, the Mountain Crow spat back something concerning the *"baashciile"*—white man—which was the only word Jonathan caught out of the short, sharp diatribe.

An older Crow Indian had appeared ahead of them, raising the red baton he held high. He looked at both racers, got a nod from each, and lowered the baton sharply.

Fire Sky was like the starter in a sprint—he was off and ahead five paces before Jonathan had gotten into his own stride. Briefly, the Mountain Crow turned backwards and ran along that way, waving to his friends before he got serious about the race. And when he did, a very powerful stride sped him on his way. But it was a two-mile race, and Jonathan, grinding his teeth together, clenching his fists, was able to stay relatively even, though he could not pass the Crow warrior no matter how hard he tried. But then, Calvin had advised him to stay on Fire Sky's shoulder and bide his time, and so he did.

After a few hundred yards, the Indian darted off the path and raced ahead down into the forest depths. The land before had been sunken in twilight purple, but suddenly, as the trees closed around them, it became ominously dark. Running on, Jonathan doggedly followed the Crow, trying to keep his pace as the trail dipped into the heart of the forest. Fire Sky seemed to have regained his earlier speed and his bravado. He glanced across his right shoulder at Jonathan and mouthed a few mocking words Jonathan was glad he did not understand.

The path they followed now veered sharply left, and there was a depression in front of them. A seasonal stream apparently ran through here. Jonathan could not see a good crossing in this light, and so he only continued to follow the Crow, sticking near to his shoulder. Following Fire Sky, he saw the Indian slow his pace in the briefest of hesitations and then leap deftly across the dry wash. Jonathan followed, knowing that had he been the leader in the race he would never have seen the crossing and would have wasted much time looking for it.

The Crow jogged on, now weaving his way upslope through the pines and scattered oak trees, returning to the flat ground beyond. Jonathan's chest was burning, and his legs seemed to knot briefly. He was fighting to keep breathing as deeply as he wished. He had run many miles across the high mountains, quite joyously extending his legs and performing challenging leaps over rocks and declivities, but all of that seemed much different from being forced to compete with a grim adversary, which Fire Sky had become.

As Jonathan watched, Fire Sky's toes struck a protruding tree root, and the Crow stumbled for just a second or two. Jonathan, having seen where the projecting root lay, vaulted over it and continued on. He had gained a few strides on Fire Sky, he thought.

Again the Mountain Crow turned his head. Looking over his shoulder he saw that Jonathan was closer than he would have liked and increased his long-legged, agile body's speed.

Jonathan felt like halting then, but some spark of competitiveness would not allow him to do that. They again emerged onto the flats, and now Jonathan could see several small groups crowding the pathway—the friends of Fire Sky on one side, the mountain men on the other.

Calvin had advised Jonathan to stay on the Indian's shoulder and to hold a final burst in reserve to be used at the race's final stage. Jonathan was wondering if he would even finish the race, if he had anything in reserve, or even enough strength to finish the two-mile run. His legs felt rubbery now; his lungs were gasping for air.

Then, as they neared the finish line, he saw Fire Sky look over his shoulder at Jonathan once again, trying to gauge his nearness. That glance threw the Crow off his pace, as it had each time he had done so throughout the contest. A race must be run with the eyes and the head facing straight ahead. Every time the Crow had paused to look back, his stride had slowed just a little, and it did so now.

As Fire Sky looked across his right shoulder once again, Jonathan raced past the Indian's left, finding a last rush of speed in his desperate need to win. They reached the finish, Jonathan Byrd inches ahead of the Crow Indian as they passed the cheering mountain men, the scowling Indians.

Jonathan ran on for another hundred feet or so, circled, and stood trembling, bent over at the waist, trying to find relief for his lungs and pounding heart. Calvin and Stinky were there to pat him on the back and shout a few garbled words of praise. Behind them a group of grinning fur-clad mountain men approached. All of their words were a jumble in Jonathan's mind; all were meaningless.

Finally he straightened up and began to dress himself again as the celebrating trappers and fur traders stamped away, shouting gibes at the Crow in any language they happened to know.

When Jonathan had finished tying his boots he became aware of another silent presence beside him. Fire Sky, still barechested, had come across the camp, leading a quite tall paint pony oddly marked with black, white, and brown patches. He said not a word as he offered the tether to Jonathan and then went silently away again. Jonathan had shaken his head in refusal, but Stinky had gathered up the ends of the pony's hackamore.

"I don't want that horse," Jonathan said, but Stinky shook his head stubbornly.

"It's the price of the challenge—you have to accept it,

otherwise you will shame Fire Sky."

"That makes no sense," Jonathan said, still panting shallowly. "I didn't make a bet on the race. I'll tell him he can have his horse back."

"No you won't," Calvin Gunnert said loudly, taking the horse's lead from Stinky. "Mr. Reginald Foote here is right—and, being raised a Crow, he should know." Stinky blinked as if he were unfamiliar with his own proper name. "Fire Sky has already embarrassed himself in front of his people. Returning the prize he had wagered on himself to him would be totally inappropriate—a man pays his debts."

"I don't know," Jonathan said, his breathing now more nearly regular. "But if both of you say I should, I'll take the pony and be glad to have him."

Leading the horse back to their campsite, Jonathan glanced back once and he could see the malevolent eyes of Fire Sky fixed on him. Calvin noticed the look on Jonathan's face and told him, "Look, it's too bad if the man has hurt feelings because he lost his pony, but the race was his idea in the first place."

"Sure," Stinky added. "Fire Sky had made his brags to his friends back there. It's not your fault—besides you didn't come here to make friends, did you?"

No, Jonathan had to admit to himself, he had not come to the Rendezvous to make friends, but neither did he wish to make any enemies among those there, and it seemed he had.

His legs were beginning to stiffen up on him by the time they reached camp, and Jonathan decided he had had enough of the day.

"Are you all right?" Calvin asked as Jonathan sagged heavily onto his bed.

"Just sore—don't ever prompt me to do something like that again, Calvin."

"No, I won't," Calvin said seriously, "But look here, if you're not up to going out tonight, do you mind if I do?"

"Go on and have your fun," Jonathan said. "You can do that or stay around here and watch me sleep."

Calvin Gunnert smiled, lifted a hand, and trudged off toward wherever he meant to find his entertainment on this evening. Jonathan knew it would include whisky, but that was Calvin's business. It was his money and he had no one to apologize to for spending it as he chose.

After tying the tall paint pony next to his gray saddle horse, and breaking some hay out of the bale they were carrying on the old cart, Jonathan left the two animals to get acquainted, withdrew into the forest a little, and rolled his bed out there, only slightly screened from the dancing fires, the shouts and drums, the shrieks of laughter, and the booming curses in the clearing beyond.

# Chapter Two

## Discovering Shywater

Jonathan awakened early, the new silver sun piercing the gloomy night shadows beneath the pines. He walked first to his horses to make sure they were still there. Both seemed at peace with their place in the horse world, and patting both, running a hand along the sleek neck of the paint, he went to join Calvin at the morning fire.

Calvin was not there. This should have been no surprise since Calvin had more or less announced his intention to go roistering, but it left Jonathan with a vaguely abandoned feeling. Why this should be, he could not say. After all, had he awakened this morning in his familiar high-mountain cabin he would have been equally alone.

Across the vast encampment, people were stirring early. The smoke from scores of campfires clouded the clearing. There were shrill cries from the children. The mountain men who had not completed bartering for their furs would be up already; the fur traders would be active, looking for prime ermine, beaver, and bear pelts. Along the river, men would be loading the boats; in the stores trappers and Indians alike would be searching through the wares for needed items. And the drums would begin again as whisky flowed, and the games of a hundred kinds from races to axe throwing, wrestling and dice playing, would rise to the levels of a pagan fair.

The thought of all this activity suddenly made Jonathan weary of the place, the antlike, frenetic movement.

Jonathan Byrd felt the need to be away from it, as he had when he had—only once—visited the bustling city of Billings, where he and Calvin Gunnert had gone looking for a new horse to replace their old black mare, Bess, which had been killed by a grizzly bear.

He visited the horses once again. Calvin had taken his own horse with him wherever he had gone. Jonathan's gray watched his approach stolidly, content in its own horse's land of plenty. It had rest, food, warmth after the bitter reign of last winter, and wanted for nothing. The tall paint pony he had won from Fire Sky was younger, more eager to move about, and it watched Jonathan with a mixture of uneasy eagerness and unhappy anticipation.

The horse stood at fifteen and a half hands high, and that alone was enough to distinguish it from the usual runty Indian pony. Its distinctive markings made it stand out from the herd. Its muzzle was splashed with a chocolate brown, which spread over its face like a mask, then at the skull and down its neck there was a blotch of deep black. The pattern, if it could be called that, continued down its flanks, overlaid on a glossy white. It had one white ear, one black. Its tail was white except for a touch of black at its tip. It had been well groomed and well fed; obviously it had been Fire Sky's pride and joy.

For a moment Jonathan felt guilty about having the animal; he even considered trying again to return the horse to the Crow, but if what he had been told was true, that would be a great insult to the *Awaxaawaxammilaxpaake*. It would symbolize that the Crow Indian had gone back on his word, his promise to surrender the horse to any man who could outrun him, so assured was he of victory.

No matter—Jonathan shook the thoughts off. He had not designed the rules of the game, nor set the price. The horse was his now, although he had no doubt that Fire Sky was the faster man and had only lost due to cockiness and inattention. Now what mattered was that he had a fine young horse in which he could take pride.

Would the paint stand for outfitting? Jonathan meant to find out. After a few minutes stroking the tall horse's muzzle, running a hand over its flanks, Jonathan reached for his saddle.

The animal amazed him by accepting saddle, blanket, and cinch without much more than a quivering under its skin to indicate that it might be slightly annoyed. Sweet-talking the horse a little more as it stood, saddled, Jonathan slipped it its bit, a contrivance far different from the horse's accustomed hackamore.

The paint pony, after tossing its head once in annoyance, accepted the steel bit as well, though it seemed confused at the turn of events.

"I'll show you how this is going to work," Jonathan purred to the paint, slipping a boot into the stirrup and swinging aboard, prepared for a violent, bucking response as he would have gotten from any wild mustang. Instead the animal only stood, shuddering to be sure, shifting its feet uneasily, but it allowed Jonathan on his back. Fire Sky had patiently trained the horse, it seemed, although it could never have worn bit or saddle before.

Fire Sky had, indeed, made a large wager on the swiftness of his own feet by using the paint as his offered prize. Now that was all to Jonathan's benefit, and he started the horse forward with a nudge from his heels. Uncertainly at first, then with accustomed ease, the horse began to mind the reins, and Jonathan guided it down the wooded slope away from the wakening Rendezvous grounds.

The sounds of the encampment fell away as he entered the woods and passed through them. Again he could hear bird song, the subtle whispering of the breeze among the high pines, the rustling of the oak leaves. Solitude, Jonathan realized, was what he had been missing. He was already tired of the vague corruption of the drunken camp. It was what had pulled him into the mountains in the first place. Some of the mountain men, he knew, were men without a country, with evil deeds behind them—these were hiding away in the mountains. Some men used the mountains as a last desperate resort, others as a sort of penance.

Jonathan relished the free, nearly brutal solitude of the far places; why, he could not have said. Being alone was to him a natural state of existence, a coveted way of life in which he did not long to reunite with the society of the old, to hastily, almost desperately, reconvene with those he had left behind, usually with good reason.

The pine forest thinned and Jonathan rode the big paint pony out onto a little valley with a flowing stream at its bottom. Silver-blue in the morning light, it meandered its way along its traditional course past yellow grass, which was only now beginning to show signs of spring green. On the opposite flank of the hills facing the meadow there was a wide swath of golden aspen, which again became smothered by the deep forest-blue pines and cedars growing there in endless progression.

Along the stream, sprinkled across the grassland, purple mountain lupine, white star flowers and black-eyed Susans grew. The horse lifted its brown muzzle and urged Jonathan forward, having identified the sweet smell of water ahead, and Jonathan let the big animal make its way down the morning-fragrant golden slope toward the creek.

Above and opposite him, Jonathan saw a broad bench of land where . . . where a house could be nicely situated to overlook the entire valley and the miles of rolling land beyond.

Behind him the bulk of the Grand Tetons showed clearly on

this fine morning, their gray, snow-streaked peaks appearing stark and indomitable against the crystal-blue background of the sky.

He already knew. Not once in a lifetime does a dream appear so solidly, so fully formed.

Jonathan guided the Indian pony toward the creek, swung down, and stood gazing in all directions, laughing out loud as a brightly colored grouse took to startled wing not far from him. The stream, he saw, was placid and sluggish, but it would run more strongly once the spring melt began. There were striations along the cut bank indicating the normal levels of its seasonal flow, like layers of eternity.

The horse had lowered its head to drink, and Jonathan, on an impulse and perhaps with a memory of "Stinky" Reginald Foote, removed a thick bar of yellow lye soap from his saddlebags, undressed, and eased his way slowly into the cold rushing water of the stream, downstream from his mount.

The shallow stream was clear, icy, exhilarating in a pagan way. He stood half-soaped, shivering in the creek as his eyes roamed over the wide land. Grassland and valley, hills studded with pine trees and cedar, with a flourish of yellow aspen, and he realized again this was the right decision for him. He would live here; here he would stay.

Of course he felt obliged to first discuss his decision with Calvin. The older man had been his working partner, his father, his friend. He respected Calvin's opinion of matters even if he did not always see eye to eye with him. Besides, Jonathan thought, if he was determined to leave the fur trade, Calvin might feel the need of another partner, and here at the Rendezvous was the place to search one out. He did not wish to abandon Calvin. He was somewhat fearful of the task he had set before himself, but it seemed that events had taken their own course, had made the decision for him from the first moment he had seen the empty land spread peacefully around him, beckoning.

When Jonathan found Calvin Gunnert, he discovered him half-drunk and half-sleeping, seated against a wheel of the empty cart. Still, it was as good a time as any to broach the subject. Jonathan slumped to the earth beside Calvin.

"I want to go off on my own, Calvin."

"What? Leave me?" Calvin took a drink from the whisky jug he was holding. "Then have I offended you? I know I act a little different here than back home, but the long winters leave a lingering chill, and the loneliness can eat at a man, you know."

"No!" Jonathan rushed to explain. "It isn't anything you've done or could do, Calvin. It's just that I have my sights set on a new way of living."

"Oh?" Calvin opened his eyes lazily. "Hasn't the fur trade done right by you?"

"It has, you have, but there's a point in a man's life when he feels the need to strike out on his own."

"Is there? And in what direction exactly did you mean to strike out? Don't tell me that like that Robert Pyle you mean to sell off your cart and join the fur company to sail down to the big cities?"

"No, it's nothing like that, Calvin. I mean to make myself a home out here. I've found the very place for me."

"And what'll you do for goods, for cash money, Jonathan? The summer might pass pleasantly as you've your dream and some cash money in your purse, but what after that?"

"I don't know what after that," Jonathan had to admit. "I mean to try it, to make my start."

"I'll see you back before the next winter snows come in," Calvin predicted.

"I don't think so; I hope not. I mean to have my try at doing things my way."

"Aye, young men must dream their dreams," Calvin said around a yawn. He was unable to keep his eyes open for now. "Tell me all about it in the morning, Jonathan, will you? Just think carefully about what you are wishing for. Some men even attain their dreams. For now . . ." For now Calvin Gunnert dozed off into his old man's dreams and Jonathan, after listening to the fevered sounds of the rowdy Rendezvous, the drums, the shouts and challenges of half-drunken men, fell asleep among the cool pine trees. Rising again the following morning, he felt a sluggish intensity building slowly in his blood. Then, as he came fully awake, he almost let out an unconscious whoop of joy, as wild as that of any Indian in the encampment, for he realized that his dream was a waking dream. He had the money and the skills, and he had found the site. All that was needed now was patience and hard work.

And a lot of good fortune.

Calvin was at a low-burning morning campfire when Jonathan reached him. The older man was crouched low, studying the flames with bleary eyes. He only glanced at Jonathan as if it hurt to move his eyes.

"You see," Calvin Gunnert said, "that Robert Pyle is the fool. Selling his cart and sailing off on a flatboat for St. Jo!"

"What's wrong with that?" Jonathan asked, reaching for the coffee pot with a folded rag. "He wants to get out of the high-up mountains. He's had enough of their cold and the uncertainty of life up there."

"Why, don't you know what those big cities are?" Calvin asked morosely. "Nothing but dens of iniquity and bacchanalian savagery—the whisky runs free day and night. No, sir, that's why I could never kennel up in a place like that."

So saying, Calvin took the whisky jug at his side and poured a neat complement of it into his coffee.

"I guess it wouldn't suit everyone," Jonathan said, sipping at his black coffee.

"It suits no one. Ask that Reverend Mr. Blaylock. I stopped and listened to him a little while yesterday. He's right when he says that liquor is a beautiful, enticing, deadly seductress. What does it profit a man to drink his life away? And look what it does to the Indians when they touch a drop of it." He drank from his laced coffee cup again. "Yes—I did say it was enticing, also deadly. But trying to put it aside is like trying to persuade yourself you should leave that evil woman when she's got her hooks in you." Calvin was silent for a few minutes.

"Anyway, once I'm back in the high reaches, there'll be no more whisky for me. You know me, Jonathan. This is the only time of year I drink, and when I get home and out of her clutches, I'm as hardworking a man as any. It's just that it's too easy for a man to be tempted. That's why I say, what does that young pup, Pyle, think he's going to find in the big city? Misery, that's what I think."

"I suppose he has other dreams that we don't know anything about. As you said last night, Calvin—young men dream their dreams."

"Did I say that?" Calvin rubbed his whiskered chin. "Well, it's true, I suppose. Did I hear you telling me last night that you were going to quit me, Jonathan, or was I dreaming?"

"That's what I told you, but I wasn't sure you were listening. I found a place I want to settle, Calvin. As a matter of fact, I was going over there today, and I'd like you to ride along with me and give me your thoughts."

So, after giving Calvin another hour or so to recover his vagrant wits, the two men started out again toward the valley Jonathan had stumbled upon. The sights, the sounds, the smoke of the encampment fell away as they filtered through the forest.

Jonathan could feel a peace settling over him as they neared the long valley. That, and a kind of excitement like an eager competitor on the day before the race, when he knows there is nothing that can be done, but is eager to get the task begun, to test himself.

Jonathan drew up the paint pony he had chosen to ride again on that day at the forest verge. Calvin halted his horse beside him and, squinting into the morning sunlight, the old trapper said, "Is this it, then?"

"This is it. Have you ever seen country so beautiful, Calvin?" Jonathan's eyes were glowing with visions. Calvin felt he should say nothing negative, but as they started down into the broad, yellow grass valley, he did say, "Don't seem to be much water flowing through here."

"It's not that time of year yet," Jonathan said accurately.

"No. But even when you get spring runoff, what's to keep it from just flowing away to the far bottom? There would never be enough usable water for farming, for greening any hay. That is, if you meant to grow stock."

"I don't intend to do either," Jonathan said as they walked their horses toward the creek.

"It would be a wonder if a man could do either. The land slopes away too hard for irrigating crops or tending them. As far as horses or cattle, there isn't a ranch within five hundred miles of here. They learned early on that the Indians would pick off their stock."

Calvin glanced at Jonathan, who seemed to be visiting some future rosy time when he would live like a lord on this open land. In fact he was, and Calvin decided to hold his negative remarks back.

"First thing, of course, is the house. You can see where I mean to build it, Calvin—up there on that bench."

"It's a nice setting," Calvin said, still unconvinced about the wisdom of his partner's plan. "How exactly do you mean to build this house?"

"You can see that stand of pines," Jonathan said, waving his arm toward the vast spread of pine trees on the far hillside.

"Logs? Well, yes that's all the material there is, isn't it?"

Jonathan was still studying the flank of the hill as if choosing lumber. "You know I'm good at notching and fitting, Calvin."

"How long do you figure it would take you, working alone as you will be?"

"I'll be through building before winter comes back," Jonathan said with confidence. He had halted his paint pony again. Their passing had disturbed a flock of meadowlarks. He watched them go and smiled. Calvin was showing signs of boredom, impatience, or of being in the need of another drink.

"It's a large task you've set for yourself, Jonathan."

"I know that—but I've set it for myself." Jonathan Byrd smiled.

Calvin shook his head doubtfully. "How do you mean to even raise the roof beams?"

"With a horse and a ramp. The pony will draw the logs up."

"Seems downright reckless to attempt alone," Calvin commented.

Jonathan lowered his eyes and narrowed them. "Many things seem reckless, Calvin. To me, now, the wish to find a place of permanence seems the safest decision I can make. I no longer want to tramp the high peaks, half-frozen, hoping for a good trap line."

"I always thought you enjoyed it."

"I did enjoy it, Calvin. Now I don't think I would. I'd be thinking of that perfect valley I walked away from because I was frightened to try making it my own."

Calvin could only shrug—he was too old to have such dreams. Jonathan was still planning.

"How much land can I claim, Calvin? And who do I see about obtaining it?"

"Who do you see?" Calvin grinned. They had started their horses back toward the Rendezvous site. "Who is there to see? There is no one. This land has never been surveyed. The territory is a part of the Louisiana Purchase, so the Frenchies have no say in matters. This land has never been a traditional camp of any of the local Indian tribes. The fur trappers would want nothing to do with it. There's no beaver down this low, no good furs of any sort, not in any numbers. Washington, D.C., is a thousand miles away, maybe more, and they've not yet attempted to extend eastern law to this land—they've never seen it, have no use for it."

"Well, then, what do I do about laying claim?" Jonathan asked with some frustration.

"Well, in Texas in the early days on that vast flat land, what a man would do was claim the amount of land he could ride his horse around in a single day. He'd build monuments at the corners, and that was his land. They didn't have eastern law in Texas either at that time. A man's claim was never challenged.

"Sometimes these early men would place a notice in an oilskin pouch and put these inside of the stone cairns they built as markers. They'd say something like, 'This is the southeast corner of Jonathan Byrd's property, claimed April so-and so.' If you're of a mind to do something similar it wouldn't be a bad idea," Calvin said. "Though I can't imagine a time when there will be another man in this territory looking for a slope-sided piece of land that's so shy on water."

Jonathan laughed, but it was a short one. "I think that's what I'll do, Calvin, if you think it's best."

"If you're sure you really want to go homesteading and leave the high mountains."

"I'm sure. I have to even if I really don't know why. I want to finally own one thing on this earth. What's the date today, Calvin?"

"All I can tell you is that it's the year 1834—and I'm not even sure of that. I was told that. Someone among the fur companies will know. Those men run their lives according to the calendar."

"I'll ask when I go over there. I need to buy provisions, anyway, and tools, a lot of them."

Calvin Gunnert was frowning again. "What are you going to do when the money runs out, Jonathan?"

"Keep living," Jonathan said with determination, "So long as I've a rifle and powder, I can eat."

"I know you can, but you might get tired of a life living off nothing but game. We've always at least had flour and beans. We've done all right."

"Yes, we have," Jonathan admitted. "If things go seriously wrong and winter sets in early, Calvin, you might find me knocking on your door for work. Until then, though, I mean to make my life down here on this shy water claim of mine."

As day groped toward evening, Jonathan was still resting in the camp, leaning against a massive pine tree's trunk, his planning mingled with the dreams in his mind. His legs still ached from the unaccustomed running he had done the day before. Calvin was gone, presumably to see how drunk he could get. His only visitor was that mongrel white dog who had been trying to snatch furs from their cart.

The fur trading was proceeding briskly; the white trappers purchasing their essential foods, the Indians bartering what furs they had for what they considered a valuable commodity—wool—along with novelty items. Every man bought or traded for lead balls and powder for their guns. That and whisky.

Both white and red men got all the whisky they could afford

from the fur traders. Although a law had been passed in 1822 forbidding the sale of liquor to the Indians, men out here were either ignorant of those eastern goings-on or refused to accept the law as a commandment.

By noon, therefore, half of the camp was drunk and the other half awaiting its turn. By that time of day, Jonathan knew the men would grow more friendly, romantic, nostalgic, and then belligerent. He disliked it all and regretted having been dragged along to this year's Rendezvous. He began to wonder if he disliked all men, but found the idea insupportable and switched his focus.

He had a constant, waking dream of walking the broad, empty land of his own possession where his house loomed large on the bench where it had been constructed, and of a series of trouble-free, peaceful days passing in slow progression without a whoop, a curse, a battle—large or small—ever occurring.

The clamor of the camp became a compelling force, and Jonathan rose, dressed, and started toward the fur company store where he had business to conduct. Foodstuffs—for a year if possible—meaning flour, salt, a side of bacon, dried beans, cornmeal, along with his own needful supply of gunpowder and lead balls, since he intended to feed himself for the most part from game. Also vegetable seeds could be useful—squash, beans, and corn as the Indians grew. Along with these he would need tools—a good double-bit axe, a bucksaw, a hammer, and what nails he could find, candles . . . his list was long. He had spent a part of the morning trying to write a list of what he needed—not what he would like to have—and totaling the price.

The sum was too much, no matter how he looked at it, no matter what items he trimmed from it. He thought that as a last resort he would try to sell the paint pony. After all, that was inherited money, as it were. The other problem was transporting the goods he had in mind to purchase. Calvin would probably let him borrow the cart they used, but his partner was unpredictable as Jonathan well knew, and might decide suddenly to strike out again for the high mountains.

He thought of the man called Robert Pyle, whom it was said had made the decision to sell off his gear, including his cart, and had joined the fur company, sailing downriver to St. Joseph to work there. Jonathan had never known the man, but had him pointed out to him. How much would this man take for his gear?

Jonathan was thinking along these lines when he passed the camp of Stinky and Dave and veered that way. He found both men collaborating on some kind of stew they were stirring in their iron pot. Stinky grinned as he saw Jonathan approaching.

"Come to supper?" Stinky asked.

"No good," was all Dave said, then the half-breed strode away.

"He doesn't like my cooking," Stinky said, "tells me it smells bad."

It did; how was Stinky to be the judge of that, having no sense of smell himself?

"I'm looking for Robert Pyle. Do you know him, or have an idea of where I can find him?"

"Bob Pyle?" Stinky wiped his hands on his pant legs. "Sure, I know Bob. If he's not in his camp, he'll likely be down along the river, bothering the boatmen. You weren't thinking of joining him?"

"No, it's his cart I'm after. Do you happen to know if he's found a buyer for it yet?"

"I couldn't tell you that. It's likely to be a difficult item to sell. Everyone here has his own cart or they wouldn't have gotten here. What do you and Calvin need with another cart?" Stinky asked, tasting his concoction with a long-handled wooden spoon.

"This one is just for me," Jonathan said, shaking his head when Stinky offered him a taste of the stew. "I mean to strike out on my own."

"Is that so?" Stinky asked with some surprise. "Not getting along with Gunnert, are you?"

"No, it's nothing like that. Could you take me over to Pyle's camp so I could talk to him?"

"Sure," Stinky agreed. "Let me tell Dave that I'm leaving so he can keep an eye on supper."

They did not find Pyle at his camp, but the cart was there, and Jonathan gave the wooden-wheeled contraption a hasty inspection. It was in as good shape as anyone else's. Carts were used only once a year, to transport furs from the high country to the trading camps, and seldom showed signs of hard wear, although the weather did some inevitable harm to those that had to be left without shelter over the winter.

"Well?" Stinky asked after a minute.

"I'd like to have it, if I can afford it."

"Let's see if we can find Bob, then."

# Chapter Three

## Brown Bess versus Hawken

Instead of crossing the main area of the camp where fires burned with a sparking flourish as Indians danced crazily around them, Jonathan and Stinky started for the quieter, untroubled fringe of trees to the east. Reaching a clearing in the woods, they found a party of Indians waiting for them, facing them deliberately, eyes and expressions fixed.

"What's this?" Jonathan asked in a whisper. "Friends of Fire Sky?" They were dressed in the fashion of the Mountain Crows. There were three younger men, their hair done in twin braids, and one older individual whose gray hair hung loosely over his scrawny shoulders.

"Shaw-at-Duan," Stinky answered, not bothering to lower his voice. "He's an important man among their people."

"Well, what's he want?"

The old man had stepped forward from the group of young braves. His eyes went to Jonathan's and then flickered toward the rifle he carried. That weapon was a .54 caliber Hawken with a maple beavertail stock. It was the most accurate rifle in the mountains. The old man was clutching his ancient Brown Bess musket. He said something to Stinky, whom he seemed to recognize.

"He wants a shooting match with you," Stinky told Jonathan.

"Not for my rifle?" Jonathan replied with a hint of anger.

"Not for your rifle," Stinky said, calming him. "It's a challenge, just like the one Fire Sky offered you. He's named the prize, and if you win, you win. If not, nothing—he will have won his pride from you."

"It makes no sense," Jonathan said. "He knows my Hawken is the superior weapon. He knows I am younger, probably have a better eye. He just cannot win, Stinky. Tell him that."

"I can tell him, but to an Indian that will just sound like bragging."

"Then don't tell him anything but that I accept his challenge. The sooner it's over, the sooner we can be on our way."

The men moved in a group. Shaw-at-Duan led the way, the two white men following, the Crow braves trailing in silence.

At a smaller clearing well away from the camp, they watched as a target area was set up. The target area consisted only of a large pine stump where two of the Crow men placed a pair of similarly sized white rocks down and expressionlessly moved far to one side. The rocks were about the size of a human skull and Jonathan was placed behind a firing line about fifty yards away. Jonathan, who knew his rifle and his shooting skills well, felt this to be no challenge at all. The old man stepped forward first with his Brown Bess, took deliberate aim on the rock to his left, and fired. The rock exploded. It was a satisfying shot to the old man, but little of a challenge to Jonathan, who took his turn, shouldering the maple stock of the Hawken, easily drawing back the rear trigger of the weapon, which set the front trigger to the lightest of fingerings. He aimed carefully, placing the blade sight of the Hawken on his intended target, barely touched the hair trigger, and similarly blew his target to dust.

Stinky emitted a faint cheer, but the shot was not even worthy of his feeble approval.

The targets were now replaced by two hand-sized stones. Shaw-at-Duan, who had reloaded his musket, stepped to the line, aimed carefully, and fired, converting his target to stone dust. Jonathan then stepped to the line, feeling almost reckless—was he overconfident? He cautioned himself against that attitude and stepped to the mark again. At the lightest of touches to his hair trigger, the Hawken .54 spoke again, its rich echo reverberating throughout the clearing, and his target was reduced to chips.

Again the targets were changed. Now side by side on the stump two rocks the size of hen's eggs rested awaiting their fate. The Crow stepped to the line, shouldered his weapon, and sighted down its long barrel for what seemed almost a minute, yanking the heavy trigger back.

And missed his mark. Jonathan toed the mark.

When Jonathan again triggered off his Hawken, his target exploded into shards behind a smoky cloud. Lowering his rifle-musket, Jonathan smiled at Shaw-at-Duan, nodded his head, and offered his hand, which the Crow took only briefly before turning, waving to his entourage, and tramping away. They left behind only a single observer, a girl in a beaded white elkskin dress who stood at the perimeter of the woods, her small hands clasped before her. Stinky glanced that way, but said only, "Nice shooting, Jonathan."

"I could have done it at a hundred yards with this gun," Jonathan answered honestly. "I wonder why the old man chose me to challenge. Let's go and find Robert Pyle before it gets dark."

They retraced their steps and started across the camp toward Pyle's campsite. They found him just as he was arriving from the trading post, new woolen city clothes folded over his arm.

"Hello, Stinky!" Pyle who was a young, somewhat dumpy dark-haired man said. He was wearing a wide smile, happy to be leaving his old way of life, it seemed.

"Hello, Bob. I've brought you a man who wishes to buy your cart if you're still decided to sail downriver to the hellhole of the big city."

"I am! A hellhole is it? St. Jo sounds fine to me. I've just sold my furs, have my pockets full of silver, and a new job from Mr. John Astor. Now you've brought someone who'd like to purchase my cart? It's been a wonderful day, Stinky."

"My friend, Mr. Byrd, here might be interested."

"Well," Pyle said shaking hands with Jonathan, "I've only had that cart out in two winters, Mr. Byrd. It's in good condition . . ."

"I've already looked it over," Jonathan said. "I'd like to have it. It's only a matter of how much you were asking for it."

"Of course. I'm not really in a position where I should dicker. As you know, every man who might need a cart already has his own, and I no longer have any use for it at all. You give me whatever you think is a fair price."

So that bit of business was finished quickly and amicably. Jonathan said he would be by with his horse in the morning to pick up the cart—he had a lot of shopping to do at the fur company stores tomorrow and the cart would come in handy.

"Let's be getting back now," Stinky said as the sale was completed with a handshake.

"I've left Dave alone with my stew for too long. He's likely changed the recipe by now."

They returned then through the large camp while purple settled across the western skies. The campfires were even brighter, the men louder, the dancing more frenetic. They again saw the Reverend Mr. Blaylock trying desperately to save souls that had no wish to be saved. His audience was somewhat larger this time: three fur-clad mountaineers, only one of whom was passed out beside his jug of corn liquor; and five or six young Indian boys, older than those Jonathan had seen before. These listened intently—was it out of thoughtful curiosity, some religious stirring, or simply out of boredom? There was no telling. The boys were old enough to have adopted the stony expression of their elders.

One of the mountain men shouted something, made a rude noise, and walked away.

"She's still there," Stinky said, and Jonathan glanced at his smelly companion without understanding.

"What are you talking about?"

"The girl is still back there. Don't tell me you didn't see her following us to Robert Pyle's camp."

Now Jonathan paused and looked behind them. The slender girl who had been observing events in the clearing where they had held the shooting match was a hundred feet or so behind them. When they stopped, she stopped.

"What's she want?" Jonathan asked, proceeding on his way.

"I know you don't want to hear it," Stinky answered as they came near enough to his camp to smell the stew, which now, indeed, had been flavored differently. "But I think she's the prize from the shooting match. I think you just won her from the old man."

"Preposterous," Jonathan grumbled.

"Not to them," Stinky replied as they entered the pine forest. "I heard a little of what those men were talking about. The girl is Shaw-at-Duan's daughter. He doesn't think his health will allow him to live through one more winter. I think he decided to marry her off.

"He wanted to find a young man who was strong, quick, a good hunter . . . and rich. By their standards, you are a rich man, Jonathan. You've just sold a year's worth of furs. You won Fire Sky's best horse from him. I think the old man wanted to lose his match with you. Not enough to miss on purpose, but he saw your Hawken and figured he could not win."

"I won't have any part of this! Tell her to go home, Stinky."

"It wouldn't do any good, Jonathan. In her mind, in her

father's mind, she is your woman now. She has no home to return to. If you could send her back, it would be a huge insult to her, to her father, to the tribe. It would mean you did not find her suitable, useful."

"Well, that would be right! I do not find her either of those. I have my plans now, and they don't include a child bride."

"A woman can be useful," Stinky commented.

"A woman can also get in the way a lot. I have no need to take in a child, to feed two mouths. Tell her to go home!"

Was that a smile on Stinky's face as he turned toward his own campfire? If so, it ought to be slapped from his face. Jonathan Byrd tramped on as quickly as his legs would carry him toward his own camp, winding through the trees whose dark shadows were settling and pooling as evening came on.

Calvin had returned to camp and he greeted Jonathan with a somewhat mournful face and a cup of coffee.

"Well, how did your day go?" he asked.

"I accomplished a few things," Jonathan said, accepting the cup from Calvin. Both men sank down to their haunches, Calvin poking aimlessly at the low campfire. "I bought a cart from Robert Pyle. Guess I'll have to do my shopping in the morning. The stores were closed except for the whisky peddlers."

"Then you're decided. You're leaving the fur game?"

"I've decided," Jonathan said firmly. "It's like this: my choices are to wait out another week with you and return to the high country to trap or to step off on my own. Into failure, or to success, whichever it will be. Toward the life I want to make for myself."

"I can't see what kind of life that is, Jonathan," Calvin said, wagging his head heavily as he stared down into the fire, "but maybe that is just a kind of stubborn blindness on my part because I don't want to lose the best partner a man could hope to have."

Jonathan did not respond. He was distracted by a shadowy figure standing at the edge of the clearing. Calvin saw his look and glanced that way himself, his eyes narrowing.

"Who's that, Jonathan? Don't tell me you've gone and got yourself a woman."

Then, after a sip of coffee and a heavy sigh, Jonathan leaned back on one elbow and told Calvin Gunnert of the day's events. "Now Stinky tells me I can't refuse to accept her without offending the girl, Shaw-at-Duan, and the entire Mountain Crow population."

"He's right, Jonathan. After the race with Fire Sky, I thought you'd learned your lesson."

"I never agreed to that, either, and that was just a horse!" Jonathan said.

"I understand how you feel, but you know our thinking isn't the same as an Indian's. Well," Calvin said after minute's thought, "it could be worse—you'll likely find uses for her."

"Calvin! I have no use at all for a little Indian girl. What am I supposed to do? Make a drudge of her, assign her tasks, and feed her? I'm starting out alone, and I intend to have some success. I intend to make it on my own, and by myself, without extra concerns. If you want her, you take her. If I can't give her back, she'll have to stand around until someone else rescues her."

"That sounds pretty final."

"It is final. I want nothing to do with her ever. If I could tell her so, maybe she would give it up and go home."

"To live with her shame, with her father's shame?"

"I can't be concerned with everyone else's feelings right now," Jonathan snapped, picking up his blanket, making his way to his bed. When he awoke again it was nearly midnight. Calvin had gone off again somewhere to try to manufacture his amusement from a whisky jug.

Something caused Jonathan to look out over the clearing as he sat up and rolled over.

The girl still stood there in the shadows of the cold pines. She might not have moved in the hours he had slept. Small, meek, hands clasped together, her huge brown eyes now caught a faint moon gloss.

Jonathan rolled over and pulled his blankets tightly around him. He was too disturbed now to fall back to sleep and enjoy his dream of the distant, imagined splendors of Shywater. An hour later he sat up sharply, and with a loud, irritated voice called to the vast, cold night.

"Damn all! Go away!"

# Chapter Four

## The Return to Shywater

Morning was clear and bright, although a few bunched clouds seemed to be gathering above the distant mountaintops. It seemed possible that it would rain. Jonathan did not let the possibility of rain shadow his thoughts on this morning. This was the day he was moving. It might have been easier to load his supplies today and begin his move tomorrow, but no—he had to be gone, to leave this place of the old and travel on to the place of the future.

He paused only long enough to boil some coffee. The Rendezvous camp was silent except for a few Indian kids shouting with the pleasure of waking to a new day, the yapping of a few dogs running along with the boys celebrating life. Calvin snored loudly in his bed beneath the cart, a whisky jug within reach. Probably his condition was similar to that of most of the men across the camp.

Best of all, the girl was gone. Probably she had become cold and tired and gone home to beg her father to let her into the hogan; most likely Shaw-at-Duan had decided he had made a mistake and that the censure of the tribe, if any, was preferable to the loss of his young daughter.

Jonathan put all thought of her aside, sipping his coffee until he was able to hear the sounds of commerce down along the river. He looked again at his much-altered shopping list, making a few other small changes. This was going to cost him all he had—a year's wages, he knew—but what did he care? Where else was he to spend money, to have any use at all for it in the coming year?

Eventually, with the new sun low and brightly beaming through the pine woods he untied his gray horse from where it waited and led it off. He had stopped to stroke the paint pony's muzzle for a time, but that paint had taken its exercise the day before. The gray was used to its occasional job of cart horse; besides Jonathan had the vague idea it might upset Fire Sky to see his prize hunting pony used to pull a cart.

Robert Pyle was as alert as Jonathan when he reached the man's camp. The squat man was grinning widely, wearing lighter work clothes instead of his usual furs.

"I'm glad to see you," Pyle said, shaking hands with Jonathan, "I'm worried about a hundred things just now, and making sure the cart was sold was one of them." In a burst of enthusiasm, Pyle told him, "Today is the beginning of a new life for me." He glanced around the wide camp briefly. "I'm off to St. Joseph. I'll work the river, be paid every month, have heat when it's cold and a safe bed every night."

"I'm sure it will all work out," Jonathan said. "Just so you're sure it's what you want."

"Is it! No more mountaintop camps in winter. I understand they haven't so much as glimpsed a grizzly bear in St. Jo for fifty years!"

"Or gone hungry in that town," Jonathan suggested.

"There's a restaurant on every street and there's a thousand streets!" Pyle said with continued enthusiasm. "Come on; I'll help you hitch your horse to the cart. Then I'm going down to the river. I don't work today, but I like to just sit and watch it flowing away toward promise and plenty."

Jonathan's own ambition was not so much on display this morning, but he felt somehow superior to Pyle. Where the man had chosen to travel ensured that he would be subject to the largesse and whims of others—a wage-slave, in fact—Jonathan's new world would have no such sharply defined horizons. He would be his own man on his own land, leading life as he wished.

"I wish you the best of luck, Robert," Jonathan said, meaning it.

"The best of luck to you, too, Byrd. If you ever take the notion to see civilization, find me and come on by." Then the man paused, looking up sharply with questioning eyes. "Does that one belong to you?" He was pointing toward the forest verge. Jonathan turned his head to see the woman, Shawn-at-Duan's young daughter, standing at a respectful distance, watching the two men.

"I only ask because I thought I saw the same girl with you when you and Stinky were here last night."

"She follows me around—I don't know why," Jonathan answered shortly.

After a few more words, Robert Pyle and Jonathan Byrd parted company. Jonathan led his horse and cart to the huge tents the fur company had set up for sales and trading.

The stores were not open yet; only the whisky peddler was working, and he seemed to already be doing a fairly brisk business. In front of the stores a queue of stodgy Indian squaws had formed, each in her tribal dress, each clutching what could have been hardly more than a few hopeful cents. Off to the side three nearly toothless old men sat against the dry grass, waiting to sell or trade a pile of furs—those the traders had rejected. It was a futile sort of attempt at earning some money. Of all the places in the world to market furs, to try selling them to men whose business was furs was the worst.

Yet Jonathan had seen a few flatlanders—tourists actually—who might want to pick up one of these poor furs as a memento of their journey to the Rendezvous. That must have been the hope of the Indians, though Jonathan saw no whites in unusual dress around.

The line for the stores was not long, but he did not know how long he might have to wait for them to open. Leaving his cart where it stood, he walked to the whisky dealer and purchased a jug of corn liquor. Returning, he sorted through the discarded furs the old Indians had before them and found a buffalo hide with patchy fur and a damaged black bear pelt.

He offered the silent Indians the jug, miming that he would take those two furs, and they agreed eagerly. The problem of his winter bedding was solved without him having to pay the high prices they asked for woolen goods this far up the river.

He had just thrown the hides into the back of his cart when the wood-framed door of the tent swung open, and Jonathan entered with the rest of the people. Consulting his list and his purse he moved along carefully, letting nothing that was not listed catch his eye.

There was a young, helpful half-breed willing to assist Jonathan with his goods as they became too much for a man to carry in a single trip. Foodstuffs, hardware, one new shirt, and a pair of new boots later, he was loading his cart, now piled high with assorted goods. He looked back into his purse, which was much lighter. Only three silver coins remained, but what had been spent had been properly spent, and he had only exchanged useless metal for the implements to build a home and the provisions needed to sustain him as he did. That thought was a little unsettling as it passed through his mind—what *was* he going to do when nothing was left but game and roots?

He would continue to live! Jonathan concluded. Thousand of generations of men had lived on this earth before the concept of a market had emerged. He had his rifle; he had his youth and his strength. He only needed a place to stow his purchases for now as he built his house. The wild things would certainly vie for some of his goods if he let them, and the weather would destroy any supplies vulnerable to rain and snow. And time. Jonathan reflected that he was now in a race with time.

He covered his goods with the tarpaulin he'd purchased for that purpose and started his walk back to the camp. Only twice did he catch himself looking around to make sure he was still alone.

He watched the crowd as he made his way homeward, but did not catch sight of Calvin Gunnert. They had been a long time together, and he did not wish to leave without saying goodbye to the old mountain man. Even thoughts about Calvin and his old trapping days seemed to have drifted into the past. This was a new day, the first day, and although he was tired, Jonathan meant to make a definitive break from his old life as soon as possible. He did scratch out a note to Calvin in which nothing was said. Then he gathered up his bedroll and tied the paint pony on to the back of the cart and started the gray horse down through the pines, toward home.

Silent, empty, and wide, the land beyond the pines somehow carried a different feel than it had only the day before. Then it had been a distant dream; now it was a barren land carrying a hundred chores that must be seen to before it could be made livable. It had emerged from the silent world of dreams and assumed a mantle of reality, where the work was something that had to be planned on, labored at. Somehow, Jonathan found this truth made the land more his own. A dream can be held, but not altered. This land now—Shywater—was a reality that could be molded, formed to his liking, tended as he hoped it would tend him in future years.

When he reached the shelf of land where he meant to build his house, he unhitched the gray horse and set it free to graze alongside the paint pony. There was no point in unloading the cart when he still had no place to store his supplies.

It was still early, the sun bright, the breeze cool. With a sort of eager trepidation, Jonathan hiked the short distance to the forest. He carried his new axe in hand. The time to start building his reality out of his dreams was now.

Jonathan Byrd rose with the sun. He examined his finished work. Four low walls of notched and fitted pine logs. All of three feet high, with the logs in front cut for a doorway, it had now entered the building phase when Jonathan knew he would have to use a ramp and a horse to lift the timbers. For only one man, this would be a risky balancing act, but he had made his choice. From time to time he found himself wishing for a helping hand and thought that maybe Calvin or even Stinky Reggie Foote might stop by and help him out for a day or so, but those men were long gone now. It had been a week since Jonathan had heard drums from the Rendezvous site or seen the fires burning in the encampment. One day, seemingly far distant, he had heard the shrill hoot of a steamboat's whistle as it proceeded downriver carrying its load of precious furs to the merchants of the large cities. And whisking Robert Pyle away into his own new world.

Well, Jonathan was happy for Pyle, but did not envy him. Pyle would find himself absorbed and embraced unwillingly in the smut and noise of the big city with his days, and his nights, regulated by his new home's own sluggish, unchangeable rhythms. A wandering hunter, a visitor to his mountain cabin, had once showed Jonathan pictures of some great city—St. Louis, perhaps—and extolled the benefits of city life. Jonathan had listened, but heard nothing enticing in the traveler's descriptions. The description of life in a city always seemed to center around food, drink, entertainment, and little else. That seemed hardly enough to cause a man to turn away from the beauty of the raw, far country.

Talking to his horses—who else was there to talk to?—Jonathan and his ponies decided to work that day on the stone fireplace. He was trying to keep up with the framing. A chimney would be much more difficult to construct all at once. He was aware that most cabins—his own old home included—used only a smoke hole, those being easier to construct, but Jonathan meant to be at home in that cabin for a long time to come, and he desired the permanence of a stone fireplace and chimney. In the winter when the north wind blew, he would be grateful to the younger Jonathan Byrd who had built it for his warmth and comfort. Hopefully he would not be plagued in any sort of weather by the smoke that collected in a room having but a simple smoke hole in the roof for ventilation. Jonathan had heard of entire poor families out on the far plains who were killed in that way as they tried to keep warm on a bitter winter night.

Jonathan had built a primitive sledge from log ends, which he used to move stones up from the creek, and now he prepared the gray to haul the stones. The paint pony watched him with seeming impatience or annoyance, perhaps wishing for some work to do on this day as well, but the paint had been well-used also, particularly on that early day when Jonathan had set out, heeding Calvin Gunnert's advice, to mark the four corners of his land.

Load by load, Jonathan loaded the hand-selected gray stones onto the sledge, sometimes forced to clamber up the slick riverbank with a heavy stone in his hands.

He had begun working on the arch of the fireplace when the scrabbling sound reached him. He got up from his knees, grabbed the Hawken from its resting place, and stepped out into the yard. It was not the first time he had heard the menacing hiss, and he stood silently studying the forest verge as the chill wind flowed down from the mountains, ruffling the tall pine trees, bending their upper reaches.

The horses had heard it too. Just now both of them stood, ears alert, eyes studying the woods. Jonathan did not see what he believed to be a cougar, and there was no sense in going after it through the trees. This was the second time he had heard the big cat moving around near his property.

The cougar was probably thinking what a fine neighbor he was, having brought him two fat animals to prey on. The mountain lion seemed to be a fact of life on Shywater. Jonathan knew he would one day have to track and kill it, but for now all he could do was take notice that the cougar was still in the area. The horses had shaken off their uneasiness and, after moving a little way farther from the forest, they returned to their grazing.

Jonathan's full attention was not on his work when he returned to the interior of the unfinished house. Twice his arch collapsed on him before he could insert the keystone.

He was not a skilled mason, and the work tired him mentally as he tried to fit the stones primitively. He believed he was wasting time that could have been better spent felling and hewing his timbers, but that was probably only because he was more familiar with woodworking and less so with stonework. Nevertheless, he had made his plan for the day and he stuck to it through the long afternoon. When the arch was firmly in place, he was able to go more quickly. By the time night had begun to settle across the land, he had a chimney standing as tall as his shoulders.

He went outside once more. His eyes had flickered that way throughout the day, but the horses seemed completely at ease now. Perhaps the cougar, not liking Jonathan's man-scent, had given up the idea of dining on horse flesh. Jonathan stood in the cool twilight, thinking that he should start his campfire. The prowling cat would like that even less.

The first real sense of urgency had touched Jonathan—the

need to have his house built as quickly as possible. He had been planning only on protecting himself from the cold of winter, for which there was plenty of time, but now he had begun thinking of other sorts of protection the house would offer.

*Where were the Blackfoot raiding this year, for instance?* he thought as he crouched to build his fire. He had no way to hear the rumors, the accounts of the rogue tribe's rovings. For the first time he began to regret his complete isolation in the mountains, to feel the need for some companion.

It was early in the morning of his fourteenth day on Shywater, with the dew still on the grass as a red sun crested the eastern horizon, that his sense of unease was given a second jog. It happened as he was transferring the last of his goods into the cupboard in the mostly finished house—only the roof and interior were incomplete—that he saw the tawny flash of movement in the deep forest. It flickered past his vision like a shadowy illusion, but there was substance to it, he knew. The prowling puma must be eliminated before it became too habituated to the area. Sooner or later when the winter snows made its hunting more difficult, the cat's thoughts were bound to focus on Jonathan's two horses, despite the man-presence it must have noted by now. Desperation emboldens recklessness.

Neglecting the remainder of his plan for the day, which had included using horse power to place the roof beams, Jonathan picked up his Hawken and trudged warily into the woods. The big cat had to be driven off or killed. It had already cheated Jonathan of a fine fat buck deer the week before. The cougar was a worrisome presence at least.

Even more troubling were the tracks Jonathan discovered as he searched the forest floor for cougar tracks. Imprinted clearly in a ring of soft dark earth beneath the pines were the prints of Indian moccasins. He followed these for a short distance before the tracks became lost among a rocky stretch of the trail. Then he gave up and crouched, frowning.

Who then? A Blackfoot watching for plunder or a scalp? The wild idea struck him that perhaps Fire Sky had returned, seeking revenge and the return of his pony. Simply some aimlessly wandering man? He did not think so. Whoever it was he had been skulking through the woods, not approaching the house as a friend.

The next day and the six that followed, Jonathan worked in some haste, his Hawken never far from his grip, his eyes constantly shifting to the forest verge. The loyal gray horse, by far the more tolerant of his two mounts, he used to tow entire logs onto the peaked roof of the house, while Jonathan scrambled to place them on fixed pegs. He did not like having to work like that, his attention always diverted, but there was a watch to keep—for the wild things, both animal and human, and his survival depended on it.

It was fortunate that fear and anxiety had driven him to such a pace, he reflected later, for the clouds to the north were building and growing menacingly closer, although it was still only the middle of September. The wind gusted heavily as he stood on the porch of his house, tugging at his shirt sleeves, chilling his perspiring body, but the last log had been set. There was a variety of chinking yet to do, but his house was secure, and he thought as he entered through the split pine door, it was warm, a safe haven from the wilds beyond.

He dropped the heavy bar across the door he had fashioned from the planks of the cart bed, and walked to the fire glowing brightly, still weaving crimson and gold tendrils of flame beneath the heavy black iron pot; Jonathan had regretted buying the pot from the traders due to its size and cost, but since then he had found it indispensable. At any given time, a few pounds of dried red beans and venison were simmering over the fire. There was always something to eat, no matter how inferior the meal.

There was his bed in one corner, an awkward-appearing contraption fashioned from four pine logs that acted as uprights, two split rails, and webbing made of leather provided by the deer he had hunted. Over this was his bison hide and the bearskin. The bed might suit no one else in this world, but when Jonathan tumbled into it after a day's grueling labor, his stomach filled with his own warm, inexpert cooking, he never tossed and turned, worrying about tomorrow, but slept in a cocoon of warm satisfaction with his progress. Sometimes little enough is plenty.

The following morning, feeling that his heavy work was finished for the time being, he lightheartedly began building an enclosure and the roughest sort of lean-to shelter for his horses, both of which watched his endeavors with curiosity. He was not concerned with their wandering, for they had always remained before, only going to the creek to drink, but the saplings erected as a poor pen might be enough to deter any prowling wild beasts. The paint pony, still without a name, did raise a furious uproar when anything like a skulking coyote neared it, but a little more security might be helpful. Besides, it was light work and Jonathan was in no mood for muscling logs around. That was done with! He reflected briefly and pridefully on that.

Finished for the day, he stood for a minute looking out across the long, funnel-shaped valley and its golden grass, the slender ribbon of the creek making its way to the far-off places, the orange-tinted western sky and the ominous, but no longer menacing, black clouds slogging their way southward, their bulk blocking out the view of the far Tetons. He found himself satisfied with his progress, with his life, small as it might seem to others.

In the morning he had little planned. He would bring buckets full of mud from the creek bottom, and take care of closing the few chinks he had noticed. After that, with deer hanging, and no need to go hunting, he would organize his pantry and hard supplies, preparing for the long winter to come.

And in the spring? He no longer worried about the coming times. He was not planning on returning to the site of the Rendezvous. There was no reason at all to do so. He considered he might like to visit with Calvin Gunnert, but that conversation would most likely be concluded after only an hour or two, neither man having much to say. No, that was all a part of the old world. He would be better off planning and testing the feasibility of building feeder dams and ponds on the Shywater so as to conserve enough water to be used for other purposes. He could grow beans, squash, and corn when he had a steady source of irrigation. And he considered other food crops. He had been saving his apple seeds—these took a very long time to grow into fruit-bearing trees, but then, what hurry was Jonathan in?

He ate a small meal that evening, following his supper with a cup of pine-needle tea, a necessary addition to any diet in the wild country where scurvy remained a possibility.

He was swinging the kettle away from the fire, preparing for bed, when the paint pony whickered loudly, not with great alarm, it seemed, but with the warning that someone, something was prowling.

Jonathan retrieved his Hawken, opened the plank door, and stepped out into the cold, starry night. He saw nothing at first, and then the stealthy shadow separated itself from the general darkness and walked silently toward him.

"Who's that?" he challenged.

"Only me, my husband."

Jonathan paused, befuddled; then, as the visitor approached, he saw that she was feminine, quite small and recognizable. He groaned inwardly. A medium-sized yellow dog slunk forward at her heels. Now, in the glow of firelight, he could make out her features. It was the Crow woman, the one Shaw-at-Duan had given to him after the shooting match challenge.

Her words were halting, garbled by a heavy accent.

"I have come for you to want me. You have made a fine lodge." She nodded as if quite pleased with herself, her English. Her eyes were huge, fire-bright, her mouth slightly curved as if waiting to smile but afraid to do so.

"What are you doing here?" Jonathan demanded in a voice that sounded cruel even to his own ears.

"You have made a fine lodge, husband," she said again, giving Jonathan a fair idea of how much English she had learned in the past months.

"Thank you. It is a fine lodge—for one man. You must go back to wherever you have been."

"I am with the Reverend Blaylock, husband. He offers shelter for unfortunates."

She seemed proud of that last bit of information, obviously transmitted from one of the Reverend Mr. Blaylock's speeches.

Jonathan looked around at the night. The skies were beginning to blow coldly and clot with darkly massed, tumbling clouds.

"Come inside," Jonathan said, relenting. He would have done that little for anyone else.

"Thank you, my husband," the woman said, bowing slightly and following him inside.

She stood, hands folded, in the center of the room, looking around approvingly.

Jonathan stowed his Hawken and sagged onto his bed. He looked the girl up and down, tried to read her wide dark eyes, failed, and jumped right in, saying, "Look. Whoever you are—see? I don't even know your name—we have to get this straight first: I am not your husband; I don't want a wife. You have to go home."

"Is this not my home?" she asked very carefully, enunciating each word as if reading from a school lesson. The yellow dog had seated itself at her side, slobbering heavily, watching Jonathan with hopeful eyes.

Jonathan repeated more forcefully: "I am not your husband! You have to go away. Go back to wherever you have been."

"You are my husband. My . . ." She fumbled for a word. "My father gave me to you."

Jonathan rubbed his forehead with the heel of his hand. He felt sorry for the girl, but could do nothing for her—not even explain matters. "Go back to Reverend Blaylock."

"Now I have found you," she said, exasperating Jonathan.

Maybe the girl knew more English than she was letting on. She had had—what?—five or six months of intensive lessons in it. He tried another tack.

"What's the yellow dog's name?" he asked as the cur began wagging its tail loudly, whacking it against the floor of the cabin.

"Yellow dog?" the girl asked brightly, placing her small hand on its wide skull.

"Yes, what is the yellow dog's name?"

For a moment she considered the question thoughtfully. "Yellow Dog," she answered finally, patting its broad head. She smiled briefly, brightly, at Jonathan, an expression of mingled hope and misunderstanding. He gave it up.

"You have to go home."

"I am home," she said almost sharply. "My husband, his lodge—"

"I am not your husband," Jonathan said, coming sharply to his feet. He ran his hand back over his hair. Her eyes were still hopeful, though she was obviously hurt by his response.

She answered with disturbing ambiguity. "I am a good girl. I learn English. I will learn more English tomorrow." Another lesson from Blaylock's home for the disadvantaged. Was that it?

Did the woman think she had now learned enough of the language to make her husband accept her? Jonathan looked down into her eyes, which now struck him as pathetic, fearful, a child's, as she watched her dream fade away. He had to bolster himself to look away and tell her once more.

"I am not your husband; you have to go away. Leave!" He kicked out at nothing, caught the corner of the bed with his toe. "And take Yellow Dog with you." He made unmistakable shooing motions with his hands. "Just go. There is nothing for you here." She would be much better off with the Reverend Blaylock, anyway. They had teachers and food and at least a few other young Crow people she could be with. He strode to the door, deliberately chilling his heart to the girl's sadly expressive eyes.

"Get out!" he roared and then halted her as she trudged forward to obey. Outside it was roaring with thunder. Lightning flickered, playing among the dark clouds, and a heavy rain had begun, driven down by a tormenting wind.

"You can't go out there," he said, turning his back to the door to close it. "Not in that weather. I don't know how far you would have to walk, but it's obviously too far for anyone." He paused and seated himself on the bed again, rubbing his thick-knuckled hands together. The girl watched him with a sort of uncertain fear.

Jonathan decided. "You may stay here. For one night only!" He held up a finger and the girl nodded. "In the morning I expect you to go—you and Yellow Dog both."

He decided to act as if the girl had already gone, that he was alone in his cabin. As the fire burned itself down to dully glowing red and yellow coals, Jonathan undressed and rolled into his bed, pulling the bearskin up over him. The girl was an Indian, she had slept in worse conditions. She had the warmth of the still glowing fireplace; there was a roof over her head that leaked only a little. Let her make the best of it.

It was near the hour of midnight with the storm still blustery, the night dark and cold, when Jonathan rolled over in his bed and found himself not alone. Someone soft, warm, and trembling was sharing his bed. He did not pause to analyze the situation. The night would be long and cold, and under his bearskin it was quite warm and very pleasant indeed.

A brilliant red glow touched Jonathan's eyes the following morning. How? He sat up in bed and shook his head. There was dawn light bleeding through the slightly ajar heavy door to the cabin. Had he neglected to drop the bar? Unthinkable. As his head cleared itself of the night fog, he realized he was alone. He had been alone on many mornings, but this was a different sort of aloneness. It was loneliness. He sat up as in a daze.

Getting to his feet, he walked toward the door in confusion. This made no sense, but then again it did. Something had happened during the night, and now he felt as if a half of his heart was missing. That should not be, could not be, but it was. There were tracks in the mud beyond the porch. They explained matters clearly. The storm had broken. The yellow dog was gone.

His wife was gone.

# Chapter Five

## The French Visitor

The winter started early and remained hard. On fine days Jonathan would return to his light groundskeeping, which included making the horses' lean-to more secure and weatherproof. The creek was an ice-fringed trickle flowing with uncertainty across the snow fields. It was fine weather for trapping, Jonathan reflected on such days. The pelts would be prime this year, thick and rich.

But he was no longer in that trade. For better or worse, he was a homesteader on some of the most desolate land on the continent. The grass was smothered in snow, and he had to wonder how long the forage he had mowed for the horses would last. Game animals were fewer, and he once went four days before he found a mule deer to take down. His firewood was also not as plentiful as it had been since he was forced to keep his fire burning day and night.

Well, what was there to complain about? He had anticipated all of this, expected it, but the harsh reality of this new life was still daunting. Jonathan told himself it was only his first winter alone. He would take stronger measures in the future to prevent a recurrence.

On the days and nights when the snow swirled down in heavy blankets, there was not much to be done except a trifling bit of cosmetic work on the cabin's interior, which seemed trivial and not worth his while. He wished for someone to talk to, even old

Gunnert, whose tales he must have heard a hundred times. He had always dreaded these days in their high-up cabin when he and Calvin had been penned in by heavy snow, unable to even open the door to go out. Now he decided there was little worse than being snowbound alone.

Inevitably he thought of his "wife," knowing that such thoughts were foolish. He even considered going to find her one lonesome day, but he did not even know where Reverend Blaylock's rescue mission was located, probably miles away. He could hardly jump onto his horse and start riding aimlessly across the long snowfields with more storms continuing to settle in. He'd had his chance with her; he counseled himself that he had made the correct decision in sending her away from him.

But at times he had to wonder and doubt that a man was ever meant to be alone.

One night a sound awakened him, the close snapping of a tree limb, he thought, and he leaped from his bed and went to the door, looking out hopefully into an opaque, swirling world. She was not there, of course. Why would she ever return? He had beaten her down like a dog, snuffing out her single hope of finding home and husband.

Shaking that thought, which now seemed shameful, aside, he returned to his empty bed.

One day in what he judged to be early December—he had long since quit keeping a tally of the passing days—Jonathan heard the bellicose whickering of the paint pony, a sure sign of an intruder, and he went to the door with his Hawken rifle. He opened the door to a stormy day. The snow was three feet deep in the yard, swirling down in a heavy veil. And through the tangle and twist of the storm he saw a solitary figure tramping his heavy way toward the house.

"Hallo, the house!" the man walking his way called out, stopping briefly in his tracks as he saw Jonathan in the doorway. "Is it all right to come ahead?"

Jonathan did not recognize the oddly accented voice, or the figure who had shouted, but this was no time and place to be overly cautious.

"You'd better come ahead or freeze," he called out.

*"Tres bien!"* the man called back, identifying himself as a Frenchman.

Jonathan frowned and stood waiting in the doorway, the cold wind twisting his hair as the man, making heavy going of it, plodded on through the snow.

"Come in," Jonathan said as the man reached the porch. "I'm losing heat through this door."

The stranger entered the room and went directly to the fire. Removing his heavy coat, he turned one of Jonathan's puncheon chairs to face the warmth of the hearth. The two chairs and accompanying table had taken Jonathan a month's work to fashion. The result had been unsatisfying, but the furniture was serviceable and strong—he expected few visitors to criticize his skills.

The man's coat, now hung on an iron hook on the wall of the cabin, was unique enough to pique notice. Of some heavy dark fabric, it was lined with sable. The hat his visitor had placed over it was odd as well. Wide brimmed, soft appearing, it was lined with the same fur. There was a shiny blue band around its crown. So, the Frenchman, whoever he was, was not a man of the mountains nor, apparently, a French-Canadian.

"If you'd like some coffee, I can boil some up in little enough time," Jonathan said as the man, warming himself, remained silent.

"Excellent—you don't have tea, I don't suppose."

"Only pine-needle tea, and you wouldn't like the flavor much—I know I don't."

"Coffee would be fine," the Frenchman said. He was young,

perhaps a few years Jonathan's senior, brown haired, even featured, with clear blue eyes. Handsome, Jonathan supposed, though he never took notice of other men with that consideration. Dipping already-ground coffee from his sack, he scooped a roughly measured amount into his small, one-quart pot.

"You picked an odd day to go out wandering," Jonathan said, seating himself in the other rough chair across the table.

"I lost my horse. This morning was nearly calm; I thought I could make up some ground," the Frenchman said thoughtfully. He turned to face Jonathan across the table. "A man has done me a serious wrong, you see. I once boasted that I would find him if I had to ride to hell to do so. I really didn't have an idea how big this country was! I thought I did, but it seems to go on forever. And the mountains! They defy a man."

"Yes," said Jonathan, who had never been more than a hundred miles from where they now sat. He had never felt the need to.

All right—so the man was no Canuck; he was a wandering European looking for someone who had wronged him, searching across the vast American West. It seemed an impossible task.

The coffee began to boil and Jonathan went to his cupboard to bring out his only two tin cups, which he placed on the table. "How long have you been looking, Mr. . . . ?"

"Excuse my rudeness! I have not even introduced myself, have I? My thoughts were so far away." Jonathan waved off the apology, and the man went on, rising and offering his hand. "I am Louis L'Enfant—perhaps the family name is familiar to you?"

"No, sorry."

"Oh, well—fame is always fleeting, is it not?" He added dismally, "And even more so is fortune."

The young Frenchman was weighted down with troubles, it

seemed, but Jonathan did not need to hear them. For now he rose again to his feet, poured coffee for the two of them, and listened to the storm raging beyond the walls, a very heavy wind indeed.

"I saw that you have two horses," the Frenchman said. "Would you be willing to part with one of them?"

"No. Absolutely not."

"I felt compelled to ask. How long can a man travel afoot in this country? Do you know of anyone nearby who might have an animal to sell?"

"Afraid not. I don't really even know of anybody who lives nearby at all."

"A town, perhaps? A ranch? A trading post?"

Jonathan shook his head with each question. He told Louis L'Enfant, "I am the only human being around for fifty miles, and I like it that way. Now there is some sort of Christian rescue mission, but I can't tell you where it is. It must be over the next ridge and south quite a way. They don't have any horses, either, I don't believe."

"Alas," the Frenchman said. "I truly am in the wilderness."

"You truly are," Jonathan said, sparing some sympathy for the ill-equipped man. He walked to the door, briefly opened it to the cutting wind, and closed it again quickly.

"I'll tell you this, Louis, wherever you hoped to be on this night, you are not going to make it. You'll have to stay with me."

"Is there a place I can stay?"

"You're here already. This house is small, but it's large enough to shelter two men. I'll not send any man out on a night like this. If you're inexperienced, it would be the same as a death warrant."

Louis was silent for a moment, turning his coffee cup in his hands. "I thank you, my friend. May I have your name as well?"

"It's Jonathan Byrd," was Jonathan's answer.

"And your estate, does it have a name?"

Jonathan blinked at having his claim termed that, but only replied. "Jonathan Byrd of Shywater."

They spoke of many things that night. For his part, Jonathan was pleased with the company. Through Louis's accented English, with his imperfect knowledge of international affairs and history, Jonathan came to understand this much: Louis's father had been quite a well-known man, Pierre L'Enfant, the architect who had designed Washington, D.C., for the federal government. In the course of time, L'Enfant failed to receive payment for his years of work and died in virtual poverty. He had only around forty dollars at the time of his death.

This was the result of the somewhat complicated machinations of two men: Abel Robert Avery, a French monarchist; and a thief named La Fortune.

Louis had many details, most of which Jonathan could not follow, such as La Fortune's association with the Sixth Coalition. Jonathan listened with interest, but most of the story went way over his head. At any rate, after Pierre had died in Maryland, Avery and La Fortune succeeded in appropriating the L'Enfant family land outside of New Orleans, Louisiana, chiefly because the two brought suit claiming the large chunk of land had never been included in the Louisiana Purchase and that, anyway, the Purchase itself was illegal because of Napoleon's uncertain status at the time. The court obviously could not negate the Louisiana Purchase, but eventually, based on the flimsy evidence of forged legal documents, all written in French, the court ended with Avery and La Fortune in possession of a thousand bottomland acres in Louisiana in addition to the L'Enfant family plantation house.

"All rigged," Louis exploded as they sat at the table. "All spurious. Mother died as she appealed to Washington, D.C., for which my father had performed such a great service, as well as to Paris. Who was there to listen to her in either place? Washington said it could not interfere in a court decision; in Paris they were trying very hard to forget the entire Napoleonic era.

"My mother passed away," Louis went on, having regained his temper. "Without a home in this country, my three sisters all sailed for France. I would not leave," Louis said proudly. "I had a small amount of money given to me by my mother and an enduring hatred. I vowed to spend the rest of my life, if necessary, meting out judgment to these two land pirates.

"La Fortune got himself killed in a duel after involving himself in another shady deal in New Orleans. Avery fled to the West after we had a confrontation. He knows I am after him, and so he will continue to run, but I will never give up my pursuit. Never!"

Jonathan did not understand the whole matter, nor did he know if he had received the entire truth from his visitor. It did not matter to him. He had heard worse stories.

The next day continued to be blanketed in falling snow, as did the next, and the next.

In the morning the two men would go out to tend to the horses in their lean-to accommodations. Jonathan thought Louis was admiring the tall, three-colored paint pony a little too much, but said nothing.

Louis tried to teach the French card game, aluette, to Jonathan, but Jonathan did not grasp the nuances of it and quickly grew bored with the game.

At some point during the evening after they had eaten their poor meal, the subject of the horse came up, and Jonathan went on to tell him the story of how he had come by it and of all that had happened afterward.

Louis's interest seemed to lift as the subject of Jonathan and Shaw-at-Duan's daughter was related to him. "Lovely is she?"

Louis asked. Apparently his French blood had been stirred.

"She is only a child," Jonathan protested.

"Yet, you let her spend the night in your bed." Louis, damn him, was smiling.

"It was a cold night; there was no place else for her to go."

"That is an old story, I believe. I have heard it many times." Louis continued to smile and leaned back from the table, both of his hands flat on its surface. "Where is the girl now, Jonathan?"

"I don't know. I sent her back to the orphans' shelter. I suppose she must be there still."

"You never felt curious enough to go see?"

"It's a long ride, wherever it is, and it's none of my business what has happened to her."

"Quite cavalier," Louis L'Enfant said in a low voice, and now, since the candle was guttering low and Jonathan's own ire had been lifted, Jonathan turned into his bed, Louis to his blankets beside the fire, hopefully to dream of other things.

Louis was gone in the morning. Jonathan's first thought upon opening the door wide to the stunningly bright, clear day was of his horses, but walking that way, Jonathan found that Louis L'Enfant was as much the gentleman as he appeared to be. Both of his horses remained where they had been, watching him over their flimsy fence. Deep footprints in the snow marked Louis's course away from the house toward the far pine hills.

Jonathan pitched the horses some of his dwindling supply of grass and wished L'Enfant luck on his impossible excursion.

The day was still, bright, the long snowfields glittering brilliantly as he returned to the silent house. It was not until the afternoon, when he was making up dough for his pan bread, that he found that L'Enfant had left payment for his lodging and meals. These glittered in the dusty flour canister: four gold forty-franc Napoleons. Jonathan removed the coins and dusted them off with a cloth. He had no idea how much they would be worth out here, or where a man could spend them. There were, of course, Frenchmen among the fur traders, and the coins could be spent there. Jonathan could use some supplies. But he had lived so poorly for so long that he thought it would hardly be worth going to Rendezvous, even if it were to be held here again the coming year.

Somehow he did not wish to return to such a setting. In some vague way it seemed like that would be an admission of failure. He knew that made no real sense, but so it seemed to him. It would be good to see Calvin again, but their conversation would not last for more than an hour or be extended by retelling tales of their past lives while Calvin Gunnert grew drunk and hearty with liquor-fueled joviality. Nor, he suspected, would Calvin long wish for Jonathan's sober company.

Jonathan tucked the gold coins away. Into every life sudden, unexpected trouble arrives. He would save the money for such a day. He already feared that, as much as he might wish it, this house, this home he had made for himself, would not last forever.

# Chapter Six

## Vashti and Angelica

Winter labored on toward spring, the time of the Rendezvous Jonathan would not be going to. Day after day passed in contented, if tedious, sameness. Then, with the shift in the wind from the north to the west, with the ever so gradual warming of the nights, summer announced itself as having struggled its way as far north as the high country.

The woman appeared in the middle of a sunny day as Jonathan Byrd, shirtless, worked at his haying in the long fields. He frowned, wiped at his eyes with his scarf, frowned again, and stood leaning on his scythe as his wife approached the house.

"You see I have returned," the woman, appearing taller, more womanly mature than he remembered, said.

"Yes," Jonathan said uncertainly, "you have."

"Do you have shade and something to drink to offer us?"

*Us?* Jonathan's eyes automatically strained across the funnel meadows toward the distant pine forest fearing possible trouble, but the woman was alone.

Or nearly alone. As she started on toward the cabin, walking ahead of him with long, silent strides, Jonathan was able to see the board tied to her back, a striped woolen blanket swaddling its tiny occupant.

"It was time to bring your daughter home to you. Don't tell us to go away again. She would not understand."

The woman's grasp of the English language had improved.

She must have devoted much study to it in the long months since he had last seen her. True, her voice had an odd, almost birdlike, lilt in it, enough to indicate she was not a native speaker, but it was not strong enough to even be called an accent.

The door was closed, but she opened it and preceded him into the house as if the cabin were hers as well. Without asking permission, she placed the baby, still on its board, onto his bed and sat down beside it.

"Well, as you see, we are back. What must be done first? Can you fashion a cradle, or should I prepare a hammock for the child?"

"Sort of rushing into things, aren't you?" Jonathan asked, dipping cool snow-melt water from the pail provided to drink from.

"I don't think so, no. I have thought long and hard, and I believe I have considered most things." She was close beside him now, and as she reached around to take the dipper from his hands, drinking from it, he had a sudden rush of warmth, and oddly, of *belonging.* "Excuse me, but I have walked long on this day," she said, "and I am very thirsty."

Jonathan turned away. Keeping his back to her as he stared down at the tiny person now occupying his bed, he asked, "Did you consider, for one thing, how I would feel about having you here, if I would allow it at all?"

She sat down on one of the puncheon chairs, still holding the dipper. "Oh, that," she said negligently. "There is no choice about that, is there? I am your wife and this is your daughter."

"I've told you before, you are not my wife!"

"My father told me I was. Did my father lie to me?"

"No, but . . ." Jonathan glanced around helplessly, looked into the huge dark, determined eyes, and said, "For one thing, there's no room for you. There's hardly room for one man."

"You will figure out what to do about that. Besides, I was raised in much smaller lodges. When the child is bigger she will spend all of her time outside in the sunshine and clean air. As she grows larger we won't even see her except at mealtimes. She will be wandering, running, climbing. For now she takes little space and no food to care for." She cupped her breasts and smiled at him impishly—or was it mockingly?

"How do I even know she is my child?" Jonathan asked.

"Who else's?" she asked, shocked. "I am your wife, Jonathan. That means much to me. No other man may ever touch me."

"You're kind of pleased with yourself, working this all out, aren't you?" he said, trying to remain gruff. The baby stirred. He saw a tiny fist lift and try to wipe away the edge of its blanket. Its eyes blinked open suddenly, tiny and dark, and seemed to settle on Jonathan's face, showing surprise. The baby girl made a small sound and her mother walked to the bed.

"Yes," she said as she sat beside the small child. "I am rather pleased."

"Yes," Jonathan said weakly as he watched her remove the infant and uncover it.

It was too much and too sudden for him to admit it to her, but as he watched her lift the infant to her bared breast and smile at Jonathan, he, too, found himself pleased with matters. The baby's mother was watching the tiny nursing baby and considering.

"At nights when playtime is over and in the winter, she will have to be taught. I will help her, though I still need to study myself. I have taken away from the sanctuary three books—one on English speaking, the Bible, and the other on white man's number work. What do you call that?"

"Do you mean arithmetic?" Jonathan asked.

"Yes, I could never say the word."

"Well, I can pronounce it. I just have trouble doing it."

Ciphering had never been one of his strong points—that had been Calvin's job when they were together

"Well, you know more than a baby does. You can help her and maybe learn some more yourself while you study. I must help her with the English, because there is still a lot I do not know. She will grow up very good at both."

"You've got everything planned out pretty well, don't you?"

"Yes," she said without false pride. "I am very good at that." A little sadly she said with more thoughtfulness, "I hope that taking those books from Reverend Blaylock's shelter was not a sin."

"Could be, I suppose, but it was only a small one if it was. You meant to do a right thing."

With the sundown light coloring the western skies to a gaudy burnt orange and vermilion above the mountains, flushing the yellow grass in the fields, Jonathan and the woman sat at the table, sipping at thin coffee, which she obviously had no taste for.

"You look troubled, Jonathan."

"Not deeply. I'm just out of my element. Do you realize you have never even told me your name?"

"Which name?" she asked, smiling.

"Your true name, the name you prefer a husband to call you," Jonathan said with some impatience. Was she deliberately trying to confuse him?

"It is no mystery," she answered, shrugging with one shoulder of her white elkskin costume. "The lady, Olive, who might be Reverend Blaylock's wife, told each of us there to pick a name from the Bible we wished to be called by. I found one I liked: Vashti. Olive said that that was the name of a bad woman in the Bible.

"I simply said that maybe a bad woman has had her name before, too, but she would not listen to me. It was because of the baby, I think. I think sometimes she thought the baby's father might even have been The Reverend Blaylock, since I was the oldest girl in the shelter, and there were no boys even close to my age. I don't know. I know she did not believe that I was married.

"Vashti was a bad name to her; that was all there was to it. She decided for me that my name would be Veronica. I don't know if that was a good woman's name or not. I do not know if Vashti was bad. I wonder why was she such a bad woman."

"You're asking the wrong man. I'm afraid I don't know much about the Bible."

"I tried reading it all, but those people were so far away and had such different ideas of life that I could not understand them well," the woman said.

"I had that trouble myself. Let's forget that. What name were you given at birth?"

"Vashti," the girl said, looking away toward the low-burning fire, glancing at the baby asleep in its elkskin hammock suspended from the roof beams. "That was why I was so pleased to find that name in the Bible, too."

"I understand that more than I understand Olive's way of thinking. What does Vashti mean?"

"Well, my true name is longer than that, but I was always called just Vashti." She paused, sipped at the coffee, made a bitter face at its taste, and looked up at Jonathan. "It means 'Encircling Heart.' "

Jonathan watched her in silence for a long minute, studying the wide amused eyes, the shadow of determination there, her full lips always hoping for the opportunity to smile, and finally replied, "I think that is a lovely name. I'll promise never to call you anything else."

His words seemed to calm her. She relaxed and glanced again at the child. "Now, what shall we call our daughter?"

Jonathan was slightly perplexed. "I don't know. I thought Indians were named by their mothers almost at birth, after the first memorable thing they saw after the baby was delivered. After a sky, a cloud, a skulking animal or a clumsy horse, the weather . . ."

"That is true for male babies. I must have known a dozen Red Clouds, and these men often change names after some exploit to commemorate their deeds, but the girl child is usually named by both parents, out of some hope for her future character or fortune."

"Like Encircling Heart?"

"Yes, just so," Vashti said with a little nod. "So what shall we name her, Jonathan?"

"I like the name Angelica," he answered with almost no time for consideration.

"That sounds nice? Does it mean anything?"

"Exactly what it sounds like, I always assumed." His voice lowered a little. "That was my mother's name—Angelica."

"Then we shall do that so that you may not forget your mother." Another pause followed. Outside they heard the paint pony whicker, but not with alarm. Stillness reigned across the valley. The evening sky was a wash of crimson and orange, now with a shadowing of purple. It was a lovely, mysterious, and altogether satisfying twilight.

"What can you tell me about your mother, Angelica?" Vashti asked.

"Not much. I barely knew her. I have only vague memories now, no real image of her face. She died when I was young, less than a year after my father passed away. I don't feel like talking about all of that now." His hand had reached across the table to enclose hers.

"Then we shall not," Vashti said. Now she did smile, but faintly, and with a bit of sorrowful understanding. "The day is losing to the night," she commented, looking out the door toward the approaching dusk.

"Yes, it always does," Jonathan said philosophically. "Shall we stand on the porch and watch the last color die?"

"If you wish," she said, rising from her chair, her coffee still unfinished. "Shall I bring Angelica along?"

"Yes," Jonathan said, although he was not sure why he was so certain it was the thing to do. It just was.

They went out and spent long minutes studying the shifting mass of colored sky, studying the long valley and the way the shadows settled in the deep woods beyond.

After a while, Vashti looked up at him, cradling the baby in her arms. "It is a good land, husband."

"Yes, it is," he replied, his eyes fixed on the distances, long, dark, and slumbering as the land awaited the dawn light. "It is ours," he said, slipping his arm around Vashti's slender shoulders. "We all have our names now," he said with a faint smile. "But we no longer need them, the three of us. We are simply The Byrds of Shywater."

Vashti leaned her head against his shoulder. "Yes. From now until the dawn, until tomorrow, through the summer into winter, until forever."

★ ★ ★ ★ ★

# Part Two: To the Far Mountains

★ ★ ★ ★ ★

# Chapter Seven

## Prairie of Despair

The day was all grayness, cold dripping water and mud inside and outside the square-cut sod house standing alone on the broad Kansas plain. Looking up from her constant mopping as the rolling skies plodded rather than passed by, Beryl Byrd saw that her husband had not risen from his chair in the only warm part of the soddy, in front of a fire smoldering and stinking with the fuel of buffalo chips. The smoke rose unfragrantly toward the smoke hole overhead, while water still leaked through it.

It had been raining for seven days and the weather would soon turn to snow and ice with nothing to look forward to on those long winter nights to come but silent deprivation.

Beryl Byrd started to straighten up from her back-breaking work and shout some scathing comment at her husband, but she knew there was nothing, really, that he could do to improve their situation. She began to hum an old song, softly, but not tunefully.

Annoyingly! Seth Byrd thought, not shifting his head to glance at his sorrowful wife. She was humming only to annoy him, he felt. She was working in near-darkness although it was only four o'clock. They had only a few candles remaining, and these must be saved for the dead of winter. They had only a small stack of buffalo chips remaining for fuel as well. When the winter set in, there would be no way of retrieving them from beneath the snow. Now they were only sodden masses that burned fitfully and provided little warmth or heat for cooking their small store of remaining provisions.

The baby, Precious Byrd, stirred in her cradle and gave out with a tiny lonesome cry.

What was the child's life to be? Seth wondered, although he knew—forty years of rugged, tragic life and an early death. Plains women did not last long. The weather, the poor diet, the unhappy burdens of marriage, the lack of laughter, all combined to smother them and drive them to a cold, early grave.

The door to the sod house opened only briefly and their son, Cason, slipped into the room, shivering and wet to the bone. The boy sat as near as possible to the fire, across the stone ring from his father. The boy's eyes were wide, his cheeks hollow, his demeanor prematurely sour and truculent. His face reflected none of the happiness a boy of twelve should have, but only the knowledge of what was to come: starvation, deprivation, hopelessness.

On the long, sagging, and bleak face of Seth Byrd, the same expression was reflected by the barely burning, smoky fire.

"I have made up my mind," Seth announced, not rising from his chair with inspired confidence, but causing it to appear as if he might do so. Some renewed vigor, some hopeful confidence, should have stirred him to rise, but it seemed there was no impetus behind his words but only weary hopefulness. Beryl glanced at her husband as she picked up the crying infant girl. She tried for a patient smile, and discovered such expressions were only a part of a barely remembered younger woman.

"We have to do something," Seth said slowly, carefully, as if talking to himself. His gaze was turned down toward his chest. Beryl made no answer. *That much* had been clear to everyone for a long while. No primitive Indian among the poorest of people lived the way they were forced to live. Year after year, living on the borderline of existence. Failed crops, failed schemes, failed lives.

"I been thinking about that letter that come through last year," Seth said to his chest. And how long had it taken that letter to reach them, traveling by means of coach and wagon, at the hands of strangers? The writer had mentioned summer was nearly upon them when he wrote it.

Of course, having any letter actually reach its destination across the long, rugged miles was something of a miracle. Mail was the most haphazard means of communication imaginable. Seth had read the letter to them at least a dozen times—for Beryl could not read, nor could the boy. There was no school around for a hundred miles. Any mail from the outside world was something to be treasured and reread, but Seth had worn out the letter as he wore out everything. Beryl knew the letter word for word.

"We got to go back to Missouri, to St. Jo," Seth said, looking up for the first time, his face almost haunted in the glow of firelight. "We will all die here."

"The farm!" Beryl exclaimed, placing the quieted child back in its cradle. "We can't just abandon it." The farm that had been Seth's promise of a good life to the younger Beryl when he had taken her for his wife all those years ago.

"The farm's already abandoned; it's already dead," Seth said, briefly letting his eyes, filled with fear, sorrow, embarrassment, guilt, and anger, meet hers.

"What's in St. Joseph?" Beryl asked, tired still, but vaguely hopeful. "For us? Except everything we gladly left to come out here."

"Why, everything," Seth said, finally rousing some emotions. "St. Joseph is the hub of the west. The big river reaching into the far places, with much traffic, endlessly. It's a place where the Oregon Trail can be accessed—all of those wagons rolling west every day, going to the new lands."

"Look where moving west got us," Beryl said, now showing some exasperation.

"I don't like boats," Cason said in a complaining voice. Seth glanced at his son with irritation. Children were not welcome to interrupt while their elders were speaking.

"You've never been on a boat," his mother said patiently.

"Don't butt in," Seth told Cason in a voice that was low, but carried an admonishing tone. Cason understood the implied threat and returned his sulky gaze to the fire. Precious had begun to stir again, but perhaps she too understood Seth's words and fell silent again. Seth's word was the law in his own house; there were no two ways about that.

"Going to St. Joseph seems risky business," Beryl said, thinking about how little she actually had to lose. What did one more of her husband's impractical schemes matter anyhow? "What has the old letter got to do with it?"

"Don't you remember it? Weren't you paying attention?"

Inattention was the exact opposite of Beryl's experience with the often repeated contents of the letter, but she said only, "What has that to do with us, Seth?" She sat down on one of the kitchen chairs, noticing that it was damp, and leaned forward, her hands clasped between her knees.

"No, you weren't listening at all," Seth decided, as if that gave him some sort of temporary superiority. "You have to try to understand."

"I'm trying to," Beryl said.

"My cousin has become a wealthy man—didn't you take that from the letter? I suppose his wealth came from the fur trade. Those men do very well. He has married, built a house, and now owns five square miles of land in the mountains! How many acres is that, Beryl?"

"I don't know. I'm not very good with figures."

"Well, just try to imagine it then. Picture five miles of land up and away. He certainly has room for other people to live there."

"We haven't a house there," Beryl pointed out.

"Well, I guess we'd have to stay with Jonathan and his wife in the meantime. I'm sure he'd help me out all he can."

"When's the last time you saw him?"

"Ages. Truthfully I barely remember him, but his mother was my father's sister. Family ties run deep."

"We weren't even invited," Beryl pointed out.

"Don't you see? That was exactly what Jonathan was doing. He has all that land and money and wants to share his good fortune with us. I'm probably his only living relative, after all that happened to us when he was young."

"We weren't invited," Beryl repeated stubbornly. The fire had burned down to a smudge pot. The smoke in the soddy was thicker than ever. Cason was attempting moodily to prod the fire to life again. Beryl was not trying to dampen her husband's ambitious plan to move to Wyoming. God knew, they had nothing here; she only wanted to have a clear and well-reasoned plan to consider. Not that she would have much choice if Seth Byrd had decided on what they were to do.

"Well, he won't turn us away from his door, that's for sure. He seems to have done fine in Wyoming; I figure I can do just as well."

"Where's Wyoming?" Cason asked, having gathered the nerve to speak up again. Seth scowled in the boy's direction. Beryl answered for her husband:

"It's far away to the north and west," she told him. "Maybe fifteen hundred miles from here."

Cason, who could not conceive of any such vast distance, nodded his head. His lips screwed together into a frown. "Then why are we going to go east if it's west of here?"

"Another one who doesn't listen to me," Seth said gruffly, then with more volume, "Can't you even understand that? You really aren't too bright, are you, Cason? I told you we have to go to St. Jo because that's where all the transport has its start.

"And we'll all have to get some sort of work there. The wagons won't be rolling up the Oregon Trail for maybe six months, when the snows have ended. By then we'd better have the money for supplies, a sturdy Conestoga wagon and a yoke of six oxen."

"Or, maybe we could go up the Missouri on a boat," Beryl said. She was already dreading the rigors of being in a wagon train for that long.

"I don't think boats upriver take passengers," Seth said. "Those are mostly merchant craft, like the ones the fur traders use."

"We could ask," Beryl suggested hopefully.

"On a boat we couldn't take all we need to start a new home. Food, iron goods, bedding . . . everything, practically. Tools . . ."

Beryl heard Seth mutter as if still mentally cataloging everything they would need in the far country, everything that must be left behind here, the cost of it all.

"I'm sure Jonathan would let you use his tools," Beryl said uncertainly.

"For how long? He'll need them himself, won't he? Besides," Seth said with a touch of his former dignity, "I'll not go to my cousin as a beggar, even though he has invited us to his spread."

Beryl glanced at Seth, his face red in the firelight. She did not remember the point in the letter when Jonathan Byrd had extended an invitation to them. Probably the man in Wyoming had merely had one of those occasional urges to contact what was left of his family, to indicate, even brag a little on, his own luck.

"You mean I'm going to get to work, too?" Cason Byrd asked.

"I mean you'll have to, son," Seth answered. "We're going to have to scrape up all the money we can just to outfit ourselves."

"I could go for a cowboy," Cason said hopefully. "There were two boys I met down at Acton Camp who were off for Texas to do that."

"You're not going to Texas, and you're not going to be a cowboy," Seth said in a tone that brooked no argument. "You're going to St. Jo with us. I want to know where your wages are going, and they're going straight into the family pool with whatever your mother and I can earn.

"I can sell the farm on the cheap—I'll take a big loss, of course, at this time of year—then we can head out before the big snows hit." He flicked a sorrowful glance at Beryl. "It has to be done, you know? Or we'll die here."

The roof continued to leak mud; the sky outside the sod house remained black and blustery; they each dragged themselves into their cold beds beside the dying fire and dreamed their different dreams for tomorrow.

# CHAPTER EIGHT

## The City of Lost Hopes

St. Joseph was filled with failed farmers; exploring men from the east; those involved in huge commercial endeavors, with wide-eyed pilgrims from the east; displaced Indians; poverty-stricken wanderers; and robust, wealthy businessmen—all moving west, all crowded up against the great Missouri River. There were tinsmiths, blacksmiths, hardware stores, restaurants, hotels, sellers of ladies' finery and men's rough work clothes, gunsmiths, and criminals.

The noise the town exhaled was banal, raucous, brassy, and exquisite. Men shouted, cursed, drank, and seemed to try to ride each other down with their horses and heavy wagons. The sidewalks were crowded narrow wooden lanes where people waited for their chance to run the gauntlet of the street.

"We'd better find us a place and fast," Seth announced before they had even stepped down from their swaying stagecoach. He was watching the milling crowds, the jumble of workers along the stinking, mammoth river wharves. "With all this activity, there's bound to be a lot of hiring down here. Let's start uptown and find someone who can tell us where to find lodging, Cason, grab up that trunk!"

"It's too heavy for the boy," Beryl said.

"He's big enough. I've got to carry the rest, and you've got your hands full."

Beryl looked down at the baby, Precious, in her arms and

nodded, saying nothing more. Precious had been very good on the first part of the journey, but now had a colicky cough and was restless, cold, and hungry. Cason failed in his first attempt to shoulder the trunk, dropped it, and tried again.

"Don't frown so, Beryl," Seth Byrd said. "I've brought him here to work; it's time he began learning what that means."

After weaving their way through the tangled throng for most of the morning, asking any passerby who seemed patient enough to stop and answer their questions, they found a single room in a low white frame building where it was not much quieter than it was outside. Seth took not a moment to settle in, help unpack, or take a deep breath.

"I'm going hunting for work. For every minute I delay, there's six others looking for the same job. The boy can help you for today," he added. "Come tomorrow he's going out with me to look for a job. Don't forget your part," he said sternly. "You'll have to find something as well, Beryl. We have to have everything done by spring melt, and that means gathering in as much money as we can before then."

"There's the baby," Beryl said.

"Well, of course I don't expect her to earn her way yet," Seth said in what Beryl supposed was supposed to be a joking tone. "Try to find some situation that will tolerate you having the child around."

He did not tell her what sort of situation that might be, or where she could possibly look. He was set on his own business, and Beryl could only stand in the center of the empty room and watch as her husband swaggered out confidently toward what he was certain would be success.

She sat down on the sagging, stripped wire bed and tried to comfort Precious. Cason stood staring out the fogged window at the bulk and gloom of St. Joseph while urgent, bunched crowds of people rushed past within inches of them.

How, Beryl wondered, could she already be missing the scant comfort of her sod house on the prairie? "Things will be better when we find Uncle Jonathan in the Wyoming country," she told Cason, who did not turn to face her.

Would things be better?

They still had a winter to endure and fifteen hundred miles yet to travel to find a man whom they only knew through a letter written long ago. Well, one thing at a time, Beryl thought as she again wrapped Precious in her blanket and placed the child aside, looking around to see what she could do to make this wretched place a home.

Seth Byrd stepped out into the cold streets just as it began to snow and people who had a place to go scurried toward shelter. Where, he wondered, should he begin looking for work. It did not matter, he decided. He was still young, still strong. If the bosses along the river needed someone to unload bales of cotton or wool, he could do that. He would accept any work that an unskilled man could do, but he had to find it quickly, he reflected gloomily as he eyed the sky. He had little enough money. The land they'd owned had sold for a pittance. In that country at this time of year it was a miracle it had sold at all. Beyond that they had the nickels and dimes Beryl had made selling their old ironware, her spinning wheel, and a set of dishes to their neighbors.

He started away from the river for no particular reason, stepped nearly into the path of a freight wagon with six-foot-tall wheels, and received a cursing for his inattention.

"I ought to knock your block off," the burly teamster driving the rig shouted at him.

"You ought to try it! I haven't had my exercise yet today."

Seth, out of stubborn pride, watched the wagon pull around the corner, shrugged, and started on his way. At the opposite sidewalk he found the teamster waiting, fists clenched. He had pulled around the corner, stepped down from his rig, and walked back.

"What'd you yell at me?" the man asked challengingly. He had bulky shoulders, a deep chest, and wore a leather hat and a belligerent expression on his meaty face.

"Maybe I was talking to your horses," Seth said, hardly afraid of a fight—he was very good at those, he knew—but he had places to go, and men to meet he had never seen before, who might be put off by torn clothes and a bruised face.

"All right," Seth said finally, "just let me pass, will you? I've things to do."

"Sure you do—but you're going to do them with your tail dragging," the teamster bragged. He smelled of raw whisky, Seth noted. People streamed past them, apparently used to such arguments in the big town, paying little attention. There was one almost scrawny-looking man with red hair showing beneath his hat brim who stopped to watch, but he was probably a man with nothing to do and nothing else to entertain him.

"I'm willing to walk away," Seth said in what was the closest to an apology he had ever come in his life.

The big man sneered. "Sure you are!" the teamster scoffed. "It's better than having to be dragged away, isn't it?"

The snow continued to fall and Seth Byrd's blood was heating up. He was not the man to back down from a challenge, never had been. He was not brought up in a way that made backing down acceptable.

"I'll give you the count of three," the teamster said, stepping forward so that his barrel chest nearly touched Seth's own. "Then, by God, you'll apologize, or I'll drive you down. One," he began.

"That's enough," Seth said. In a rage he threw himself at the larger man, slamming his right fist into the teamster's jaw, kneeing him in the groin, then throwing an uppercut punch that landed solidly on the big man's chin, twisting his jaw sideways. The teamster blinked like a great, confused fish out of water and fell on his back against the sidewalk.

Seth, breathing in deeply, stood over him, his fists still tightly clenched. "Get up and finish counting," he said to the bulky, still figure. Behind Seth someone laughed.

"Pretty handy, aren't you?" the man with the red hair said, smiling grimly.

"I get by."

"Like to work for me?" the stranger asked.

"Right now I'd like to work for anybody at any job I can get," Seth said honestly.

"A lot of men would just tell me 'no,' " the narrowly built stranger said. As he thrust his thumbs into the pockets of the red, embroidered vest he wore, Seth could make out the outer edge of a town constable's badge. "I'm in law enforcement, you see."

Seth was still panting hard. He smiled and thrust out his big hand. "Just tell me when to report and point me in the right direction," was his answer.

"Seth," Beryl gasped when he returned from the streets in less than an hour and gave her the word that he was now a part of St. Joseph's law enforcement team. "That sounds terribly dangerous!"

"I figure it is. I also figure I can handle it. Look how long I might have had to walk these streets without finding half as good a chance as this. Tomorrow I'll meet Huggins—he's chief constable—at his office, and pin on my badge. Then one of the more experienced constables will show me my rounds and instruct me on my duties. I tell you, it's a sweet, lucky circumstance to fall into, Beryl."

Looking at the floor, she muttered, "Men get killed on that job, Seth."

"Ah, they can't kill me! I've got places to go and things to do yet. Six months on this job, Beryl, and we'll be ready to travel west." He looked at Cason, who sat on the windowsill across the room. "That is, so long as the rest of us get to work, and soon."

"Shall I bother to unpack?" Beryl asked with light mockery. Seth paid her no attention. He lay down on the bare bed, staring at the faded ceiling with a look of satisfaction on his face as beyond the window snow swirled down coldly, unpromisingly.

Beryl walked the streets of St. Joseph day after day for over two weeks with no luck at finding work. She trudged through the fallen, dirty snow, seeking out dressmakers, laundries, restaurants, and once even a saloon, trying to find any job she could think of. Many of the people she met were congenial at first. When they asked where she meant to leave the child, she had no answer, and when she asked if she could bring it to work, the answer was always the same.

No.

Desperate, under Seth's glowering eyes, she listened again as he read the want ads in the newspaper to her. Not knowing the town was a disadvantage. On more than one occasion she started out for what might be a suitable job only to find it was too far from the center of the city to be reached.

In a bakery one morning she overheard two black women talking. "Miz Jasper—her bondswoman took off on her, ran away with some quadroon fellow with slicked-down hair. Don't know what she'll do now."

"That old lady don't need half as much help as she always lets on."

"Maybe not. The thing is she don't have anyone to talk to and her living alone in that big house, it kinda eats away at her."

Beryl gathered her courage and interrupted. "Excuse me. Where can I find Mrs. Jasper's house?"

Cason Byrd was exhausted at day's end after working in the sawmill for twelve hours. The labor itself was not so debilitating to him. What wore him out were the hours spent in being kidded, ordered around . . . and trying to catch a decent breath. Most of the workers wore scarves over their nose and mouths the day long as sawdust swirled from the singing, buzzing wheels of the big blades of the steam-powered saws. The two large saws were twelve feet in diameter, sharp as Satan and as unrelenting. These were the rip blades, which cleaved the long trees—mostly northern pine shipped downriver on huge timber rafts—and later ripped them again, the first step in the process of making finished lumber for which there was a great demand on the mostly treeless plains to the west.

Cason worked in another division of the huge manufacturing building, stacking finished boards by the thousands onto iron shelves for future transport. His slight distance from the whirring, cutting wheels did nothing to make the breathing any easier, and by his second day on the job he too adopted the bandanna as a necessary part of his work clothing. On a busy day it looked as if a hundred outlaws roamed the floor of the sawmill.

Sawdust lingered constantly in the air and coated the floor, shelves, and men.

After the huge saws fell silent, which they did each day from Monday through Saturday at precisely eight o'clock in the evening, Cason Byrd joined a small team—perhaps twenty men—in cleaning up the mounds of sawdust, bark, and tailings.

Mounting the trestle, they would clean the sharp precision blades of the saw and all of the running gears. Later, the technicians with their tool chests and cans of machine oil would sharpen and polish the demon circular blades for the following day. In the yard, men would begin unloading the logs from the huge timber wagons that had transported the fresh green lumber from the river ports. This operation could not be carried out in daylight when the saws were running. If the logs on the saw tram had not been exactly clamped and secured, there was the danger of a back kick, which could send a fifty-foot pine trunk flying across the yard with deadly menace.

Cason did not mind this night work so much. It was quiet after dark, lanterns burning brightly, and all of the bosses had gone home. There was no one yelling at him to speed up, slow down, be more careful. Instructions such as these he had learned to hate and fear growing up on his father's little farm where nothing he ever did was good enough to please him. Also at this time of the night, the workers could drop their masks and actually converse with their fellow workers—something that was confined during the daylight hours to gesturing and pointing, shrugging or glaring.

As at any job, most of the men were friendly enough, even the sullen, silent men whose lives seemed destined to end here. Those were mostly the older men who had already made their boasts of future accomplishments, only to see them wither and die on the floor of the sawmill, splintered and swept away with the dust. There were some young, energetic, and still-hopeful boys in the mill. Most were amiable if distant, as if they were watching their doubtful futures creep toward them.

Thomas Pearl was an optimist when it came to his own life. Cason did not like the young, bright-eyed man with his pink cheeks and thin, arrogant mustache. As they swept out under the conveyer, Pearl smiled and without being prodded, announced, "I mean to have a place like this for my own one day. Not necessarily a sawmill, you understand, but some enterprise a man can be proud of."

Cason didn't answer. He looked at Pearl, who was not much

in the way of muscle, whose trousers were out at one knee. Didn't the kid know how the world worked yet?

"Ownership is the only sensible road to travel," Thomas Pearl said as if he believed his own words. "Look around here. The lumberjacks in the north woods make nothing for their labor, nor do the timber barge crews. And they run the risk of having a hundred-foot tree falling on them or running up on a reef and capsizing! Does our lead saw man make enough money? He doesn't go home to a white mansion like the bosses do, I'll guarantee you. It's those who control the means of production who get rich—ask any economist."

"I don't know any," Cason Byrd said with a little irritation. Straightening up beneath the feeder brackets, he had bumped his back on support iron. "Anyway, how can you make the money to buy if you aren't making any money working?"

"Patience and frugality," Pearl said as if he were some lecturing economist. "For example, where are you going to spend your money? I save almost every penny I earn, because I can see the bright future ahead."

"Good for you," Cason muttered. He, himself, was not going to save any money at all from his labors. It all had to go into the family pot, and was counted before it was dropped in. The way Cason saw it, he was working only for his father's dream, which seemed to be to buy a wagon and team and go . . . somewhere in the hazy, distant future.

If it were up to Cason, he would save enough money to buy a good saddle pony and then ride off toward the Texas lands to work cattle. Once he had said as much to Thomas Pearl, who had, predictably, laughed.

"That's no good, Cason. Don't you see? The same principle applies there. The boss might reap the profits, but they're none of your own," the perfect capitalist said.

Cason answered, "Me, I just want to make the dollar a day

men are making down there, to be free on the land, on my own, alone."

Cason stopped there to consider what he had said. Was that all he wanted? To be free of his father, to be alone where no man was looking over his shoulder, directing his every move? He pondered the thought, although the question was still moot at this point. He would not have any money, could not buy a saddle pony, could not ride to the Texas land. His fate had dimmed behind his father's decision. When spring came, Cason Byrd would be a reluctant, indentured laborer traveling the long, dusty trail to a wholly uncertain future of his father's choosing. He sliced his forearm rather badly on one of the massive ripsaw's blades on that night.

# Chapter Nine

## Mrs. Jasper and the Captain

The parlor was quiet and cool on this morning in Woodland Hills, as it always was, set apart from the tangled bustle of the city and its noisy, crowded ways. Beryl Byrd placed Precious in the crib Mrs. Jasper had had sent over from one of the finest shops in town, next to the exquisite French country-style settee upholstered with dark-blue velvet.

Mrs. Etta Jasper had no qualms about allowing the baby to visit while Beryl performed her own tasks, which were mostly light housekeeping. Beryl eventually concluded, as one of the women in the bakery had said, that the old widow was mostly in need of company. Etta Jasper was a woman with completely white hair, usually done up in a strange sort of bouffant. She had a tiny mouth, which she over-rouged, and twinkling periwinkle blue eyes. The house she lived in on Ash Street, a mile outside of town, was two-storied with a shake-shingled roof. The blue-gray house was not of any style familiar to Beryl, although its nautical influence was emphasized by the iron-ringed turret atop the house, at its south end. There were three gables, two in the front, and one at the north side of the place.

"For viewing the polar reaches," Etta had explained offhandedly and ambiguously one morning. Beryl had only nodded her incomprehension. There was a huge oil portrait of Etta's late husband hanging on the parlor wall. "The Captain," as she invariably referred to him. Etta had many stories to relate of

The Captain as a young man, and as an older experienced sailor who had wished to retire from the sea and had this house built for the two of them in St. Joseph.

Beryl, who had never seen and could barely imagine the sea, listened to these stories patiently. The old woman had a pleasant, dreamy voice when reminiscing, and the house was warm and safe. It was certainly more comforting to Precious than the noisy, crowded room they were living in downtown with neighbors on all sides, above and below, and with drunks or merely exuberant men roaming the streets at all hours.

"It must have been a pleasant life," Beryl said one day as she wound a skein of crimson yarn into a ball. She had never seen the woman knit, though she was always saying she was preparing to.

"Ah, it seems the best of life occurs to one only after the end is in view! We had hard times, Beryl, very hard times. But The Captain always had his eye firmly on providing for us. I hated his absences at sea, sorrowed over them, but he always did what he thought a man must do to provide." The old woman added, "I suppose that be what your man is trying to do."

"Yes, I suppose it is," Beryl answered, nearly sighing. However, Seth's goals always seemed far-distant, more nebulous than the far-sighted Captain's had been. "He's trying hard. Did I tell you he was a deputy town constable now?"

"Yes, you did," Etta replied. *More than once,* but then it seemed most women needed to continue praising their men. Etta was not alone in that particular compulsion. "Shall we have our tea now, Beryl? Then I believe I shall take my evening nap while you tend to Precious."

The older woman had risen to look down tenderly at the stirring baby in the white rattan cradle Mrs. Jasper herself had purchased. "So young, so beautiful," Etta murmured, taking the baby's fingers with her own. "I wish you weren't going away, Beryl."

"That's not for months yet," Beryl said, glancing toward the snowy property beyond the mullioned front window where shivering, naked elms stood. "The wagon trains won't leave at least until the last of March."

"Well," Etta said, straightening her night dress, "I suppose there's no choice after that. We women go where our men lead."

Yes, Beryl supposed. But where was Seth leading her, Cason, and Precious? Onto another piece of useless land, this one even more remote than the last primitive Mecca? One they would not even own. She was still pondering that as she left the warm confines of the Jasper house later that evening and stepped into the cold and savage dark, carrying the bundled Precious close to her breast. Life was carrying them somewhere, but where? The swirling snow seemed analogous to her confused course through life: tangled, twisting, ultimately doomed to defeat. She shook her head and walked on. Perhaps Etta had been right—the goodness of life could perhaps only be clearly viewed when one approached life's end. What did that mean for someone so young as Precious, who deserved warmth and comfort now and not cold uncertainty?

# Chapter Ten

## The Constable

Seth Byrd had caught the night shift this week. That meant plodding through the heavy snow on the streets and spending as much time as possible simply standing inside the local saloons. "You can tell 'em you're watching the place, Seth—doin' your duty, you know," the older, more experienced, constable, Vickers, had advised him. "What's the sense of freezin' outside when there's as much crime collected in the saloons as on the avenues? Besides, most bartenders will stand a couple of whiskies for the constables. Gettin' in their good graces, you know?"

So on this night, after plodding through the deep snow along four blocks of the empty, mostly dark Seventh Street, Seth pushed in through the green-painted door of the Lucky Lady Saloon and stood dripping snow-melt from his dark-blue uniform overcoat, teeth chattering, and let his eyes roam around the overflowing room. There were a lot of men there, hiding out from the bleak weather, from bleaker lives.

Seth had never been into this place before, only peeked in the noisy doorway, but he didn't need to introduce himself—the eight-pointed star he wore on his coat did that for him.

"Rotten night, ain't it, constable?" someone said at his side. Seth turned his head to see that the man who had approached him was short, round, his hair neatly pomaded, his gray suit slick.

"It is that," Seth answered without smiling. He had already adopted a lawman's reserve when greeting strangers.

"That's when we get the sort of crowd that comes early and stays late, too late for some of them." The man smiled broadly, uneasily, it seemed. "I'm Joseph Cruz. This is my establishment," Cruz said with a touch of pride. He thrust out a small, chunky hand. "I take it you're the new constable on this beat."

"Seth Byrd," he replied, gripping Cruz's chubby little hand.

"I had the feeling Bill Vickers wouldn't be around much longer. In St. Jo everybody's either coming or going. It seems some don't even stop long enough to draw a deep breath."

"Vickers got promoted to deputy chief," Seth told him.

"Did he now? Well, good for him. He's a good man. We always got along well . . ." Across the saloon a table toppled, followed by a spurt of rough language.

"Those some of the ones you say stay too long?" Seth asked. Cruz's face became an unhappy frown.

"Yes. That's Jed Keene and his two brothers. I wish they'd find themselves some other place to drink. Can't tell you how much glass and furniture they break every time they visit. They never offer to pay for any of it, and they've got plenty of money. Their father deals in hogs, owns that big slaughterhouse down along River Street."

Jed Keene threw a beer mug across the room, shattering it as Seth watched. The man was tall, rangy, and dressed in a blue suit.

"What did Bill Vickers used to do about them?" Seth asked, his own face a tight mask.

"If I asked, he'd show them the door, then throw them out," Cruz answered, " 'The weather be damned,' Bill used to say. 'If they can't behave themselves where it's warm, they must prefer being out in the snow.' "

"Is that what you're asking me to do right now?" Seth asked.

"Get rid of them for you?" As he asked, another glass was broken at the table that other patrons had turned upright.

"I know you're new around town . . ." Cruz said. He stuttered to silence.

"That's my job." Seth said. He did not want it to appear that he was not the man Bill Vickers had been, that he might not be up to the task of throwing the three rowdy brothers out of the Lucky Lady. "I'll move them along," Seth said with a tight nod.

There was a side door near where the three were whooping it up, Seth noticed. Good; he did not want to try to herd the troublemakers across the crowded room filled with gamblers, drinking men, and working girls. The Keene brothers, he saw as he approached them, were younger than they had appeared. Eighteen, nineteen years old. That probably was the reason for their rowdiness: they had been introduced early on to beer and hard liquor and did not understand that alcohol must be managed.

"Hello, boys," Seth said, announcing his arrival at the table. Three pairs of red, belligerent eyes were lifted to him, as was a mug of beer in what might have been meant as a mock salute.

"What the hell do you want?" Jed Keene demanded truculently.

"I don't want anything from you, but the management is requesting that you leave."

"That squirt, Cruz? Let him tell us that," one of the other brothers said.

"That's my job," Seth told them. "Notice this star I'm wearing?" Seth tapped it deliberately. "You must have seen one a time or two before."

"I could smell it," the third brother said. "They got a stink about them." His brother sniggered and took a deep drink of his beer. His gaze remained mockingly on Seth. Near them a few men had turned to watch the action; a few others had departed. Seth had no intention of turning this encounter into an exchange of barbs.

"Either leave, boys, or I'll take you along for a walk to the jailhouse."

"I don't feel like doing either one," Jed Keene said, "and I don't figure you can make us, Mr. Constable."

"Somebody open that door for me," Seth Byrd said, indicating the side door behind him. Somebody did so, and a blast of chilly air filled the over-warm, smoky saloon. Seth had already moved to carry out his commission. Grabbing Jed Keene roughly above the elbow, he simultaneously kicked his chair from under him. Seth held the staggering man up and propelled him out the door into the snow-deep alley.

The other brothers were quick to react, rushing to Jed's aid. As Jed went facedown in the alley, one of the brothers lunged at Seth from his left. Seth winged his elbow back, catching the boy on the liver. The kid on his right had his hand raised, a heavy beer mug in his grip. Seth used his right elbow, aimed higher to deliver a sharp blow to the kid's face, breaking his nose. Blood streamed from his nostrils as Seth kicked him out of the saloon to join his brother. The third one, holding his liver, ducked under Seth's arm and stood in the cold alley, bent over double at the waist. Seth slammed the door shut again.

One man called out, "Good job of it," but mostly the men returned immediately to their own business. Removing the Keene brothers was a small incident in a place like the Lucky Lady.

At the front door Cruz stood waiting, a smile on his flabby face. "Good job, Constable," he said, mopping his face with a linen handkerchief. "Bill Vickers couldn't have done any better. Let me stand you a couple of drinks at the bar, if you've got the time."

Seth thought of the deep snow outside, the gusting wind, and said gratefully. "I could use a couple of drinks." Besides, hadn't Bill Vickers as much as recommended such a course of action on these freezing nights?

St. Jo, he reflected as he was escorted to the bar by Joseph Cruz, wasn't really such a bad place. Seth drank a toast to his host, then turned his back to the bar and aimed an indulgent gaze toward the merrymakers. You couldn't really blame the men for wanting to kick up a little after working all day in the freezing cold outside. True, those troublemaking Keene brothers had stepped over the boundaries, but they were young men trying not to act their ages. Almost all of the rest of the saloon's clientele was simply hunkered down against the storm as people on this earth had always done in the warmest, safest place they could find.

No, St. Jo was not such a bad place. It had given him work, a respected position. Now the owner of the Lucky Lady had given him the added warmth of a few glasses of whisky for doing nothing more than his job. A few strangers had walked up to him and clapped a hand on his shoulder. Two of them had even bought him another drink.

Once Seth had felt obliged to step in between two men who were ready to fight and separate them, but that he did calmly and without much resistance from the drinking men who had probably not really wanted to fight anyway.

Returning to his spot along the bar, Seth drank again and stared through the blue fog of tobacco smoke at the smiling faces of men who were sipping their drinks and playing cards, talking in mostly low, cheerful tones. Once he had even sat in on a card game, encouraged by a smiling Cruz, and the night, which might have been a cold, numbing horror, passed in peaceful, companionable progression.

# Chapter Eleven

## Solutions and New Problems

Beryl Byrd stood at the window of the dark, bare room they now occupied—the third such place—and stared out at the constantly falling snow. Through the cold draperies she could see only two lights across the street, late-burning lamps welcoming some struggling storm-bound worker home to dinner. In the streets, traffic had ceased almost completely. The buggies could not roll through the drifted snow. Now and then a determined single rider, or a pair of men on horseback, would buck their way through the drifts, but that was about all. One certainly saw no pedestrians trying to breach the walls of snow. She thought of poor Seth out there on this night, wading his way through the wind and cold. At least back in the old sod house he would have had the meager comfort of his buffalo chip fire, of the four walls to shield him from the gusting wind.

She turned away from the window, holding tightly to the blue knitted shawl around her shoulders. The room was cold; everything in the world was desolate and cold. The icy touches of the storm's searching fingers even managed to reach into the room where she now sat and waited, feeling as if she were the last living person in the cold universe. Could Wyoming be colder?

She walked to the sagging bed and glanced down at Precious, sleeping uneasily in her cradle. Tucking the child in more tightly she lifted her eyes and thought of the clean, cozy parlor of Mrs.

Jasper's house. The old woman was also alone on this bitter night, perhaps staring out her upstairs window waiting for the ghost of The Captain to return. Mrs. Jasper had a lonely life, but was it any lonelier than Beryl's own?

Drawing her shawl still more tightly around her, Beryl searched the empty room with empty eyes. Sitting up more erectly as the thought occurred to her, she wondered suddenly if Seth would object to her spending her nights at Mrs. Jasper's home. She wasn't of much use to him as a wife just now anyway. He was out working somewhere at this moment and would drag in half-frozen and grumpy in the morning to go immediately to bed. Surely he would not wish for Precious to grow ill again. The little girl had already suffered through colic earlier in the year.

Mrs. Jasper would not object, or so Beryl speculated. She would have to ask Seth—if he would ever stay awake long enough to talk with her. They needed, all of them, to continue working until spring to outfit themselves for the trail west. What if Precious were to get sick again and Beryl had to quit her job? What was the sense in her walking the mile out to Ash Street, the mile back every day, carrying Precious—especially in this weather? She thought Seth could not object if she put the matter to him in reasonable terms. They barely saw each other anymore, anyway.

There was Cason to consider, of course. He had not come home this evening either. He had told her that he had made a few new friends at the sawmill, so perhaps he had stayed with one of them rather than trudging home to this cold, sad little room where they had to speak in whispers if his father was asleep. One night, she knew, Cason had decided just to sleep in a cozy spot he had discovered at the lumber mill. Sadly, Beryl wondered why Cason would want to come home now anyway. He had a steady job, friends. She knew he was resentful about handing over his entire pay packet to his father—but they had no choice about that, none of them. Oxen and horses were at a premium just now with all of the westward-bound travelers arriving in the city. The cost of provisions was high. Beryl had made do for a year on what a month's trail supplies would cost them. It was because that sort of provision had to be hand-tailored for the long trail, and Beryl had neither the goods nor the tools to make compressed vegetables and dried fruit or to make up such travel necessities as butter packets sealed in bread dough for reuse along the way.

No, they needed every cent to purchase these things from local purveyors who were mostly local farm wives with the time and a knowledge of the travelers' needs. They had been warned time and again about the folly of taking iron goods—kettles, pans, and stoves—along the Oregon Trail. These, she had heard said, were invitations to disaster on the long road already littered with such goods discarded where the land began to rise and fall sharply along the path of the pilgrims' wagons, and where river crossings must be traversed. Indians who had never so much as seen an iron pot were now wealthy with found items such as those. It sounded a dangerous trail indeed; perhaps they had not given the matter enough thought. But it was the course they were now set on, and they needed everything they could earn to survive on the way to Jonathan Byrd's land in the north country.

It was all too much to think about on this cold and lonely night, so Beryl threw herself back on the bed, covered herself with two of the old woolen blankets they had brought with them, stared up at the snow-speckled window, and closed her eyes to search for the respite of untroubled sleep.

Cason Byrd woke up, vaguely eager to face the day. He could not remember at first what had caused this pleasure. He and two other boys, Tom Pearl, the future capitalist, and a stick-thin younger fellow named Andy French had curled up in their blankets in a storeroom beside the steam turbines providing power to the sawmill's saws. It was warm there and cozy, warmer than their own homes, which none of the three felt like plodding through the snow to reach. They had talked of work, fallen to teasing each other about girls, and gone off to a peaceful, warm sleep.

Cason Byrd had made a purchase from Andy French the night before, which he now unrolled carefully from a spare blanket as he sat on the floor of the mill. He let the item simply rest on his lap for a while. It was glorious, a possession that raised Cason's status to manhood, at least in his own eyes. The door opened and the annoying Tom Pearl came in to find Cason still sitting cross-legged among the blankets. Andy French, who worked the early shift, was gone.

"We'd better get this room straightened up," Pearl said. "The boss might not like us sleeping in it, and we're liable to need it again before this winter's over." Pearl had bent over, picked up a blanket, and begun folding it. Suddenly he stopped, staring at the article on Cason's lap.

"What's that?" he asked, pointing.

"Isn't it a beauty?" Cason asked. "Andy sold it to me last night after you were asleep. What it is, my friend, is a Colt's model 1837 five-shot revolving pistol. It's less than a year old."

"Why did Andy sell it to you? I mean, where did he ever get it?"

Cason's expression was a subdued smirk. "I don't know and I don't care, Tom. I doubt that his mother gave it to him for Christmas. It doesn't matter. It's mine now. I only need to stock up on caps and balls, and I'll be all set."

"All set for what?" Tom Pearl asked a little timidly. The heavy pistol in Cason's hand was intimidating even when aimed at nothing.

"Well, for the Texas lands, of course. You know that's where I'm planning to go."

"You spoke of it," Tom said, returning to his task. "But I thought you were going to buy a horse first."

"Well, that's what I figured on, but it would be pretty expensive to buy a horse and gear around here. Besides, by the time I had ridden it all the way to Texas, it would be pretty well beat down, wouldn't you say. I've changed my mind. I'll take a boat downriver and make my way across from there."

"That sounds like a better way to go if you're determined," Tom Pearl said, folding another blanket, stacking it neatly in the corner of the room. "But what about your family and the trip west? Aren't you going? And what will your father say about you spending your money on a revolving pistol?"

"Nothing for now," Cason said. "For the last couple of months I have just taken my pay packet unopened and dropped it in this metal lock-box we have at home for our contributions."

"But he's bound to notice it sooner or later and want to know where the missing money is. He might give you a whipping like you never had before because you're holding out on the family."

"I suppose he might. That would just start me on my way sooner, Tom."

"I don't know," the cautious Tom Pearl said, folding up the last of their blankets. "It seems to me that it's a dangerous game you're playing."

"That's too bad. They're telling me I'm man enough to work, but not old enough to make my own decisions. I'm for Texas. What about you, Tom? Are you still going along with your family?"

"Oh, yes. I intend to find some good timbering country even if I have to wait until we reach Oregon. Then I'll hire a crew and set them to cutting. I'll find a few partners and we'll start our own sawmill—larger than this one," he said, waving his hands around. "A man who goes about it properly can make a fortune with sawn lumber in the northwest. It's as good as gold."

"I suppose so," was all that Cason had to say on the subject. He had to give it to Tom Pearl. Here he was without much money, with no timber and no crew to cut it, with no partners he knew of for this difficult project, yet he was determined, convinced he would become a wealthy man in no time. Cason did not have that kind of ambition. He was, in fact, glad he did not. He slipped the Colt's revolver in between the folded blankets as the morning whistle blew and started off to his work, his dreams swarming his mind.

The next night was no less stormy, no less cold than the ones previous. A shivering Seth Byrd, the collar of his blue constable's coat drawn up, tramped up onto the plank walk in front of the Lucky Lady, stamping the snow from his heavy boots. He glanced up and down the street, studying the drifted snow, watching for foot traffic, of which there was none, saw a man lurch toward the Lucky Lady's front door, and followed him into the smoky warmth of the saloon's shelter.

Joseph Cruz was not in evidence, but Seth did not need the help of the saloon's owner to find his way to the long bar. Unbuttoning his coat, Seth signaled to Willie Leroy, the balding, red-headed bartender, and was served a double bourbon. Leroy stood before him, watching, waiting as Seth drank it down.

"Waiting for something, Leroy?"

"It's customary to pay when you drink," the bartender said

almost apologetically.

"You've seen me with Cruz. He always picks up the tab, doesn't he?"

"Well, as you can see, Mr. Cruz isn't here right now," Leroy said, wiping a damp spot on the bar. "He never said nothing to me about that courtesy being considered as an open invitation for all the free booze you could drink."

Leroy looked down at the floor as he spoke, his face leery, as if he did not like speaking to the law about such matters. Seth Byrd simply stared at the man, his expression cold. Then he produced a few silver coins and slapped them on the bar as if saying, "Well damn you, then."

Seth had never thought of himself as a diplomat, but he probably could have handled that encounter better, he thought, as he went out again into the snowy night. The streets were still empty, the cold wind still gusting.

"Oh, the hell with it," Seth thought, and he returned to the bar. There he purchased a bottle of whisky and seated himself at a round table in the far corner, brooding over what he knew was an unintended snub.

By the time Seth left the Lucky Lady, returning to that cold white world outside, it was nearly time for him to return to the station and sign off his shift. The night was incredibly cold at this first hour before dawn and Seth wove his way gingerly across the stormy streets. Feeling more than a little unsteady, he stumbled to the icy ground while crossing Third Street. A few early-rising newspaper boys hooted at him. A cop in distress seems always to make people laugh and mock.

Seth pushed himself slowly to his knees from the snowy ground. Once on the soles of his feet, he started after the newsboys, meaning to teach them a lesson, but he slipped again as they dashed away, bundles of papers under their arms. He fell quite hard this time, catching his forehead on the edge of the sidewalk. He must have briefly passed out, for the morning sun was in his eyes when he again managed to rise, make his way onto the sidewalk and sit at the curb. A few men passed him on their way to work, and there were more comments made.

Seth Byrd was an hour late checking in, which did not go unnoticed. The day shift had already reported for duty. Bill Vickers, in his new role as deputy chief constable, was giving the men their assignments, reminding them of certain trouble spots. His eyes flickered to Seth as he staggered in, and braced himself upright against the wall to the office.

One knee of Seth's uniform trousers was torn out; his hair was wildly disarranged. He had lost his cap. After the day shift constables had filtered out of the room, sparing glances at Seth, who now sat on a wooden bench normally reserved for arrested men, Vickers slapped a logbook shut, placed a fountain pen neatly aside, rose, and walked to where Seth sat sagged on the bench.

"You're late, Constable Byrd."

"Yes, sir, I know it," Seth said, looking up with watery red eyes.

"Get into a fight, did you?" Vickers asked, seating himself beside Seth. When there was no answer, Bill Vickers reminded him, "You're still on probation as a constable, you know."

"I realize that."

"The chief doesn't like this; doesn't like it at all," Vickers said, watching the opposite wall.

"Surely you wouldn't report me for one night's mistake, Bill."

"It hasn't been just one night, Seth, not from what I've been told. I've kept quiet about it until now. They tell me you're at the Lucky Lady every night, trying to drink as much on the cuff as any paying customer."

"You told me once—!" Seth erupted.

"Yes, I told you once. I was trying to make your way a little more comfortable. I didn't mean for you to take up residence there."

"But you used to have one once in a while there yourself, Bill. What's the difference?"

"You just said it," Bill Vickers said, rising to his feet now. "Once in a while! Besides, I have eight years on the force. You—you're a new hire, a probationer. When I have men like Joseph Cruz coming into the station to complain, what can I do? I told him to cut you off, and he promised he would. But that didn't stop you from propping your feet up in the saloon with a bottle in your hand, trying to ride the storm out, providing no effort in return for the town's pay."

"All right," Seth said, unsure if he was angry or feeling guilty. "I'll bypass the place. I'll spend every shift out in the cold. Will that make everything all right?"

"I don't know," Bill Vickers said with some sympathy. "You understand, Seth, there are a lot of men without work in St. Jo right now. Constable is a pretty plush job for those who can stand up to the work. You can be easily replaced."

"But you wouldn't . . . ?"

"I wouldn't do anything, Seth. We've had citizen complaints about you. It's up to the chief now."

Seth tried to rise from the bench, failed, and was seated again as Bill Vickers walked away, shaking his head. Stunned by events, feeling affronted, Seth remained on the bench for another half hour as the constables, some escorting prisoners, bustled around him. He started to stand, to shout out how badly he had been treated, but the force of that impulse died rapidly. In the end he just rose heavily, shakily, to his feet and plodded out of the station. He needed to get home; he needed to sleep.

★ ★ ★ ★ ★

When Beryl Byrd reached home after her day's work at Mrs. Jasper's house, she found her husband, still fully dressed, sprawled on the bed. His mouth drooped slightly open. He was sound asleep. Placing Precious in her rough cradle, Beryl poked at her hair and went to the kitchen table. There was little light at this hour, so she lit a candle, placed it on the center of the table, and unlocked the strongbox to place the envelope with her wages inside. Cason, she saw, had already put his pay packet in the box. Seth had not. Perhaps he had his wages stuffed into his coat pocket still. Unusually, disturbingly, there was a half-empty bottle of whisky sitting on the floor beside their bed. Poor Seth; his work must have been very rugged and dangerous. Maybe he had felt the need for a quick drink after a cold night wrestling with criminals.

She wondered idly how much money they had saved in all. Spring was not that far distant, after all. She and Seth had made a rough budget out for their trail needs. How near were they to their goal?

The wagon and oxen were a prime consideration, of course. Earlier in the week Beryl had tried talking to one of the companies that specialized in outfitting westward-bound settlers. She had inquired about the possibility of acquiring a used Conestoga wagon in good shape to try to save some money.

The man she talked to had laughed. "Lady, the people who buy these prairie schooners and strike out on the Oregon Trail aren't likely to return them to us. And as far as being in good shape, any wagon that has traveled fifteen hundred miles out and fifteen hundred back wouldn't be fit for anything but firewood."

They also needed to have more than the absolute minimum of supplies with them. It was true there were few places to stop and reprovision, but Beryl had heard there were trading posts along their route where certain men were growing wealthy on overpriced goods. Well, she supposed, that was only right. The traders had to pay to have their supplies transported over the long trail to where their stores stood. There had to be profit in it for them as well.

Beryl counted the contents of the strongbox carefully once, and then counted it again.

They seemed hardly ahead of where they had been the week before. True, Seth had not yet added this week's pay, but on a somewhat guilty impulse, she looked into Cason's last pay packet and found it light. That was disturbing. Cason knew how much the entire family was counting on him to contribute what he could. Perhaps she would speak to him about that; perhaps not. She didn't wish to have a confrontation with him. She certainly did not want to start more trouble between him and his father.

Perhaps in the end Seth would realize that they would not be ready this spring and would delay the pilgrimage for another year, though he was fiery in his determination. Beryl would not have minded the waiting; she would have welcomed an extension of her time as caretaker for Mrs. Jasper. She enjoyed her days there, and the baby was always safe and warm. Beryl knew that infants did not always travel the long trail easily. Precious would be a year older next spring, and the going would be easier, less likely to contribute to the infant's illness. She knew Mrs. Jasper would be pleased if she stayed at her job.

But Seth . . . Seth had his mind made up, his program made mentally. She watched him now as he slept on the bed. He himself had a good position now with the city. Maybe he would be more amenable to the idea of remaining in St. Joseph for a while longer.

For now, after feeding and changing Precious, there was little for Beryl to do but to crawl into bed in the scant space Seth had left for her on the edge and try to sleep as the cold winds blew outside.

Seth Byrd awoke with massive cobwebs in his head. His mouth was dry; his tongue felt glued to the roof of his mouth. Opening his eyes hurt. The feeble sunlight from the gray skies beyond penetrated deep into his skull. With an effort, he fought through the headache and desire to sleep for another hundred years, although his sleep had been restless, and sat up on the side of the bed. His left hand clutched at his shirt, his right dangled toward the floor and brushed something cool, smooth, and familiar.

His fingers gripped the neck of the bottle eagerly, and he held the bottle in front of his eyes. Squinting at it, he saw that it was not empty. Well, it would be.

"The cause is the cure," Seth thought as he picked the whisky bottle up, uncorked it, and shakily poured the liquor into his mouth so greedily that it seemed to go directly to his throat, where it ignited a small fire, before descending to his stomach, where it threatened to turn it. Bile rose and he swallowed it down, forcing another swig of whisky into his stomach.

He then sat unmoving on the edge of the bed, watching the dull gloom of the winter light shining through the curtains. He only then noticed that Beryl and the baby were gone. He had been asleep so soundly that her rising, dressing, the baby's crying, could not have awakened him. She must have wondered why he had been abed so early the night before. Well, it would not matter; he would tell her about it later, dressing the story up a little, of course.

For today his course was set. He would dress, go out, and find another job, a better job.

One that involved only honest daytime work. For a moment

Seth considered the possibilities, but there were hundreds of jobs available in St. Jo, too many to think about. He raised a trembling hand and the bottle that it held to his lips and drank deeply. His headache seemed to have subsided somewhat. His stomach no longer turned over, but he was hardly ready to wash, dress, and go out into the snow. Not just yet. He decided to take the day in small stages. One thing at a time; only one thing.

The first thing was to get his hind legs under him and clear his mind. There were, by his reckoning, only two more drinks left in the whisky bottle. He doubted that was enough to get him started on his way, but it would be a further aid. He would go out and find himself another bottle of supplies, enough to finish his awakening and send him on his way tramping through the snow to look for work. He finished the bottle in one choking swallow.

The cause was the cure.

Rising finally, feeling a little shaky yet, Seth went to where the family lockbox was hidden. He would need at least a few dollars to help him make it through the cold, hungry day. He sorted out some change from the box, not feeling guilty or ashamed. A man can't steal from himself, can he? The money could quickly be replaced with the three of them working. At the worst, he would have to trim some inconsequential item or another from his budgeted supplies.

Going out into the snow, Seth thrust his hands deep into the pockets of his coat and trudged toward the riverfront where most of the city's businesses were located. Halfway along his legs began to feel rubbery and his vision became blurred. The dull throbbing of a headache re-awoke at the base of his skull. When he reached the Lucky Lady Saloon, he found it already humming with early drinkers. Seth glanced scornfully at the poor wretches. This was a habit with most of them; a way of life. The day bartender was unknown to Seth. He purchased a fresh bottle of whisky and decided to sit down for just a little while and let his legs revive and warm themselves.

Sitting alone, he poured a large amount of the amber liquor into a glass and sat back to comfortably nurse it. Around him a small, sad troupe of whiskered faces sat staring with bleary eyes at their own glasses, reaching for them with trembling hands. Seth pitied them. This was a different sort of men from those who haunted the Lucky Lady at night. These men were quiet, disinterested, surrendering to their fate, it seemed. Seth found he preferred them for company. They sat; they drank; they left. The bartender whistled as he wiped the glasses to a bright polish.

In one corner sat an older woman, her hair hennaed but badly arranged. She wore a dark shawl across the shoulders of her shabby dress. Her face was bloated and shrunken at the same time. Her eyes might have been made of opaque glass. She toyed with her glass of liquor, wanting it but apparently unwilling to see it completely emptied, not knowing where her next one might come from.

Feeling suddenly depressed, Seth corked his bottle, stuffed it into this coat pocket, rose, and went out into the bitter weather. He reminded himself that there was much to do on this day, and his excuse for not getting to it was now gone.

Reaching the dock, he saw a newly arrived steamboat with its tall, flower-petal stacks mooring. Its white paint seemed whiter than the new-fallen snow. There was gingerbread molding strung on the eaves of the passenger deck. Seth saw a man in a city suit and scarlet cravat standing at the rail of the second deck, two young women beside him, one on either arm. The women wore silk dresses, one of yellow, the other of a grass-green shade.

The young man—Seth guessed him to be either a riverboat gambler or some Louisiana cotton magnate—smiled fondly at each woman in turn.

Working men rolled barrels of molasses along the pier, and carried flour and vinegar, sugar and farm produce. A little farther along Seth saw a plain, flat-bottomed riverboat that smelled to high heaven, unloading a herd of hogs, which were then driven up a chute into a processing plant near at hand. One pig made its escape, and Seth took a minute to watch the beleaguered workers try to catch it again. The amusement didn't last long as one of the processors grabbed the pig by its hind legs and muscled it back into the chute as if this were an everyday thing, which it probably was.

Seth stepped a little way behind the corner of the gray meatpackers' building and unstopped his whisky bottle. After taking a little liquid courage, he determined it was time to start looking for work. He could not go home without having found a job.

Circling to the front of the building, he noticed a short line of hopeful work applicants standing there. He joined the queue.

"They pay much?" Seth asked the stout man in front of him in line. The man shrugged.

"Who cares? A man has to at least eat."

From the inside of the building the cries of terror-stricken hogs emanated, and a terrible stench continued to fill the air. The office, when Seth was finally admitted, was small, white, and smelled of cleaning disinfectant. Two young men sat behind the employment counter, passing papers between them and speaking. Seth watched as more than one man left, dejected.

Seth put on his best smile and stepped to the counter when it was his turn. One of the young men behind the desk looked up, smiled, and nudged his companion with his elbow. Both of them burst into laughter.

"Constables report to the back entrance!" Jed Keene said loudly. Seth blanched. He had forgotten that the Keene boys he had thrown out of the Lucky Lady were the sons of the slaughterhouse owner.

Both boys continued to laugh. Jed craned his neck and looked behind Seth, crooking a finger. "Next!" he called, and a bewildered man brushed past Seth Byrd to go to the employment window. Seth turned and went out, the hoots of the Keene boys still in his ears. Angrily he pushed through the employment line and tramped up the narrow street there. He paused at the next alleyway to duck inside it and uncork his bottle again. As the liquid warmth settled, Seth returned to the docks, feeling better.

To hell with the Keenes. Seth Byrd was not made for a slaughter man anyway.

He came to a warehouse with a neat little office attached, and glancing toward the river, saw a line of men marching from a riverboat toward the rear of the building with bales of furs on their shoulders. Seth decided to follow the working men. Passing through a service alley between two buildings, the men turned at a cross-alley and proceeded to a loading dock there.

Well, Seth thought, it was worth a try. Holding back for a minute, he took another swallow of fortification and then proceeded to the fur exchange building. He mounted the low wooden loading dock and found himself in front of a warehouse storeroom where furs of all sorts were being distributed along rows of racks. A heavy man carrying a shotgun approached him with suspicious eyes. That, too, he should have expected. The fur warehouse was more likely to concern itself with thievery than the slaughterhouse.

"Steady, friend," Seth said with whisky-bright bonhomie. "I just came around looking for work if I can find it."

The burly guard's expression said that if it were up to him, he wouldn't hire Seth if he owned the place. "I wouldn't know," the man muttered, still examining Seth with suspicious eyes.

"All that sort of business is taken care of around front in the office. I wouldn't think there's much of a chance unless you have a personal letter from Mr. John Jacob Astor."

Seth figured he was supposed to smile at that, so he contrived the expression for his interrogator.

"You'd better just amble along," the bulky guard said.

"I intend to," Seth replied. A line of men crowded past him, returning to the boat at the dock. He asked impulsively, "Tell me, is there anybody around who knows these north country trappers well?"

"Not me, that's for sure. I don't know if any of the riverboat crew does. They generally keep their distance from those mountain men. They're a rough bunch."

"Oh, well." Seth shrugged. Seeking to ingratiate himself, he said, "I've a cousin in the fur trade up Wyoming way."

The man with the gun briefly reappraised Seth, shrugged, and said, "There's nobody around who might know him. As I've said, the riverboat men generally steer clear of those mountain types. They're a shaggy, half-crazy bunch. I maybe could ask around—what'd you say your name was?"

"Byrd. Seth Byrd. My cousin's name is Jonathan Byrd. I thought maybe someone had met him up that way, being he's in the fur trade."

The guard shook his head heavily. "Not me, that's for sure. I've never been that far north. I like my indoor life here just fine."

Seth thought that remark required another smile, so he flashed one for the big man.

From one side of the aisle where he now stood, a younger man starting to go to fat, dressed in a brown town suit and red vest, appeared. He had small dark eyes and wore sideburns that trickled down his jaw. He strode toward them clutching a sheaf of papers and a pencil.

"I thought I heard voices," the new arrival said, "and the mention of a familiar name."

"Good morning, Mr. Pyle," the guard said. "This man here is named Byrd. He was asking about a relative of his." Seth and Pyle shook hands briefly.

"That's the name I thought I heard," Pyle replied. "Jonathan Byrd. Are you a relative of his?"

"Yes, I am. His cousin. I was wondering if someone here might have news about him."

"I haven't been upriver myself for years," Robert Pyle answered, "but I knew Jonathan. Not well, but I knew him. Mr. Byrd, would you have the time to step into my office for a moment? I'd be happy to answer any questions I can about Jonathan." He dismissed the guard with a small motion of his hand.

Seth followed the man along another corridor and they made their way to a small, uncluttered office with two wooden filing cabinets, and a blue ledger book on a scarred desk. Robert Pyle seated himself beside the desk, smiled, and looked steadily at Seth Byrd.

"You have been concerned about your cousin's well-being?"

"Well, Mr. Pyle, it's not exactly that, but we were planning on traveling his way. I wanted to make sure he was still there, still healthy, and well set up in his affairs."

"I see . . . Call me Robert, won't you? As I said, it's been some time since I've been into the north country myself. I gave it up for an easier, more settled way of life. I was a fur trapper, you see. It can be killing work. Now I grade and sort furs for Mr. Astor. I much prefer it."

"But I imagine it paid well while you were at it," Seth said, looking without interest around the office. He wanted another drink, but did not think that this was the time or place for that.

"It paid well," Robert Pyle said with a nod. "Most of the trappers tried to see how quickly they could spend it once a year at the Rendezvous."

"I'm not familiar with the term."

"It was a gathering held every year for the mutual benefit of the mountain men and the fur company traders. For the few years I was there, it was held in the meadows near Granger, Wyoming, though it's been moved around from time to time. The mountain men and even some Indians bring their take to the riverboat camp and trade what they have for cash, supplies, and whisky—a lot of whisky. They sing and dance while the fur boats are laden, and it seems that almost everyone goes home happy, though there have been some unhappy occurrences there."

"So Jonathan was among that crowd?"

Robert Pyle shook his head and began tugging at one sideburn. "The year I left was the first time I had ever seen him at one of the gatherings. It was more usual for him to stay at home in the far-up country and let his partner, a man named Calvin Gunnert, take care of the trade business."

"Saved himself a lot of money doing that, did he?"

"I wouldn't know about that, but it stands to reason. I never saw him spend any money until the day he was planning to leave. He bought my used cart and stocked up on supplies. He was going to strike out on his own, but not trapping."

"What then?" Seth asked. He felt he should know all of these things. He had a lot depending on Jonathan Byrd's past dealings.

"Well, from what Stinky—pardon me—a man named Reggie Foote told me, your cousin had staked himself out a five-mile-square piece of land, married a woman, and meant to build a house and settle down there.

"That's the word I had from him," Seth said. "Except—a wife? Where would he have found a woman out there to marry if the country is as rough and wild as you say?"

"That one? I saw her, but never did learn her name. Stinky didn't know it either. She was an Indian, a Mountain Crow. Stinky told me Jonathan won her as a prize in a shooting contest."

"Won a woman in a shooting contest? But . . ."

Pyle was nodding, "As I told you, things are different that far away from civilization. I've met many men who've purchased wives from the Indians. There's a man down at Harris Fork—that's a tiny settlement right on the Oregon Trail—who has himself three Shoshone wives. I've wondered about that from time to time," Robert Pyle said, contemplating the problems and possibilities of multiple wives.

"But that's really about all I can tell you, Mr. Byrd," Robert said, rising. "The last time I saw Jonathan, he was in good health, about to settle on his land, had a new bride, had made all the fortune he cared to make from those Rocky Mountains, and intended to build a house."

Seth rose as well, thoughtfully. He told Robert Pyle, "That's about all that I heard from him when I last heard. Except for him having a wife."

"Well, none of us is meant to live alone," Pyle said, opening the door for Seth. "For me, I prefer them with just a little powder and lace."

Seth felt like asking Pyle about the woman he had apparently found himself, but decided not to. He was feeling the urge to be outside once more, to help himself along with a quick swallow of liquor. But since it was what he had come for, he asked Pyle as they walked toward the loading dock, "Any chance of finding work here?"

Pyle shook his head. "I'm afraid there's not much of one, not if you don't already know something about the fur trade. Astor and the American Fur Company both are pretty strict about that. Unless you would like to go river boating. You could get a start on a fur expedition."

"I guess not," Seth, whose thoughts were already elsewhere, said. "I'm meaning to take my family up the long trail on a prairie schooner once this weather breaks."

"Going to visit Jonathan along the way?" Robert Pyle asked. They were standing on the loading dock. The cold wind lifted the flaps of the coat he wore and mussed his dark hair.

"I sure hope so," Seth replied. "It's what I have in mind."

The two men shook hands, and Seth slipped down to wander the alleyways again, stopping around the first corner to take a deep drink of whisky before starting toward home. This evening he was going to have to face Beryl with the news that he had lost his cushy job and had yet to find another, but he was hoping that somehow she would be more interested in what he had learned that day about Jonathan Byrd.

It was a little after five that evening when Beryl Byrd reached home with Precious after walking the snow-lined road from Mrs. Jasper's pleasant house on Ash Street. It seemed that the storm was finally breaking, but it was still terrifically cold on the dark streets. Precious was growing, and carrying her added weight made it more difficult to walk than when the baby was inside her. Constantly shifting Precious in her arms to her hips, the mile walk over ice and slush was treacherous and tiring. Twice she had been splashed by passing wagons, and once a trio of young men had paused to hoot something at her. She never paid any attention to that sort, but simply plodded ahead. They were only a part of the plague of cities.

Seth was asleep on the bed, though Beryl could see that he had been up and about that day. She placed Precious down and sat on the wooden chair, watching Seth. She looked around the poor rented room, longing for the comfortable warmth of Mrs. Jasper's parlor with its low burning fire in the hearth, the trinkets and ornaments scattered about, the sweeping draperies, The Captain's oversized portrait on the wall, Precious sleeping in her wicker cradle.

One night the weather had been so foul that Mrs. Jasper had not allowed Beryl to depart for home. "Your husband is out working, anyway. And you've got the baby down for the night. Stay with me."

Beryl was shown to an upstairs room where a soft bed with a coral-colored bedspread and two pillows in matching frilled cases beckoned. There, while the storm raged outside her window, Beryl spent the warmest, most comfortable night she could remember in her life. If only . . .

She would have to again ask Seth if it was necessary that they travel on to his cousin's estate that spring. Finding a match, she lit the smoky kerosene lantern that provided the only illumination in the room. It was little better than buffalo chips, she thought. Beryl noticed that the bottle of whisky still stood near at hand beside Seth's bed, but oddly, it seemed to have more liquor in it than it did the night before. Or was that the same bottle? They had no money to waste on such, although she knew that Seth's work was cold and rough and he needed a small drink before going to sleep.

He would be out in the cold and dark again this evening among the rowdy, dangerous men. She could hardly chide him about his drinking. He was trying his best.

With little else to do, Beryl again opened the lockbox, and again unfolded the list of needed supplies for their trek westward. She saw that Seth had scratched a few items from the list, probably to save money, to make sure that they met their difficult financial goal before the first wagon train was ready to strike out along the Oregon Trail. She had heard the imprecations of traveling with an overloaded wagon herself; still, she did not want to strike out on the long trail without enough money for the basic necessities. There had to be a little money left for when they reached the occasional way-station. With that in mind, she settled in to do her bookkeeping, considering whether to keep her own next pay packet secret—Mrs. Jasper had generously promised her a little bonus.

An hour later she wearily slapped her pencil onto the table. She had double-checked everything, down to counting the change in the box. They were not gaining ground. As a matter of fact, there was less there than there had been only days before. One part of her grew very angry; another side of her mind saw this as a way to delay the beginning of their journey until the following spring.

But where was the money going?

When Seth stirred, he swung his feet to the floor and reached first for the bottle of whisky positioned there. Before he had hoisted the bottle to his lips, he saw Beryl sitting at the table. A bright, mischievous, false smile lit up his face.

"You're home, Beryl! It's fine to see you." He took a drink from the whisky bottle. "Things won't go on like this much longer. I'm going to take a daytime job; then we'll be able to spend more time together."

"They're putting you on the day shift?" Beryl asked, rising to walk to where Seth sat on the flimsy bed.

"Oh, this wouldn't be with the constabulary. Oddest thing happened early this morning while I was finishing my shift. I was checking the businesses along the docks, and guess who I ran into down at the American Fur Company warehouse—an old friend of Jonathan Byrd."

"You don't say," Beryl said, placing her hands on her husband's knees.

"I do! He confirmed everything we learned from Jonathan's letter. He has a spreading estate up north. Made his fortune in the fur trade and then decided to settle up there and build a fine house to live in."

"Well, we knew all that," Beryl said. Or rather, they had assumed all of that from the scant lines scribbled in the letter. It was nice to have it all verified by someone else. Jonathan Byrd had become an almost mythical figure in their lives.

"Yes, well here's something we didn't know. This man, his name is Robert Pyle, who is pretty much in charge over there and has all but promised me a day job making more money now that Cousin Jonathan has taken a wife. Well, not exactly a wife, I don't suppose . . ." Seth's words trailed off, and he took another drink and looked thoughtful. Beryl waited with patient excitement.

"Come on," she urged when she could wait no longer.

"Well, I don't see how she could be his actual wife—I don't think they have such things as a Christian church wedding out there in the wilds."

"I wouldn't suppose so," Beryl said, now frowning. "Where do you suppose he even met the girl, way out there?"

"Things are different in the mountains, Beryl," Seth said solemnly. He took another drink from his liquor bottle. "Pyle told me that men usually just buy themselves a woman out that way."

"Your cousin bought himself a woman!" Beryl said, flabbergasted. She had never imagined things like that happened on this continent. Seth was smiling. He now got to his feet, reaching for his pants. Beryl had forgotten that her husband needed to go to work that night.

"Pyle tells me that this was a little different," Seth said, smiling thinly. "Jonathan apparently won this one at a shooting match."

"He won her at . . ." Beryl grimaced, started to answer, then slowly let her features settle to equanimity. "Well, it certainly is a different world out in those wild lands." She got to her feet with a small laugh and went on, "Well, at least she's in no position to legally inherit his estate."

"No, no she isn't." Seth smiled at the closed window as he pulled on his coat. Sometimes he and Beryl did share the same thought patterns. That was precisely what Seth had been thinking when he heard Robert Pyle talk about Jonathan's Indian squaw. She could not inherit Jonathan's vast holdings. She was probably an ignorant savage who would just wander back to her tribe if something ever happened to Jonathan Byrd. His property would fall to his next of kin.

Deciding to carry the charade a step further, Seth Byrd kissed his wife on the cheek and started out the door as if he were on his way to work. There were warmer places to drink where no one cast glances of aspersion your way and the conversation was more interesting.

As the door closed behind Seth, Beryl turned back toward the small table where her accounting figures lay spread across its face. She had forgotten to ask Seth about the dwindling funds; she had neglected to ask him again if they might not delay their trip west for one more year. She had been more interested in hearing about Cousin Jonathan and his savage bride.

Why would a man do such a thing? Well, Beryl knew why, of course, but still it seemed pagan in the extreme. She had vaguely admired Jonathan Byrd, or the image she had had of him. Still a young man, he had been a successful fur trader and was now a landowner, holder of a large estate.

Seth had not fared so well, but all of life was a matter of opportunity, and of chance. Jonathan had apparently made good use of both. But Seth was a hardworking constable with the St. Joseph's constabulary, struggling to make things better for his family. And Jonathan was . . . a squaw man!

Precious had decided to have a restless morning, so Beryl

rose earlier than she wanted to. Outside the sky was clear. Much of the previous days' snow had melted. More people were moving along the streets than had been usual. The early sun over the eastern buildings shone brightly. When Beryl opened the swollen window to their room, the air that came in was cool, but not chillingly so. She made a mental note to ask Mrs. Jasper if she didn't think that today might be a good day to air out the big house some after the long winter.

Beryl paused, seated on the bed for a minute or two before beginning to dress. She really did like working in that house. Mrs. Jasper was very kind, the work light. Going to the house in the mornings seemed very much like going home.

The weather outside was both promising and threatening. If it held, Seth would be getting anxious to move on. She could tell that much, even though he was excited about his new job at the fur company warehouse. At least there he would be safe from the ruffians who prowled the streets after midnight. He would, nevertheless, want to take the first wagon train west.

Well, Beryl thought, pulling her dress on over her head, it was what they had all planned, agreed on, worked and saved for. She supposed her own feelings were caused by the natural preference for known comfort rather than uncertainty; besides, who knew but that tomorrow might mean the end of her employment. Mrs. Jasper could become very ill with something Beryl was unable to cope with. The old woman could simply grow tired of Beryl's presence. Her family might decide that she could no longer live alone. She sighed and stood, a half-smile on her lips. No, she would continue with Seth Byrd as she always had. At least Seth could not fire her.

That led her thoughts to the time. Seth should have been home by now. Perhaps he had stopped to talk to the man at the fur company or to inquire at the wagonwright's.

She walked again to Precious's cradle. The baby had eaten

and fallen contentedly back to sleep. Now it was time to bundle her up for the travel out to Ash Street. Before she had reached the baby, the door to the room swung open, very hard, banging the wall, and Seth staggered in, his face bruised and cut. There was a trickle of blood from his eyebrow winding across his cheek. He stumbled to the bed and flopped down.

"Oh, dear!" Beryl gasped. She moved to the bed with a damp cloth and sat beside him. "I hate that job of yours, Seth! The thugs out there won't be satisfied until they've killed you."

"It's a rough town, all right," Seth muttered as Beryl blotted at his torn eyebrow.

"Even if it's a job you can't keep for long, things will be better at the fur company warehouse."

"At the . . . ? Yes, better . . ." he said indistinctly. He had taken a good beating somewhere. He lay on his back, fully dressed, eyes closed. "Did you see the weather outside, Beryl?"

"Yes, I have. Quite nice, is it not?"

"I'd say this week will see us traveling on. I'll see about finally buying our wagon and stock today, find a place to store the wagon, and then we can start provisioning it."

"You shouldn't be out doing that until you're feeling better," Beryl said, feeling her reluctance turn to a physical knot in the pit of her stomach. She was always that way when a long expected event was suddenly upon her. They were actually going! There was a huge job in front of them, a long hazardous trail to she knew-not-where.

"I'll be late for work," Beryl announced, rising with the pan and bloody cloth, which she placed on the table.

"You won't need a job much longer," Seth said, opening his eyes to watch her. The expression in them was cloudy, yet determined. "You might as well let the old lady know so she can start looking around for someone else."

"Shouldn't we wait until we see that the weather's going to hold?"

"They're already organizing the wagon train. Everyone who wants to be among the first settlers is crowding their office just now. Wait?" He shook his head heavily. "I'm just a little tired of this waiting, Beryl."

Well, yes, of course he was. Who wouldn't be? The town life had not gone well for Seth. She looked down at his haggard face.

"Do what you must do, Seth." She leaned down to kiss him, smiled faintly, and picked up Precious from her cradle.

"Beryl," Seth said in a more muffled voice. "It's what we have begun; we can't turn from it now."

"No, no we can't. I'll talk to Mrs. Jasper." She paused, baby in arms, but Seth said nothing more. She frowned only slightly as she went out the door and down the corridor, the scent of Seth's whisky still in her nostrils.

# Chapter Twelve

## Preparing for the Pilgrimage

An hour later Seth was still awake. He had been feigning sleep, hoping that it would lead him to the real thing. He was weary; his jaw still ached tremendously. He could tongue a few loose molars on the back of his lower jaw. The knee had been torn out of his twill trousers when he fell. They had targeted him, for sure.

Seth could no longer venture out anywhere near Baker Street where the Lady Luck stood. He no longer tried to enter the saloon at all, but did his drinking in other low dives in that district. But the word had been put out on him, and he was no longer welcome in the area, either because he was a former constable or, more likely, he thought, because the powerful Keene brothers had put the word out on him. The brothers would not risk another assault on him personally, but there were half a hundred workers at least at the hog processing plant who would do just about anything to curry the favor of the owner's sons.

Last night had been miserable, the night before no better. He sat up, rubbing his aching head, which had a noticeable knot on it. Damn these city toughs! Now he would have to be especially alert and animated to finish everything he had planned for the day. Wagons, oxen, storage for same, provision check, meeting with wagon train organizers. It was going to be a hell of a day.

Seth had once heard a preacher man say that God never laid

more upon a man than he could endure. Now he wondered about that supposedly comforting homily. Struggling to his feet, Seth glanced at his empty whisky bottle, winced, and went to the table where he sat heavily, needing the use of his arms to lower himself. He reached for the lockbox and opened it. Today was the day their hard-saved money must be expended. Their entire future lay inside that steel box.

On opening it, he first glanced at Beryl's accounting slip, then at the list of necessary provisions. It would do if her sums were accurate, even not taking into account the whisky that had become more essential to Seth's sense of well-being, the occasional gambling debt he had incurred in the saloons, the—once only—cost of a woman companion. These were all trivial expenses. A few dollars here or there.

He began counting the money. He counted it again, for the amount there was far short even of their somewhat pared-down needs—the list that Seth had shortened to cover his own borrowing.

Where had the money gone? There was little enough to work with. Beryl? Unthinkable, even though he knew she had the strong desire to wait another year before heading west. Her weekly packets, the same each time, were regular and identical—except for the money she spent on the needs of Precious, which was little enough.

Seth leaned back in his chair, slapped his forehead once, and then rubbed at the headache behind his eyes. There had to be an answer to this. There were only the three of them . . . Seth straightened, rose to his feet, and started toward the unmade bed where Cason slept. Slept, when he was home at nights, which was very seldom. And where then was the boy spending his nights? In what enterprises? Growing angry with his suppositions, Seth Byrd flipped aside the bedding and lifted the mattress.

Like a cold, sleeping snake, he saw the Colt's revolver lying there. Seth knew little about these newer weapons, but he knew that the shiny five-shot handgun must have cost a good deal—on a mill custodian's wages!

Seth sat on the unmade bed, holding the revolver across his lap. So that was it—Cason had been taking money from their savings, buying pistols and such and probably staying out at night in gambling dens and low saloons. Possibly he was even up to robbing men, judging by the weapon. What then was Cason's plan? The boy did not plan to get caught obviously, but if he was, was he going to take the rest of the money and run away to the Texas lands as he had talked about before?

It all had to come to an end, *had* come to an end at this moment. Seth placed the pistol back under the mattress—it didn't matter anymore—returned to the open cash box and scooped up the change and bills there, folding the paper money neatly in half before stuffing it in his pocket. Winter was waning. Now was the time to begin what must be done.

If his wicked son had left them enough even for the basic necessities. Seth did not slam the door as he exited the room, a silent curse twisting his features, but a glance at that face would alert any passerby to the fact that he carried hell in his heart.

"A hundred dollars a head!" Seth Byrd said unbelievingly as he stood at the railing of the stockyard fence, looking out over the thousands of oxen loitering within. "They weren't half that when we got here last fall."

"Well," the man, whose name was Fisher, answered, "there was no market for them in the fall—unless you wanted to butcher one out. The wagons west weren't rolling then. Now they are, and the price goes where the market goes."

Seth eyed the big cattle, still mentally counting the money in his pockets. They had to have oxen; that was all there was to it.

Trying one last time to find a way to save money, he asked, "Does anyone ever haul out of here with only four oxen?"

"Only fools," Fisher replied. "When you hit one of those long mountain grades, you'll need six oxen and wish you had eight. And, it'll be too late then to change your mind and turn around."

"I suppose," Seth said unhappily. "If you pick six for me right now, where can I leave them until I have the wagon ready to go?"

"I'll hold a team for you right here in my yard for forty-eight hours, no charge. If you take any longer to get your set-up ready to roll, you'll have to pay me for their keep or move them."

That was the end of their financial discussion; Seth was licked and he knew it. He would come back to hopefully get a few tips for free on how to drive the oxen. Fisher told him all the beasts were well-trained. With a vestige of pride, he said his oxen took three to four years on the average to train—the reason you couldn't just go out and find yourself some milk cows for the task of wagon-hauling. A lot of money was invested in these animals, since the oxen had to be fed and housed, and doctored all that time. A halt oxen or one that had got the fever was of no value whatever.

It was not a bargain Seth had received, but a fair enough deal, considering the market. Seth knew that; still, he left the Fisher property feeling low. He felt the urge for a drink tugging at him. He had the time, and what was fifty cents from their poke for a little whisky? First a couple of drinks, then to the wagon people. Buying a drink for himself was fair, he considered; he was the one doing all the work. As he was thinking that, he passed the sawmill where a few wood-dust-covered workers could be seen sitting out front, having their lunch. Cason was not among them. Probably he was off somewhere wasting more money.

The big open yard behind the wagon makers had as many as

five-hundred Conestogas standing there, looking undressed without their canvas tops. As Seth passed through a maze of equipment sheds and working wagon wrights, he heard the constant hum of a thousand saws, the echoing sound of hammers, and the striking of metal against metal in the smiths' sheds where iron wheels were being formed and hammered out to fit the large wooden wheels of the wagons. When Seth found the sales office, he entered, found he was not alone, and waited his turn behind a nervous looking woman in dark blue and her equally nervous husband. These two finally signed some sort of contract agreement, and it was Seth Byrd's turn to meet the sales manager, a thin, angry looking man named Profitt, who had little to do by way of persuading people to buy his product. They couldn't manufacture wagons fast enough, it seemed.

Seth sat down, nodded to Profitt, and looked over the schematic drawing of a Conestoga wagon. He objected to and asked about several accoutrements that seemed unnecessary to him, including a feed bin fixed to the wagon.

"I can't see that I have much use for this," Seth said, tapping the drawing. "Cattle know how to graze, don't they?"

"If there's any grass for them," Profitt allowed. His expression indicated he was not too happy with this particular customer. "If you're taking any smaller animals, you'll find it absolutely necessary."

"You mean to tell me that I'm expected to carry grain along with me?"

"Only if you want your animals to eat," Profitt said smugly. He leaned back, tapping a pencil against his desk top. Two more customers had entered the office and he glanced their way, flashing a meaningless smile. Seth still had his finger on the schematic. There were a couple of other items he thought were unnecessary and could be left off to save a dollar or two. Profitt listened in silence for a full minute, then told Seth, "We make our wagons one way—the right way—and we charge one price for every wagon that rolls through our gates." He scribbled something on a pad and pushed his completed price sheet across the desk to Seth. "Do you wish to do business here or not?"

The price did not totally surprise Seth, but he was still trying desperately to juggle the figures mentally. He would have an ox team and a wagon—but very little else. Taking a deep breath, he decided not to look like a piker and a man on the brink of poverty. He nodded and signed his name. A number was entered below his signature, and after a minute, a man wearing an apron came in from a back room and was given the number that would be stamped on a metal plate and nailed to the wagon.

Seth went back outside, folding the agreement and tucking it into his coat pocket. He should have felt some sort of exultation at finally having matters solidified, his preparations advancing. That, after all, was what they had suffered for through the long winter; yet he felt uneasy, even a little bit frightened. The money he had received from the sale of his property was gone, the wages they had earned in St. Joseph very nearly depleted. He needed a drink and wasn't sure he could afford it.

And Cason was out roving the town and buying firearms!

Working his way back toward town, he passed through a field the size of a fairground where all sorts of equipment and preserved food were being sold in small booths by the local people who had labored the winter long producing the goods for travelers. He only looked at the items in a few kiosks that interested him. Beryl would have to come with him to help him decide on what was needed, what could be carried . . . what they could afford.

This was it then. This was when they would finally begin provisioning for the long journey to Wyoming. Beryl would have to quit her job immediately if she had not already done so. And Cason . . . Let the ungrateful kid work up until the last moment. Seth had still not finished with his son. He wondered, having counted the money again, if Cason had been withholding money from the family treasury all this time. Greedy little pup.

Seth's anger surged anew. Muttering, he went up Sixth Street and entered a low dive where the worst sort gathered and drank whisky, glowering at anyone who looked as if he might say something to him. He would wait until Beryl got home, show her the bill of sale from the ox-trader and the receipt for the Conestoga, making it quite clear that she was to go with him to market the next day so they could start lading the wagon. And if he happened to run into Cason along the way, he would give that young man something to regret for a long while.

In the morning Seth relented as far as Cason continuing at his job went, though the boy had caught his dressing down with a few extra punctuation marks made with fists. Seth would not tolerate thievery by his own son. The thing was, he needed Cason with him today and many others to follow. They rented a heavy barrow in town from a man who was probably making a fortune providing rentals and went with Beryl to the open market. Beryl nervously selected packets of compressed vegetables and dried fruit from the women there. Most of the women were helpful, telling her about their own experiences, and explaining how unfamiliar food like prairie turnips could be identified and dug along their route. The women, for the most part, tried to be very specific and helpful concerning the storing and preparation of their goods.

Beryl tried her very best to learn what she could. Seth only grew impatient when she lingered too long with one of the vendors. "We don't have forever to get this done," he growled at her once.

"It's of no use buying these supplies if I don't know how to use them properly," Beryl spat back, looking at the ground. It was nearly tea time at Mrs. Jasper's home. She glanced at Cason, plodding along, towing the barrow with his usual sullen look pulling his lips down, narrowing his eyes. "Smile," Beryl said, nudging him gently.

As far as Cason Byrd was concerned, there was nothing in the world to smile about. His father had shoved him around pretty roughly the night before for things he had done and those he had not. He had been ordered to quit his job at the sawmill. Maybe that wasn't really much of a job, Cason thought, but he had grown used to it and liked most of the men there. Now he had nothing at all, no pay packets, no friends. His only function now was to tow the heavy barrow along like some pack animal. Then he could look forward to months traveling to some remote location none of them had so much as seen, where there would not even be the chance of meeting a friend because the country was said to be desolate and mostly uninhabited. Cason thought that if he had had a horse, he would then and there have taken off for the Texas lands and secured a job on one of those vast cattle ranches where they were always looking for help—where a boy could be a man. He thought that if he could even steal a horse . . .

Cason was thinking in this way when they rounded the corner of the market and he came nearly face to face with the girl. She wasn't very tall and maybe a little plump, but she had a slightly gap-toothed smile that seemed ready to widen if she was ever more pleased with her world than she already was. Her hair was dark, pushed away under her bonnet so Cason had no idea how it was fixed, if it was fixed at all. She was built about the average way of a fourteen-year-old girl, which Cason guessed her to be, but her eyes were deep green and sparkling, seeming to enjoy everything and everyone at the market. When she halted in front of Cason, carrying a brown paper-wrapped bundle, she seemed to notice him and include him in her world view. Her glance was warming.

"Sorry," Cason mumbled, removing his hat.

"It was my fault," the girl answered. "I wasn't looking where I was going."

"Leslie! Where are you?" an older woman was shouting, waving a hand from behind a cart full of vegetables.

"Right over here, Mother!" the girl yelled, turning that way with a slight, lingering smile. She paused, looked back, and asked: "Are you traveling with the Bixby Train? If so, I'll see you again."

Then she was gone, and Cason watched her girlish swish and sway as she departed. He watched her pause beside her mother and another woman and speak to them about something in a bubbly voice. Cason could not make out the words, but he imagined they were about him. His own mother and father had caught up with Cason, Precious crying now.

Minutes later as they continued up and down the aisles of merchandise, Cason asked his father, "Are we going with the Bixby Train?"

"Yes, as a matter of fact," Seth Byrd answered, frowning at his son. "What makes you interested all of the sudden?"

"Nothing," Cason answered. "I just thought I had better get used to all of this."

"Yes, you had," Seth said. "Because you are going with us, and the work has hardly begun."

Cason only nodded his head in response; his mind was wandering far away.

# CHAPTER THIRTEEN

## The Wyoming Trail

By the third day on the trail the oxen had settled to their task. They seemed to have adjusted to the change in their way of life more easily than their human counterparts. The wagons rolled slowly across the bleak, featureless plains as Jason Bixby, the old plainsman who had organized the wagon train, led them into the desolate wilderness.

Seth Byrd was grim. This was the goal toward which he had worked, yet it hardly made for satisfactory days. The animals plodded on at their steady pace, averaging only about one mile an hour. Most of the pioneers had already adapted to the animals' slogging pace and walked beside their teams with rods, urging the oxen onward. They had already passed the hill of heartache shortly after leaving town. On this upslope just beyond the town limits, some among the party had extreme difficulty. Those who had only a four-oxen team, for example, could achieve little on the grade and at times slid back along the few yards gained as one or another of the beasts lost his footing. Other wagons, despite all cautions, were transporting heavy items like iron goods, stoves among them, and some had heavy oaken furniture. These all had to be discarded at the side of the trail and were soon hauled away by scavengers from St. Jo who made their living in that way. The overweight abandoned goods were cleaned and sold, sometimes to the next unwary, unwise wagon travelers.

The mud was more than an irritation. Horses and oxen slipped; wagons slowed and even bogged to their wheel hubs as they followed the well-defined trail. Beryl was of the opinion that the dust was the worst evil by far. When they did reach dry ground, the dust from a hundred wagons and teams flowed past in heavy veils, smothering their breathing. The wisest, most experienced pioneers had assured themselves of a position near the front of the wagon train either through influence or bribes. The Byrds' wagon was nearly at the middle of the long column of determined settlers.

Cason usually chose to walk beside the team for most of the day. At times he would wander ahead or lag behind, watching the other wagons, looking for the intriguing Leslie Hart. Yet among hundreds of travelers there, it was impossible to find her. Men on horseback, looking free and independent to Cason, rode along the length of the wagon train freely—hired Indian scouts and camp men, friends of Jason Bixby hired for the trip—and Cason envied them their freedom and apparent recklessness. Almost all of these men were young, not much older than Cason himself. They wore buckskin shirts, had rifles sheathed in fringed Indian-decorated sheaths, sported belt guns, and had Texas-rigged saddles and fine spry ponies. They seemed to belong on the long plains; Cason did not, and he knew it.

Night camp at times offered a sort of community gathering, a place to rest and celebrate when there was not really much to celebrate outside of completing the day and being one day nearer to their goals. It was enough for the long-traveling folks.

A few of the men had brought fiddles with them, and at least one had a squeeze box. At night, around a dozen campfires, they would break out their musical instruments and play. Nearly everyone danced at least once, inexpertly, clumsily, but it was a release, and they always ended up smiling when the music was over. There was always coffee and a few of the men had brought their jugs of whisky along on the long road. These made friends quickly on those festive nights.

The flames from the campfires flickered and weaved in the night; music played and people laughed. And across the camp on one particular night Cason Byrd saw the short, animated girl, the smiling Leslie Hart. Without asking anyone, he started off across the camp in her direction.

The walk seemed to take an hour as he hesitated, then strode on steadily. In five minutes he found her preparing to dance—in the arms of Tom Pearl. Tom looked not much different than he had on any workday at the sawmill, except that he was wearing a blue suit, and his hair was combed in the middle and watered down. Cason's mouth tightened involuntarily and he slowed his approach. What was Tom Pearl doing out here? More, what was he doing holding Leslie Hart, who was the only thing making this trip west even tolerable?

Cason stood watching as the fiddles started up again and Leslie and Tom swirled into a high-stepping, cheerful dance Cason did not find in the least amusing. He turned away from the firelight and began plodding back toward their wagon, dodging the playing kids along his way. Cason leaned against a heavy wagon wheel, the music still loud in his ears, the air still heavy with lingering dust.

Surely Pearl couldn't be courting Leslie; how could she even know him? Besides, Tom wasn't even a man yet—he was only a boy with the ambition to become wealthy before his time with some wild sawmill-in-Oregon idea. That much Cason knew about Tom Pearl. Hadn't he and Andy French spent many a boring hour listening to Pearl drone on about his plans during the long nights at the mill?

How could Leslie do this to him? Cason had told her he planned on spending some time with her this evening. Or had he? No, he thought, striking the wood behind him with his fist.

He hadn't gathered up quite that much courage, not enough to tell Leslie that she was first in line for him as far as dancing went. Thinking about it, he realized he had barely said a dozen words to her, ever. But women were supposed to know those things, weren't they?

He could have waited and danced the next dance with Leslie, but he did not wish to be her second choice. Angrily he walked on toward the family wagon as the mocking fiddles played on.

"Cason!" Beryl appeared from between two wagons, her shawl pulled tightly around her shoulders. "Good. I'm glad I found you. I thought I might find your father and get him to dance a couple of jigs with me—if you would watch Precious for a little while. She's been fed and is sleeping; she shouldn't be any trouble."

Cason noticed that his mother's eyes were strangely bright, almost girlish in the pale moonlight. He muttered, "Yes'm, I reckon I can watch the baby for you."

Beryl did not hurry away. She stood hesitantly, looking at the smoky sky above the camp, and asked, "Have you seen him, Cason? Your father, I mean. He planned to step out and have a drink or two with some men he's met . . . but that's been hours ago, and I was hoping . . ."

"No, ma'am, I sure haven't seen him." Well, here was his excuse for not being at the dance if Leslie should ask. Why would she bother to ask? Cason thought angrily. He turned to walk away, leaving Beryl standing like some abandoned mission in the night.

In the darkness, the racing pony nearly trampled Cason. He lurched to one side and came up roughly against a wagon. Rubbing his shoulder, he turned and shouted: "Hey you! Why don't you look where you're going?"

The stranger reined up his horse, wheeled it, and walked it

back toward Cason. Cason could see now that the horse was the little spotted pony he had admired. It was ridden by one of the outriders from Texas—the younger one—who approached him, hat tilted back, his eyes apparently apologetic.

"I'm sorry, friend," the man said, leaning forward in his saddle. "I guess I got careless, forgetting where I was."

Cason started to say something more to impress the cowboy with his dominance, but the kid looked so sincerely apologetic and ashamed that Cason cut himself off. The slight, yellow-haired man from Texas was patting the neck of his sleek little pinto pony. Cason found himself more interested in the horse than in making threatening statements.

"Nice spotted horse," he said, almost reverently sweeping a hand across the horse's flank.

"We call 'em pintos down home," the young man said. "Yeah, I kind of like him myself."

"Is he a cutting pony?" Cason asked, meaning a horse trained to cut steers out of a herd or bunch them again.

"Can be. Old Strider here can do just about anything a man asks of him. If you mean is that the kind of work we do back at home, yes, I guess it mostly is."

"You're on a working ranch?" Cason asked, looking up at the mounted rider.

"I guess you could say!" The stranger laughed. "On the Starr Ranch. You might have heard about it even away out here."

"No," Cason answered, "I never did, but I've been looking for a ranch to hook up with."

"You've done some cowboyin'?" the rider asked with more than a little surprise.

"No, I haven't—not yet, but I mean to."

"That so? In here with all these nesters, I wouldn't have figured you for that. You ever need any hints on how to go about it, look me up. Name's Will Hecht. I expect you've seen me riding around with Tracy Camp."

"Is that his name? I've never met him. How did you two come to get fixed up with this wagon train?"

"I thought everyone knew that." Will Hecht shrugged. "The big boss, Mr. Ben Starr himself, has known Joe Bixby for quite a time—out of Louisiana, I think. Mr. Starr is a man who has never had enough. You know the type."

"I think I do," Cason Byrd said, thinking of Tom Pearl.

"Well, Mr. Starr has cows—millions of them—but not enough market. He thinks he can drive cattle up the trail to Denver where they have all those new copper, silver, and gold mines opening up, and the men will want their steaks.

"Starr sent me along with Tracy Camp to scout the area. We don't carry pots and pans and such, nothing but our bedrolls, so Starr asked Bixby if he could use a few men to keep an eye out for Indians and raiders in exchange for meals and a place to sleep. Mostly I'm just company for Tracy Camp. He's the big man on the job. That doesn't bother me. It's better than a long summer on the range, I can tell you that."

"Seems like a deal for both parties," Cason said. "But, say, Will, I'd like to talk with you some more along the way. It's me for Texas once I get myself outfitted for the trail."

"It's a good life for those who like it," Will said. More slyly, he asked, "You haven't got a sister you could introduce me to, by chance?"

Near at hand Cason could hear Precious starting to awaken and cry. "I do—and that's her you hear right now," Cason Byrd said with a grin.

"Looks like I'm going stag to the dance," Will Hecht said with a staged sigh. "We'll talk again before long. I'm the man to ask if you have any questions about cowboying in Texas."

*What a lucky break,* Cason Byrd was thinking as he wandered toward where Precious waited. Clambering up into the wagon, he checked the baby first, as he had been taught, to see that no pins were sticking her, then he tickled her under the chin a little and talked some gurgling baby talk to her to let her know that she was not alone. Then, after the little girl had fallen asleep again, Cason sat perched on the wagon's tailgate, listening to the distant music, watching the starry night and contemplating his fortune and his future.

The meeting with Will Hecht had given him reason for optimism. The two cowboys were scouting for a large Texas ranch that was contemplating future drives into the north country if they could be managed. Hecht and Tracy Camp would be looking at the available grazing, the sources of water, trying to gauge the mood of the local Indians. When that job was completed, they would be returning to the Starr Ranch in Texas. Could Cason consider riding with them if they let him? Why wouldn't they?

Because he had no horse to ride!

He had no horse and no money to buy one, and nothing to trade for one. He had his Colt's revolver, but that could not be considered for trade. He would need the pistol. He drummed his fingers on the rough wood of the tailgate. There had to be a way. They said that there always was, but a way out of this predicament eluded him completely. Perhaps he was putting the hind end first. The first thing to do might be to approach Tracy Camp and ask the trailbreaker if it was even possible for him to ride along with him and Hecht. Will Hecht would introduce them, he knew. Cason had seen Tracy Camp here and there—good, square shoulders, a ruggedly handsome face that did not look corrupted into surliness by the life he was leading. Cason decided he would do that first; at least that was something he could control.

Would his parents let him go?

They would just have to, that was all there was to it, or Cason swore he would go anyway. He knew his father was counting on him for help in building a new house once they reached the famous Cousin Jonathan Byrd's estate, but Cason saw only years of toil ahead ending, when his father died as he must eventually, with Cason being stuck alone on someone else's wilderness property, perhaps no better off than a tenant farmer.

That was Seth Byrd's goal in life, not Cason's. There was a way; there was always a way.

The following day held clear as they continued to plod their way north and west. At sundown Will Hecht unexpectedly showed up at the wagon, riding his prancing pinto pony. Cason had hoped to see the man again, but was surprised by his luck at meeting him again so soon.

"Ah," Will said, tilting back his broad-brimmed cowboy hat with his thumb. "Tracy, he went off to drink whisky and play some cards with Bixby and a few of the other men. Tracy says he only goes for the conversation, to learn all the news he can of this area from those who know. Claims he really doesn't care that much for whisky or for gambling, but you couldn't prove it by me. I got nothing much else to do, so I thought I'd drop by and see you."

"I'm glad you did. I have things I'd like to ask you," Cason told the yellow-haired kid.

"Ask away," Will Hecht said amiably. Cason studied Strider, the pinto horse, with an admiration bordering on envy. "You ever sat a real cow pony before, Cason?"

"No, I haven't. I'm planning on getting me one, though."

"Well, don't be shy, son," Hecht said cheerfully, and he dismounted from the horse with one smooth, easy motion. "Take the driver's seat; see how you like it." He handed the reins to Cason, who goggled at the chance.

"C-can I?" he said, stuttering just a little.

"What did I just tell you?" Will Hecht said. "Mount and see

how it feels up there. You know which side to approach it, don't you?"

"From the left," Cason said irritably. "Like all other horses. I didn't say I'd never ridden a horse before, just that I've never sat a pony like this."

"Just asking," Hecht said, hoisting his hands as if to ward off Cason's wrath. He was still smiling widely. "If you want, you can take him out for a turn, just to get to know each other."

"You mean it, don't you?" Cason asked with a little suspicion, as if he thought Hecht might be playing a prank on him.

"Sure, I mean it. We're friends, aren't we? Just don't run him flat out, all right?"

Cason Byrd, still unable to believe his luck, swung onto the saddle and started the pinto horse, Strider, away from the camp and onto the dark plains. He walked the horse until they were well clear of the camp, then lifted the willing little pony into an easy trot.

Cason circled the entire encampment, secretly hoping someone might see him astride the pinto. It was only with reluctance that he guided the pony back to camp to where Will Hecht waited, sitting on the wagon's tailgate. Hecht was still smiling. Cason flushed with pleasure as he swung down and stroked the pinto's muzzle.

"Strider treated you right, did he?" the yellow-haired cowboy asked, walking toward them.

"He was easy to sit, easy to control," Cason told Hecht.

"Yeah, he's a good boy. It took some time to train him, but he's all I could ask for now."

Hecht took the reins from Cason's hand. Cason asked with a kind of wonder, "That's what you get paid for, sitting Strider?"

"Oh, that would be like getting paid for sitting in a rocking chair," Hecht said with a laugh. "No, we do a lot of pretty tough work together. I'll tell you about some of it another night."

Unable to control himself, Cason blurted out, "I've got to ride with you men; that's all there is to it."

"You haven't got a horse," Hecht said. Then, seeing that he had wounded Cason, he told him: "I promise I'll talk to Tracy Camp about you, Of course, you'll ride with us if you want to, if you can get yourself situated. There won't be any pay in it for you, not if you join us up here. Back in Texas the Big Boss, Ben Starr, would have to be the one to hire you or not. He's short of men though—especially if he decides to drive north next year. If you show yourself to be a decent trail mate while we're up here, I don't know why old Starr wouldn't hire you on, though, not if Camp and I both recommend you. Everything else can be taught. Look at me! They taught me everything I know." Hecht swung easily into the saddle.

"Just see what you can figure out, Cason. Speaking for myself, I'd be glad to have you along. I've already heard most of Tracy Camp's stories over the last thousand miles."

Will Hecht walked his pinto pony homeward then and Cason watched them disappear into the shadows. Had anyone been around, they would have thought they saw starlight gleaming in the young man's eyes. Cason Byrd found himself standing at the very verge of his dream, he thought. He needed only the nerve to make the jump.

Beryl was very tired. The dust was thick, incessant. She had walked beside the ox team for the last ten miles, swatting the oxen with her rod when they dallied. She had been on the long trail since sunup, as had everyone else traveling with the wagon train with few exceptions. Sometimes she had been forced to carry Precious with her so the child could nurse. At other times she had simply trudged ahead, barely able to see for the swirl of dust, her feet burning. Breathing was difficult.

She continued to look back at the wagon as the six oxen

plodded stolidly onward. Where was Seth? He had dragged himself home to bed very late the night before. His card-playing and drinking excursion had become a marathon. On this morning he had pleaded for extra rest, and Beryl had acceded to his pitiable request, but he had pledged to be up and working by noon. Judging by the sun, it was well past midday now.

The wagons had halted around ten o'clock to allow some of the women to dig prairie turnips and pause for a comfort break, which required the women to walk out in a group and form a circle, spreading their skirts as a screen while the ones in need took turns in the center of the circle to make their necessary comforts. It was primitive, but they had all grown quite used to the primitiveness of the prairies by now, and the time when any woman was shy about the arrangement was long past.

Beryl found she was not good at digging prairie turnips, but as good as anyone else it seemed—with the exception of the single Shoshone woman who was traveling with them, an older woman loosely attached to Joe Bixby in a way no one understood, and which did not matter to them except as a matter of curiosity. Any social pretensions someone might have sheltered before the long trek began had quickly fallen away after days of endless sun, deprivation, dust, and wind scoured them. When someone needed help, you asked one of the women, not where she was from or who her parents might have been. It made the traveling easier for all of them once the women had formed their own crude democracy.

*Where was Seth?* Some time late in the afternoon, Cason had come up to meet his mother. "I think he's still asleep," the boy had told her. "I just came because Precious is stirring again, and I figured it was time for another feeding." Cason shrugged with some embarrassment. "I can't help the child, but I figure I can keep the oxen in a line, following everybody else."

Beryl placed her hand briefly on Cason's shoulder, handed

him the ox goad, and went to the rear of the covered wagon. Precious was indeed restless, Beryl found as she climbed up into the wagon. Tiny pink fingers waved at her from the blanket of her cradle.

Sighing, Beryl sat down on the only chair they carried with them, unbuttoning the top of her dress, looking longingly forward to the distant day when the child would not need her nourishment that much. Precious was already beginning to cut two teeth in front and Beryl winced as the baby began to nurse.

This would soon be over, she told herself; they would have their new home, and a cheerful baby girl living there, playing there, sitting down to her lunch at the table.

Beryl sighed, gazing at the canvas roof over her and stroking the fine hair on the baby's head.

Seth Byrd slept on. Or, if it was not sleep, it was a restless imitation of it. Her husband thrashed and rolled over. He must have had a bad night. Well, Beryl thought generously, there had to be a bad night or two interspersed with the thousands of good ones, but what was a person to expect? Things did not always go perfectly. The wagon hit a rut inevitably caused here and there by the hundreds of wagons ahead of them in line. Seth's eyes opened, and he looked around blearily.

"Where are we?" he asked. It was a question with no answer. Beryl did not know where on the broad plains they were located; they simply rolled on and on into eternity. Someone had said the day before that they had reached Colorado, but the land continued to look exactly as it had for the last month and a half. It was simply another section of the long road to nowhere.

They had, however, heard rumors passed along the line that there was a decent trading post not far ahead now where stores of coffee, salt, baking powder, and flour could be replenished. One woman had even heard there was fresh fruit to be had at these posts if one had the money. Beryl was sure they did not have money to spend for such luxuries. She was far from alone among the weary travelers in that respect. Very few had planned so far ahead with their resources. It would be a relief simply to halt and walk among the bargains offered, even if she could purchase none. They had nothing left that could be sold or traded—except for Cason's prized pistol, and Beryl could not force the boy to sell that. It seemed to be all he had left in the world to fasten some hope on.

She did have her secret fund hidden away—the bonus old Mrs. Jasper had slipped into her hand. "I won't have the baby suffering for any lack. We are given the obligation to see to our children," she had told Beryl in a papery voice. That money Beryl held sacred.

Seth awoke again, studying Beryl, baby to her breast, as if he were unaccustomed to seeing such a sight. His eyes cleared slightly. Then filled with sudden concern.

"What time is it? Who is tending the oxen?"

"It's about an hour before sundown. Cason is guiding the oxen."

"Why did you let me sleep so long? If Cason is steering the team, we might be in Mississippi by now. He never could do anything right."

Seth sat up quickly. She noticed that he still had his boots and trousers on from the night before. Beryl could pinpoint no time, no event that had turned Seth against his own son, but it seemed lately that the boy was to blame for anything that went wrong, that his own father despised him. Perhaps Seth did not really feel that way. He might just be unable to express his confused thoughts in the midst of the uncertainty and anxiety they had endured for so long. That did not excuse his behavior. How was Cason to distinguish his father's real feelings from the harsh treatment, the verbal scourging he was subjected to daily? The two would never be close again, Beryl knew, and she mourned for the dead days when Seth would proudly take his young son on his knees.

"I'd better get up there," Seth said as he hastily finished dressing. "Before the youngster runs us into a ditch and breaks a wagon wheel."

Beryl wanted to counter his argument, but she was too tired to do so just then.

Seth slid off the tailgate to the ground; the wagon rolled inexorably on. She closed her eyes and for a moment while she drowsed, imagined herself in Mrs. Jasper's warm, comfortable parlor with the baby sleeping at her side.

Twilight found Beryl sitting on the wagon tailgate in the fresh air after the stifling day. Precious had been soothed back to sleep. Cason, after a brief, useless argument with his father, had taken himself off somewhere in the settled camp. Seth had unyoked and picketed the six oxen and returned in a foul mood for a supper consisting only of Johnny cakes, gathered greens, prairie turnips, and a handful of dried apples. Their stores were growing quite meager.

"I wonder if we could trade something for a hog," Seth commented halfway through his scant meal. "Grady Kleinschmidt still has a dozen little shoats. He said his wife didn't mind moving west with him, but refused to go with him if they couldn't transport her pigs."

Clever woman, Beryl thought but did not say. The German couple was one of the few traveling "overloaded," but Grady Kleinschmidt had a ten-oxen team, and had brought the stove along with the shoats and a few other luxuries most people could not carry on the trek. Kleinschmidt had said in Beryl's hearing, "I don't mind that I know not where I'm going, but when I get there I will have something with me."

Seth turned his mood against Kleinschmidt. "Keeps those

piglets in a cage inside his wagon! Must stink like hell. He doesn't even like someone looking at them. I guess he's afraid we'll descend on him like a flock of pig-buzzards." Grumbling like that, Seth cleaned his plate, pushed it aside, and stared at Beryl.

"You're fine company tonight," he said, rising. "I'm going out to find some friends to talk to."

Beryl only nodded and picked up the utensils. She wished he didn't feel it was necessary to go through these small deceptions. Seth was cranky because he needed a drink. Why couldn't he just say so, apologize, and go out? She suspected it was because he didn't want to admit that the beast, alcohol, had wound its tentacles so tightly around him. No matter. He was happier away from her for the time being, and Beryl did not miss his sour presence.

Now Beryl sat on the tailgate, watching the delicate colors of the dying sky, the brilliant early stars. Now and then a husband and wife she knew would pass by, nodding to her as, arm-in-arm, they took their evening stroll.

The tall man on the buckskin horse came out of nowhere and halted his big animal beside the wagon, startling Beryl. She had seen the man before; everyone knew who he was, but they had never been introduced.

"Evenin', ma'am," Tracy Camp said, lifting his wide-brimmed hat a little in a respectful greeting. "I dropped by to talk to your boy, Cason. Is he aboard the wagon?"

"No," Beryl said timidly, "he isn't."

"Oh, well, probably he and Will ran off to do something or other." The man smiled faintly. "My name's Tracy Camp, you might have heard my name through Cason."

"No, I haven't," Beryl said, hastily checking the buttons of her dress top. Had she done them up carefully after nursing Precious? Buttoning her dress should have been habitual, but she knew sometimes if it was close to bedtime, fastening the twenty or so small buttons seemed to be more than her time was worth.

She looked more closely at the rider. Had she seen him? It seemed so, yes, but she could not remember anything someone might have said about him. He was tall, almost lanky, with a rather sharp-edged face and eyes that just now were squinting with what seemed to be amusement. Beryl again touched her fingers to her bodice. The man shifted in his saddle.

"Cason has been talking to us about going along with me and Will Hecht, maybe even returning to Texas with us. I thought I should talk to him and give him a clearer idea of what all that entailed."

*Will Hecht?* Did Beryl know who that was? Cason had said nothing to her about these two men. Tracy Camp continued to study her with what appeared to be tolerance. The man continued his explanation.

"I also wanted to warn Cason that he would have to make up his mind and be ready pretty soon. Harris Fork is coming up within a few days. When we reach the outpost there, Will and I will be turning north into Wyoming, not continuing on with the Oregon wagons. There will be about fifty wagons making that turn, I'm told."

"But we're going to Wyoming as well," Beryl told the horseman silhouetted against the background of stars. From along the line, a traveler whooped with apparent joy. The night fell immediately into silence after that. "My husband has a cousin who holds a lot of land there. Maybe you've heard of him—Jonathan Byrd?" Beryl asked hopefully.

"No, ma'am. I've never been in that country myself. Will and I have been commissioned to map the trail through to Cheyenne, which Mr. Starr is convinced will one day be a railhead for the entire north country, a place where he can ship his cattle."

"Then you're a *cowboy*?" Beryl said with sudden understanding. She had heard there were two Texas men performing what amounted to patrol duty in exchange for hot meals, but she had paid little attention to those bits of gossip simply because they had not interested or concerned her.

"So they tell me," Tracy Camp said, his smile expanding a little.

"Then you will be riding along with us into Wyoming—you and Will Hecht?" She had to struggle to remember the second man's name.

"You'll have to put up with us a while longer, I'm afraid," Camp said. "So you are Cason's mother. He's a likely looking lad. Too bad the kid hasn't been able to come by a horse yet. Maybe he can find one at the trading post in Harris Fork."

"Perhaps," Beryl said breathily. She knew Cason could not; there was no money for a horse. She knew Cason would be crushed if he could not find a way to ride away with these two men and seek his fortunes elsewhere. She knew that Seth would not agree to it no matter what. He was anticipating having Cason on hand to help him on the land.

"This could be the start of something big, Mr. Starr believes. There's nothing much in Cheyenne yet, it seems, but Mr. Starr believes in being first in the door so they can't show him the gate later on."

Tracy Camp's horse shifted its feet impatiently, but Tracy himself seemed anything but impatient. Beryl had no answer for the cowboy's last statement. Tracy Camp continued in a different vein.

"It's nice of your cousin to invite you folks up here. It's pretty country if it's good for nothing else."

Beryl didn't ask the cowboy why, to his appraising eye, the land wasn't good for much.

"He didn't exactly invite us up here," Beryl felt compelled to tell Tracy Camp.

"He didn't?" Camp squinted with surprise. It was enough of a risk to uproot your entire family and equip a prairie schooner when you had plans and expectations, but . . .

"Jonathan doesn't even know we're coming," Beryl said.

Tracy Camp fumbled for a reply, then said, "Well, it's sure to be a happy surprise for him." His face did not express the same conviction. "I've taken up a lot of your time, ma'am," he said at last. He asked Beryl if it would be all right if they kept Cason at their camp tonight. "If those two rascals ever do show up!"

Then, touching the brim of his wide hat, Tracy Camp turned the responsive buckskin sharply and rode off into the silence of the night, leaving only a film of dust in the air that slowly settled and gradually disappeared.

Reentering the wagon, Beryl sat in their solitary chair, unpinned her hair, and began brushing it vigorously. There was no silver among the auburn stands there, at least not many, she thought with satisfaction. Her figure, she knew, was still good . . . and why was she even thinking about these things? True, she wished always to make a good impression, but on this night it seemed slightly more important. Why?

She leaned back, brush still in her hand. Precious slept soundly, the pleasant tiny puffs of her breath reassuring somehow. Seth had not yet returned. That was no surprise.

Inexorably her thoughts returned to her night visitor with his sharp features, his tightly fitting black denims, his hawkish, amused eyes. Sighing, she placed the brush aside.

So that was what a cowboy looked like. That was the sort of man Cason wished to become!

She found herself wondering how much a horse would cost this far out on the plains.

# Chapter Fourteen

## Berry Picking

The sun seemed like a gray leaden ball this morning. The air was quite cold. Around the fires men and women could be seen, still with their night blankets wrapped tightly around their shoulders. Breath steamed from their lips as they crowded near the campfires, drinking coffee. A low mist hung over the grasslands beyond the camp. After pouring himself a cup of coffee, Cason Byrd stepped away from the general conversation and stood between two wagons, thoughtfully sipping his hot morning drink.

Leslie Hart, who happened to be passing, noticed Cason standing there and stopped, her smile bright, her hair brushed to a gleaming sheen.

"Well, you really aren't one for socializing, are you?"

"I guess not," Cason admitted, looking down at the toes of his boots.

"I noticed last night at the dance," Leslie said. "I kept looking around for you, but you never did show up."

"You must've had fun anyway," Cason muttered. How could the girl smell so soap-sweet and vital in the morning?

"Oh, I did," Leslie said, finding herself a seat on the wagon tongue. "I danced with a few of the men—and quite a few dances with your friend Tom Pearl."

"We worked in the same place," Cason said. "That don't mean we were friends."

"No? He told me that you were. He's an interesting boy—and an ambitious one! Wouldn't you say?"

"I suppose so. He told us all his ideas for running a sawmill of his own in Oregon."

*Until they were sick of hearing of Tom's plans.*

"He has other ideas as well," Leslie said, arranging her blue gingham skirt. "Something about the telegraph. He says that one day it will run all across the country from coast to coast. Tom wants to get in on the ground floor. He says there will be a fortune in it for those who get in early."

"I guess he'll be able to afford it with all that money pouring in from his sawmill," Cason said gracelessly. Leslie was eyeing him sharply. Her smile had lost some of its glow.

"Tom is a thinking boy, determined to get ahead," Leslie said, standing up, her hands on her hips now. "You shouldn't be so free in mocking him. He's the sort who will find himself living in a fine house, well-wed."

Cason could think of nothing to say to that, and in another minute, Leslie had pivoted and started off toward the breakfast fires to join her mother. Cason shuffled off toward his family's wagon as the girl chirruped like some delightful morning bird. Feeling low, it was Cason's luck to find Tom Pearl there, waiting at the rear of the wagon. There were two pails at his feet.

"Good morning, Cason," Tom said by way of greeting. "It looks like we're going to make a brief stop here. Someone has broken a wagon wheel and we're waiting for them. I've found a likely looking raspberry patch. What do you say we go along and do some picking? Your mother would be sure to appreciate them."

Cason tossed his tin cup into the wagon, heedless of where it landed. His back was stiff with an anger he could not truly define. "I'll go along if you promise not to talk about the sawmill, the telegraph, the railroad, or banks."

Off-stride for a moment, Tom finally grinned and said, "I'll promise. Who have you been talking to? I hardly ever mention my idea about the telegraph to anyone."

"You did last night," Cason said, still in a gray mood. "I was just talking to Leslie Hart. You impressed her with all this talk about things you haven't done and probably never will."

"Did I?" Tom said brightly, ignoring Cason's negative view of things. "Well, she's a girl who deserves to be impressed if it can be done. Isn't she the brightest little penny, Cason? And just about the right age for me. I probably shall keep in touch with her in Oregon, and if things go well, I might even ask her to marry me some day."

Cason's bones had turned to ice. He realized suddenly how much he hated Tom Pearl, had always hated him. If only he were traveling to Oregon as well, he would soon show Leslie something about making good, and not just talking about great success.

But he was not going there; he was Wyoming bound.

"Best of luck," Cason squeezed out between his lips. He picked up one of the pails and they started off across the grasslands toward the raspberry patch.

"Yes, that little girl is a real gem," Tom Pearl continued. "I'd like to offer her furs and jewels—and, with any luck, I shall."

Cason grumbled something and plodded on toward the thicket Pearl had found. His ears were red with the cold, his breath steamed in front of his face. Everyone had been expecting milder weather, but they had not yet met it. There was frost on the willow trees surrounding the spools of raspberry vines, and beyond the trees Cason could see a small pond, still frozen at this time of the morning. It was like a tarnished silver dollar in the poor morning light.

The berries were many, fat and mostly ripe. Tom was right about one thing. His mother would be pleased to have them, despite the work she would have to dedicate to making raspberry tarts for them. The delight of having something new and fresh to eat would strongly motivate her. Beryl was that way; newness, freshness always intrigued her so that it was almost a compulsion to her to acquire it. The old quickly wore on her.

"What of that thicket across the pond?" Tom Pearl asked, pointing that way. His bucket was already half full, but the ripe fruits were growing fewer and farther between.

Cason was dubious. "I don't know. Can we get around to that side, and how long would it take us? They'll have that wheel fixed in no time."

Pearl grinned. "Hold this," he said, handing Cason his pail. "It won't take any time at all."

Cason saw where Pearl's eyes were fixed. "No, Tom, I don't think walking on that pond is a good idea. The ice can't be very thick, and it hasn't been frozen long."

"I'll go first if you're afraid," Tom said, hardening Cason's dislike of the boy. There seemed to be a taunt in the words; deliberately implied or assumed. Cason bristled at them.

"They're your feet that will get wet," Cason Byrd said. "Do whatever you want to do."

"Nothing ventured," Tom Pearl said, taking three quick strides out onto the silver face of the pond, "nothing . . ."

And then he was gone.

There was no menacing growl of ice cracking, just one sudden jagged rift appearing across the face of the frozen pond, and Tom Pearl was in the water, thrashing, twisting, and turning, his eyes wide and turned frantically toward Cason Byrd. His bucket had spilled, leaving a trail of blood-red berries across the ice.

"Help me, Case! Find a branch!"

Cason spun and dashed to the willow woods to find a long branch. And then he slowed. What was the hurry? If Tom Pearl got a little wet, so what? He could claw his way out of the icy water and Cason would return him to camp, a sympathetic hero in everyone's eyes. Cason found a long crooked willow branch, discarded it as being too light. From the hole in the shattered ice, Tom Pearl continued to flail, to plead for help—more weakly now as his lungs filled with water. Cason Byrd returned to the edge of the pond to watch Tom's struggles.

"Case!" a gurgling voice called, then as Cason watched, the boy slipped deeper into the pond as his strength to resist was slowed by the numbing cold of the water. Cason inched his way out onto the slick, frozen surface of the pond, moving very carefully. He was not due for a bath. That simple thought caused Cason Byrd to smile. He thought it was a fine joke. Tom Pearl's arm was thrust up abruptly from his cold hell, and his eyes appeared. He gurgled something, but Cason could not understand him.

Cason managed to ease forward by going to hands and knees and cautiously creeping toward the jagged rim of the ice hole. Once he was near enough to touch the icy blue tips of Tom Pearl's fingers as they waved past his eyes, but could not grasp the man's hands.

The new ice was blue, nearly translucent. From where Cason had positioned himself, he could see the urgent writhing of Tom's body under the water, the futile stretching forth of his hands. They moved very slowly in a slow supplication. Cason did not dare go any closer. What could he accomplish but putting himself in the same situation as Tom Pearl?

As he watched, Tom Pearl's frantic motions slowed. His body drifted until he was under the shelf of ice where Cason lay. The boy's eyes were still open; he seemed to see through the ice to where Cason watched. Those eyes were still wild with panic, but slowly they glazed over until they expressed nothing at all. Streams of bubbles escaped from his nostrils and lips. His entire face pressed against the underside of the ice for a long moment, rolled, and then drifted away in the slight current of the pond waters as Tom Pearl was taken away in silent retribution of the pond gods.

Cason Byrd lifted himself from the face of the ice, eased his way back toward shore, and then, when he judged it to be safe, rose and walked away, his boots crushing the scattered berries Tom had spilled in his fall until they looked like bloody splotches on the ice.

For a while a fuss was made, and a crew of men rushed out toward the pond on what they knew was an impossible mission. By the time the broken wagon wheel had been repaired and they were ready to rumble on, only a few of them remembered to care about Tom Pearl—his stricken mother and the overwhelmed Leslie Hart, who spent some time on the bench seat of the Pearl wagon seat, clinging to Tom's mother and sharing tears.

Beryl Byrd made two-dozen raspberry tarts for her family that evening, using Lini Kleinschmidt's little iron stove, and there were no questions from Cason's mother or his father concerning Tom Pearl, although once or twice Beryl did give her son an inquiring glance.

Well, Cason thought, let them blame him if they liked. What else could he have done?

# Chapter Fifteen

## The Outpost

The trading post at Harris Fork was a solitary mud-brick building positioned in a shallow valley between ranks of gently rolling hills where a dozen or so tepees sat, tribal emblems painted boldly on their buffalo-hide walls. The sky was high, wide, and blue. The outpost itself looked like some squat beetle besieged by hundreds of yellow ants. The wagon train had halted here in the middle of the night and now those settlers waited to replenish depleted goods, to ask about trail conditions, the temperament of the Indians, and the possibility of having mail dispatched from this remote station.

By the time the store owners and their clerks arrived just after dawn, the crush of pilgrims was heavy against the door, overflowing the small plank porch. People peered in the windows, whistled, and knocked, hoping to gain admission. Those who had saved back no more money spent the time leading their oxen or horses to graze, cleaning up what could be cleaned, greasing the rolling gear of their wagons, and being a little envious of those who had been richer or wiser in allocating their funds for the long road.

"Those Indians," Cason Byrd asked, looking at the tepees along the rise, "they're all friendly, are they?"

"Well, the men running the outpost must think so," Will Hecht said. He had removed his hat briefly, and the rising breeze shifted his corn-silk hair. He smiled and rested a hand briefly on the taller Cason Byrd's shoulder. Cason was not soothed. Will added, "Tracy Camp says they're Shoshone and we haven't had any trouble with them in memory, and Tracy knows his Indians."

"They still give me an uneasy feeling," Cason said. "It wouldn't be so strong an unease had I powder and some .36 caliber balls." Will Hecht's surprise bordered on shock.

"You're not telling me that you're carrying around an empty pistol?"

"That's what poverty will do for you," Cason Byrd answered with a crooked smile.

"It can't be so," Hecht, who had acquired the Texas habit of never going anywhere unarmed, was truly shocked.

"It is," Cason assured him. "No powder, caps, or balls for this fine pistol of mine." He shrugged, "But what can a man do?"

"What?" Will Hecht asked with profound disbelief. "A man goes to his friends and asks for a loan under such dire circumstances. Boy, you'll be wandering the mountains naked, the way you're going about things!"

"Do you mean that you would . . . ?" Cason asked.

"Of course I'd loan you enough for powder and balls, son," Will Hecht said. "Me and Tracy Camp are working men still. Tracy isn't carrying a lot of money, just our trail bank, but I can get powder money from him once I explain your situation. Unless you just happen to like toting around useless iron."

Cason's spirits revived. He slapped Will Hecht on the back and grinned. Was Hecht his friend? Cason didn't know—he had never had a friend before, but Will was proving to be a useful acquaintance.

"Besides," Hecht said as they trudged toward the trading post to join with the mob there, "you'll likely be traveling on with us to Cheyenne, isn't that right? Then you'll be working for Starr Ranch, and you can pay me back what you owe me from your first pay packet."

"Things have to be settled about that," Cason Byrd said, thinking primarily of his father, "when we get to Wyoming."

"Well, then," Will Hecht said as they shouldered their way through the crowd in front of the store, "you'd better get to settling, Case." At Cason's blank look, Will Hecht told him, "We're already into Wyoming, my friend. That dirt under your boots is Wyoming dirt."

Seth Byrd had been at the front of the line when the trading post opened. Not that he had much to spend on provisions, but he still had a few of the dollars he had skimmed from the family strongbox. Now that they were splitting off from the bulk of the wagons bound for Oregon, the number of nightly community gatherings would be fewer and smaller, and men around the campfire might begin to resent the constant presence of an ungenerous man, as men in a saloon soon tired of the one among them who never bought a round, but was always thirsty. Seth Byrd had too much pride to be viewed that way. He meant to purchase a jug of cure-all this morning.

As women buzzed about looking at bolts of woolen goods and gasped over the fresh apples the store carried by the bushel, Seth found the area of the counter he desired. There was a line of tired-looking men waiting there in ragged, trail-stained clothing, and one-gallon brown jugs were being placed on the counter and taken away as fast as the clerks could provide them. There seemed to be nothing else sold in this section of the trading post but whisky, tobacco, and gunpowder. Seth waited his turn impatiently, once spotting Cason skulking from the counter with a small bag in his hands. What was that no-good kid up to now?

Of the men crowded around him, Seth asked, "Does anyone

know this territory? Anyone know where Jonathan Byrd's place is?"

"Mister," one man with a stiff red beard answered, "we're all as new as you here. If you want to find somebody, try asking the store owners, or try that man sitting in the corner. He seems to be a sort of atlas of the north country."

The man to whom Seth had been directed sat alone at a tiny round table in the farthest recess of the store. He was blue-eyed, rather handsome, dressed in a combination of buckskins and heavy tweed. He was dealing a two-handed game of cards, although he was alone. Seth started that way and stood hovering over the brown-haired man for a while.

"Aluette," the man said apropos of nothing Seth could think of.

"Pardon me?"

"So very sorry," the blue-eyed man said in a sort of purr. His accent was not American. "Usually the first question men ask me is what card game I am playing. It is a French game called aluette."

"Played like solitaire, is it?"

"Not usually, not by civilized men, but I have been wandering alone for so long, with nothing but these paste boards to keep me company, that I have adapted the game. Was there something you wished?"

The man stacked the cards and leaned away from the table. As he did so, Seth saw the edge of a shiny badge pinned to the front of the stranger's fringed buckskin shirt.

"I'm looking for a man who has a land holding somewhere north of here. I don't know if it even has a name. My wife and I are due there, and I was just wondering if you happened to have run across a man named Jonathan Byrd."

"Jonathan Byrd! Yes. There is a name from out of the past."

"You do know him then?" Seth asked, sagging into a chair

opposite the Frenchman.

"He once saved the life of a foolish young man who chose to hike across Wyoming in the winter—me. I did not know him long, nor well," the man, who proved to be Louis L'Enfant, said, leaning back in his chair, a faraway look in his eyes. "We talked the blizzard away and played a lot of aluette. I learned about his past and his wishes. I told him about my personal problems." L'Enfant waved a hand as if that subject no longer meant a thing to him. "I have frequently thought that I should drift up that way one day and visit Jonathan."

"And his wife?" Seth suggested, poking about for news.

"So," L'Enfant, "she returned to him? Good. It's difficult for a man alone in the cold winters! It is good for him to have a wife, is it not?"

"I suppose so," Seth answered moodily. He was still in need of a drink on this morning, and his spirits were at low ebb. "I heard that Jonathan bought the girl. Or won her in a contest."

"True!" L'Enfant said with enthusiasm. "Won her in a contest of shooting skill. As glorious as winning the maiden in a knightly joust, is it not?"

"I'm not that romantic," Seth snapped.

"Oh, no?" the Frenchman said, his eyelids lowering. "Too bad. I am sorry for you." L'Enfant's mood changed and his eyes brightened. "So," he said, "you are looking for Jonathan Byrd."

"Yes, he's my cousin and we've been invited to stay on his estate."

L'Enfant's eyes narrowed again, but he said nothing concerning Seth Byrd's half-truth.

"It is in his character," L'Enfant replied. "He is a fine man, a generous one. You say you are his cousin?" L'Enfant had picked up the deck of cards and was idly shuffling them again.

"That's right. Seth Byrd is my name. I am hoping to find

someone who can tell me the way to his place. They say it has no name."

"Do they? It has a name, Mr. Byrd. It is called Shywater, and I can tell you exactly where it is if my memory is not failing me," he said with a fleeting smile. L'Enfant's blue eyes grew thoughtful. "I will take you there if you will allow me to travel along with you," he said abruptly. "I would like to see Jonathan Byrd again. I owe him much. I should pay him a visit. Shywater is on the road to Cheyenne—or somewhat—and that is where my next bit of work takes me."

"Can't see why you shouldn't travel along with the wagons north," Seth said. "And we could sure use your help, once we come to the place where you say our trail deviates. Traveling alone in strange country could lead us into all sorts of difficulties, I expect."

Seth rose from the table, and the two men shook hands. Seth was eager to be going. As soon as he had made his farewell and offered his thanks, he meant to go to the rear of the trading post and pop the cork from the jug of corn liquor he was carrying. He gave little more thought to the Frenchman or the badge L'Enfant was wearing.

# CHAPTER SIXTEEN

## The Red Pony

Beryl had found her way to the paddock where a few dozen Indian ponies were kept penned. She felt extremely nervous, so much so that her head seemed to buzz with trepidation. Seth would skin her if he found out what she had in mind. A lone Shoshone Indian man, shirtless even in the chill of the morning, sat on the top rail of the corral, watching as Beryl and various other prospective buyers examined the horses he had for sale.

"I've got to get me out of that wagon," one gray-bearded man was telling a friend. "It's sit there and take splinters in my hindquarters or walk step for step with my oxen to Oregon. I can't take neither no more." His friend laughed in agreement, and they began pointing out likely looking ponies to each other. Beryl stayed within hearing distance. Most of the Indian's stock seemed too young, too frisky, to be decent saddle mounts. She should have brought Cason and his knowledgeable young friend, Will Hecht, along, but that would have ruined the surprise.

"That little roan!" the bearded man yelled at the stoic Indian. "Will he take a saddle?"

"All of 'em, you ride, or me fix 'em," the Shoshone answered in a flat tone.

The gray-beard muttered to his friend, "I guess that means ain't none of 'em used to saddle or bit, but he'll rough break 'em."

"That's all right for him," his companion laughed, "but I wouldn't want to be the man riding one for the first couple of miles—or trying to."

"No." The bearded man yelled again: "Hey, chief, are there any white men selling horses around here?"

"White man, Shoshone, all horses the same," came the laconic answer.

"I suppose he's right there," the bearded man said, "but let's keep on looking. What do you say?"

"It makes me no never mind. I got nothing else to do today. I just want to stop somewhere and have me a drink first."

Muttering, the two men strode away, leaving Beryl no wiser than she had been. If she risked all, buying a horse for Cason to pursue his dreams, she did not want to find she had thrown her money away on a pony he could not handle.

"Made up your mind?" a voice behind her asked and Beryl reflexively jumped. Her nerves were that bad on this day. She turned almost fearfully to find the tall smiling cowboy, Tracy Camp, at her shoulder.

"N-no," she said with a hesitant stutter. "I don't really know much about horses, it seems. I was looking to buy one for Cason . . . my son."

Tracy Camp's smile broadened. "Yes, I know who Cason is, remember?"

"Yes, of course," Beryl replied. "Cason has talked of nothing but getting a horse for days now."

"I know," Tracy Camp said, stepping nearer yet. His presence was both intimidating and reassuring. "The boys go on about it all the time, trying to come up with some solution. They've had some outlandish plans to find a horse for Cason."

Beryl felt a little snubbed. Why couldn't the boys have had these conversations with her, felt comfortable enough to discuss their plans? She knew the answer to that. They were afraid Seth might learn of those plans.

Tracy Camp leaned against the paddock fence, his boot propped up on the lowest rail, studying the horses there with a knowledgeable eye. "That little red roan is not a bad looking pony," he said, agreeing with the bearded man's assessment. "It's young, but that's neither good nor bad. It's all in the way they're raised, in my opinion." He was silent then for a minute or so, watching the mostly young animals in the pen.

"I think Will believes that if they mention it often enough, I'll use some of Mr. Starr's money to buy him a mount myself." Tracy removed his hat and wiped back his hair, smiling at Beryl. "I don't think Mr. Starr's instructions can be interpreted quite that loosely."

"No," Beryl said hastily. "I can see that. And I wouldn't want you to feel responsible for Cason. That's why I'm here. I have a little money I've kept tucked away, and just now Cason's needs seem more important than my own. Unfortunately," she said, "I am discovering that I know nothing about purchasing a saddle horse."

"There's nothing to buying a horse," Tracy Camp said, looking away again. "Tending him, breaking him to saddle, and rearing him can be a little tricky with some animals. Most of them, in fact."

"I can see that," Beryl said, her voice subdued as the colts in the pen kicked up their heels and pranced around, proudly displaying their youth and vigor, stirring up a fine dust that sifted over them.

"Not that anyone with a little knowledge couldn't do it. Like most things, it just takes time." Camp glanced down at Beryl. "How many horses were you thinking of purchasing?"

"Why, just the one, for Cason," Beryl said with surprise. "Why would I want more even if I could afford it?"

"I don't know," Tracy Camp said, averting his eyes now. "Just some notion I had. Pay no attention to me."

Beryl felt her cheeks grow warm. "You think that red roan might be the best of the bunch?" she asked hastily.

"From here, yes," Camp said. "I'd have to check it a little, feel its hocks for bowed tendons and such, but he seems to be one of the best of the colts."

"I wonder if I could afford it," Beryl said.

"You won't know until you ask. But, ma'am, don't take the Shoshone's first price. Bargain with him. He'll expect you to do that."

"I don't know if I'd be very good at bargaining. Seth generally dickers with salesmen and such, not me." She paused. "Would it be terribly presumptuous if I were to ask you to . . ."

"To go along and talk to the man?" Camp said with a short laugh. "Of course I will. You came here to try and do some business. Let's have at it."

They made their way around the paddock to where the Shoshone still sat perched on the top rail of the fence. The deal was closed with only a minimum amount of bargaining. The Shoshone seemed in urgent need of some cash money on that morning. Leading the prancing roan colt away from the pens, Beryl felt a strange sort of giddy exhilaration, along with an undercurrent of fear. Seth would skin her if he found out that she had spent the last of their holdout money, and what she had spent it on. No matter. Cason had his horse now. The pony danced and shook its head as Tracy led it sure-handedly along with a gloved hand. The cowboy seemed to enjoy the antics of the spirited horse.

"Well, as you can see," Tracy said as they walked their way along the line of wagons, "he's not quite ready to be ridden yet. But that can be solved. One thing at a time. Where are we taking him?"

"I don't know," Beryl said. A cold sort of remorse lingered

after the hot impulse that had caused her to purchase the animal. Nearly in panic, she realized she had no idea what to do with the horse now; she had not even planned that far ahead. "Seth will want me to return it."

"We can't have that," Tracy Camp said across the burnished back of the young roan. "Not when you are about to make a young man the happiest fellow in the world. I'll tell you what," he said, halting the colt, "we'll take it to my camp. Will and I can look out for it when Cason isn't around. Though, come to think of it, he's mostly around these days."

"More than he's at home," Beryl answered. "But I can't expect you to take on that responsibility. You have your own work to do."

"Not until the wagon train's ready to roll again, and they tell me that's going to be another three days yet to let the animals rest and put some weight back on. This young fellow can stay with us until we break camp," he said, stroking the red roan's muzzle. The colt tried to nip at him, but Tracy jerked his hand away, laughing.

"Those two young men—Will and Cason—will likely have the roan rough-broke by then. They won't be kept from wanting to ride it, if I know them."

"I suppose not," Beryl said, still doubtful. "But the animal will have to be fed."

"The grass is tall," Tracy Camp said as soothingly as possible. Well, if the Texan had no qualms about it, why not go along with the plan? She only wanted to see the look on Cason's face when he first saw the horse.

She only wanted to see her son finally happy again, as he had been as a child.

"He'll need saddle and bridle," Beryl said, realizing that she was bringing up objections to her own scheme.

"Ma'am," Tracy Camp said, again halting the horse, "let's

leave something for the boys to figure out on their own."

"Yes," Beryl said with a little laugh of relief. Tracy Camp was right; she had done all she could. It was time for Precious's feeding; she had been gone from the wagon longer than she intended. "I have to get back and see to my daughter, Mr. Camp," she said, feeling rather stiff with him. Camp smiled crookedly. She could not understand what his expression was meant to convey.

"All right. Tell Precious that Tracy says 'hello,' won't you, Beryl?"

# Chapter Seventeen

**Isolated**

The breeze was warm up the long canyons, the air dry, the weather summery. The long veils of dung-colored dust that had colored the sky were absent. The foothills were covered with new grass. Far beyond these, snow-capped mountains rose in stern, forbidding ranks. When the wagon halted, there was no sound of either man or beast across the long meadows.

The silence, the isolation, seemed oppressive to Seth Byrd. Since departing the northbound wagon train, they had seen not another human being, heard no sounds of human endeavor. No structures dotted the land, no herds of domesticated animals; there were no fences, no passing men.

There were deer, which seemed scarcely afraid of the settlers, perhaps never having seen man or gun before. Rabbits, ground squirrels, and badgers, along with ground nesting birds, fled only with the greatest reluctance before the hooves of the great plodding, stoic oxen.

Seth Byrd walked on across the grasslands, prodding the oxen without spirit. Trail-broken by now, the oxen needed no encouragement to continue on their assigned way. Seth scowled at the empty land. Well, he wondered, what had he expected? He had known that they were traveling into the remote northern lands. Had he thought they would roll up onto Jonathan Byrd's estate, passing through stone pillars on a graded road leading to a mansion on the hill? Of course not. Yet there was something disturbing about the lonesomeness of the land, intimidating about the high Rocky Mountains, bothersome about the men they now traveled with, which made Seth not regretful, but almost resentful about the decision he had made: the grand move west.

There were those two cowboys who for some reason had separated themselves from the northbound wagon train and now tailed along with Seth and his family although the idea had never been discussed. There was the Frenchman, L'Enfant, who was some sort of a lawman, and supposedly an old friend of Jonathan Byrd. The man guided them along their way not with serious intensity, but with a sort of lackadaisical air, as if it mattered not to him whether they ever reached their destination or not, and who at times seemed to not even know where he was in all of this vast land.

Cason Byrd did not ride in the wagon anymore, but now followed along astride a fractious little red pony that had appeared from nowhere as far as Seth knew. No one had bothered to tell him. He assumed the two men from Texas had given it to him; otherwise, the pony's presence made no sense unless the undisciplined boy had stolen it from someone on the wagon train. The horse was just there one morning, and Cason had stepped into the saddle as if he had always owned the animal. Now haughty and proud, Cason rode out from the wagon in wide circles, often accompanied by the yellow-haired kid from Texas.

The older one, the one called Tracy Camp, spent more time near the wagon. Too much time, in Seth's opinion. The tall Texan seemed to hover around Beryl and the baby like a bee around a flower. Camp was obviously a man who had been much alone and yearned for the little touches of home he seldom got, but it was *Seth's* home he was buzzing about, and if he had any idea of doing any pollinating there, he had better find another thought. A man who has been long alone comes up with some unsavory ideas, Seth knew.

Beryl was more worrisome yet. She beamed with delight when the man paid her any small attention, smiled in a way she had not smiled at Seth in years. True, the trail had been long and hard for her as well, with little companionship, but Tracy Camp was not the sort of companion she needed. Seth would simply not tolerate it.

Seth had much time to ponder as he walked west, endlessly west, across the long grasslands. Although he had pretended otherwise—perhaps for himself—he realized he was little more than a trespasser on this land and that his cousin, Jonathan, blood ties aside, might simply turn him away. Jonathan had his estate and his young Indian concubine; he might be content with a short visit from his cousin, but to allow him to stay on indefinitely was a different proposition, and Seth knew it.

Seth plodded on, his gloom growing deeper. It seemed to Seth that each of the men he traveled with was more sure of himself, more confident, than Seth was these days. It seemed he had lost some of his sureness back somewhere along the trail. He had noticed this before, this feeling of dwindling a little the farther west they went. The men out here seemed larger; certainly they would not be intimidated easily. Seth's self-image had taken a long, painful beating. It seemed that he had lost control of his world, of himself, in a way that was indefinable, bleak, and quite isolating. He no longer thought of himself as being in charge of his wife, son, family, or of his own destiny. He was crumbling before his own eyes.

Seth's head lifted at the approaching sound of charging hoofbeats.

The Frenchman appeared out of nowhere, riding his off-white pony rapidly toward the wagon. There was a look of excitement on his face. Seth did not attempt to halt the oxen.

That was a difficult task that would only lead to having to start them on their way again. The Frenchman rode his horse in a tight circle and pulled it to a walk beside Seth Byrd. "Just about there," L'Enfant said in a loud, raspy tone. "I found one of Jonathan's corner markers. I'm not sure, but I think I may have even caught a glimpse of his house up along the valley. We're nearly there, Seth. In just a little while, we'll be on Shywater."

★ ★ ★ ★ ★

# Part Three: The Shywater Gypsies

★ ★ ★ ★ ★

# Chapter Eighteen

There was a splendid peace across the valley. The sun was high enough to make a slithering silver glitter of the creek, low enough to paint deep shadows among the pine trees growing in stoic profusion on the hill slopes facing the house. The meadow flowers, gentian, columbine, and mountain lupine dotted the long valley. A large colony of colorful grouse had arrived this year and decided to stay. The distant gray Tetons still lorded over the land. Deer were plentiful as always, despite the lurking presence of the tawny cougar—or its grandson. Jonathan preferred to think it was the same old grandfather cat, since it had never yet disturbed the horses.

There was a shriek of joy and then from around the corner of the house, the stubby-legged Angelica came running toward him, her flyway dark hair drifting from her skull. Strong, chubby arms stretched out for her father, who scooped her up as Vashti, smiling, came toward the porch, a look of mock seriousness on her face.

"What have you been doing to this child?" Jonathan Byrd asked, Angelica clinging to him, her face buried against his chest.

"What do you think?" Vashti asked with stage severity. "It was hair-washing day, and she knew it. Now she has run away from me. I don't care anymore," she said sitting on the porch, brush in her hand. "Let the child be the dirtiest girl in the world for all I care. I give up!"

Jonathan looked down into the three-year-old's eyes. Angelica's eye shifted between amusement and uneasiness. He told her, "It seems that you have made your mother sad by running away. She only wanted to make you a clean little girl she could be proud of. What will we do if she cries?"

"Kiss her," Angelica suggested, fingering the fringing on the front of Jonathan's shirt.

"Yes," Jonathan said thoughtfully. "That would be a very good thing to do, but Angelica, my love, wouldn't it be a good idea to just do what she wants so that she would not have to cry at all? Then we wouldn't all have to waste our time, kiss-kissing, like this." He kissed the girl's nose, ears, forehead, and fingers until she resumed laughing. "Go on now," he said with artificial sternness, and he handed the girl back to Vashti.

"Thank you for scolding her, Father," Vashti said. "I know that now she will be a good girl and let me wash her hair."

They walked away then, Angelica looking back across her mother's shoulder, waving goodbye with a curling and uncurling of her fingers.

It was then that the band of gypsies caught Jonathan Byrd's attention. The approaching sounds, which were not sounds of the forest, alerted him to their arrival long before he saw the unexpected, completely out of place, caravan rolling up the long valley directly toward his house. Frowning, Jonathan considered snatching up his Hawken rifle, but then his attention was caught by someone yelling his name.

"Jonathan Byrd!"

Jonathan shaded his eyes with his hand and watched as the incoming rider on a pale horse galloped toward him. Of his own horses, the paint now came alertly to the railing of the corral, ears pricked at the sight and scent of a strange arriving horse. The gray horse stoically ignored the activity and continued to munch at his hay. The horseman approaching the house wore a blue woolen coat and a buckskin shirt with something bright attached to it. He had on a dark hat with a wide brim. He seemed somehow familiar, but Jonathan could not place him.

*"Mon ami!"* the rider called out.

Jonathan's searching mind assembled the pieces of the puzzle. He had not known the man long or well, but now he recognized and remembered Louis L'Enfant. L'Enfant pulled his horse up short a dozen yards from the porch, dismounted, and walked toward Jonathan, hand extended.

"Jonathan Byrd," L'Enfant said, holding Jonathan by both shoulders and smiling at him. "I did not think I would ever see you again."

"Truthfully, Louis, I didn't think I'd ever see you either. Not the way you seemed to be rushing after death!"

"Yes—my pursuit of the man Abel Robert Avery." The Frenchman nodded. "I'll tell you about how that turned out later on. For now, you've got guests to see to. You don't mind if I make myself a little camp up among the trees?"

"Of course not, Louis." Jonathan's eyes narrowed as he watched the slowly approaching caravan arriving from out of the low sun. "Who are all those people, and what do they want?"

"As to that," Louis answered, "I'm not so sure myself. I just happened to be tagging along. You'd be better off asking your cousin there who they all are."

"My cousin?" Jonathan asked in astonishment. "Which one?"

"The tall man walking with the ox goad," Louis said. "Don't you recognize him?"

"Not at this distance. But my cousin? It can't be!"

"This can't be the place. That can't be your cousin, Jonathan," Beryl said, riding on the wagon bench with Precious in her arms.

"Louis says this is the place," Seth answered, wiping the

perspiration from his brow. “So that must be Jonathan Byrd.”

“This is just a shack on wilderness land. I don’t see any crops growing, any herds of cattle or horses. This is a wealthy landowner, and a big fur trader?” Beryl nearly shouted. She had been trying to contain her disappointment with her lot in life for months now, but this was the final bitter pill—to have traveled so far, so roughly, toward Seth’s golden destination only to find nothing but a cabin among the pines, a trickle of a stream not even large enough to be considered a creek, making its sluggish way down a long chute in the mountain flanks in a manner too hasty even to nourish the dry grass along the slope.

It had to be Shywater; she was convinced. The place had been assigned that name for a reason. On the porch of the unbarked log house she could see a tall man wearing a fringed buckskin shirt looking their way. Beside him was a woman in a beaded white elkskin dress. There was a little girl of three or four with them, her hair damp, gnawing at a knuckle, studying them with wide brown eyes.

Seth, walking beside the wagon, looked as if someone had knocked the chocks from under the trap door of his gallows. Not too far away from them, surveying the scene with curiosity, rode Tracy Camp. He glanced only once at Beryl, and said nothing, but the glance seemed to convey pity.

Cason closed on them from behind the wagon, riding his frisky little red pony. He yelled at Seth, “Aren’t you going to even introduce yourself?”

“Yes, I am,” Seth answered in what was nearly a snarl. “Give me a hand slowing the team, circling them, and settling them for the evening.”

“They’re smelling the water,” Cason answered in a tone he would not have dared use to his father even a week earlier. Seth ignored the obvious comment and proceeded forward to unyoke the first team. Cason hesitated a long time before swinging down from his red roan to help his father with the rest of the animals.

"What are they doing?" Vashti asked as the oxen were lined up along the Shywater creek.

"Watering their animals, obviously," Jonathan answered. They stood together on their porch still. Angelica had gone off running through the sunshine, drying her hair and getting it dirty again at once. "You'll have to start braiding that girl's hair," Jonathan muttered, watching fondly as Angelica pursued a yellow butterfly.

Vashti, whose own hair was done in the two braids typical of the Mountain Crow, had not shifted those obsidian eyes from the wagon of the newcomers. Now she said to Jonathan, "I can see the animals drinking, Husband. What I meant to ask is, what are the people intending to do here?"

"To water their animals," Jonathan said with the smile that sometimes infuriated Vashti. He went rapidly on, "To rest their stock and themselves. They have come a very long way and want nothing more than to eat, rest, and relax. And then, there's my cousin Seth, if that is him as L'Enfant says. He must wish to greet me and offer his best wishes."

"If he is your kinsman, why did he not come immediately to the house? That would be more usual," Vashti said.

"He tends first to his animals. That's a good sign in a man."

"Yes, if you say so," she said. "Husband, are we expected to feed all of them?"

"It's only common politeness," Jonathan said, "to feed long travelers."

"I wonder how we are to manage it." Then Vashti laughed. "Well, at least they have brought their own meat with them."

"I don't think Seth will consider butchering one of his oxen. They have another use more vital to get them to wherever they are going."

"Where do you think that is?" Vashti asked.

"I have no idea, but it could be to Rendezvous. I saw the distant glow of a dozen fires last evening, didn't you?"

"I did, but I didn't remark upon them. I have only sad memories of Rendezvous."

"Oh, really?" Jonathan arched his eyebrows and drew Vashti nearer to him with an arm around her shoulders.

"Oh, not you," she protested. "You know better than that, Husband," she said with softening eyes.

"I do, yes," Jonathan said, lightly kissing the top of her head. "I had no liking for Rendezvous myself, but others do. Don't worry about food for all of these people. There is that young buck I shot this morning. I'll have Louis help me take it into the woods and hang it from a tree to be skinned out and butchered. We'll cook the meat over an open fire if we must. There's no time to dig a pit, and I don't have the ambition or inclination to do so."

"That alone will make a poor meal," Vashti said, worrying as any hostess does. "I think some of the ears of corn are ripe, or nearly so. The beans have not come in yet, and the squash is still very young. Angelica and I can go out and gather some hop clover and goldenrod while you visit with your cousin and the men."

"Don't exhaust yourself over one meal," Jonathan advised her.

"I don't intend to." She turned to face him, looking up with those dark liquid eyes of hers. "Just do me the favor of finding out who they are, Husband . . . and when they will be going away."

"I would think you'd be happy to have some company for a change. We haven't seen a person since that young man came by trying to find the Reverend Blaylock's camp, and that's been over a month ago."

"Which is just about often enough for company," Vashti said. She added, "And that skinny young fellow didn't eat much."

"I was just thinking you might like to have someone to talk to besides me," Jonathan Byrd said. "Look there. One of the travelers is a woman, and she's carrying a baby."

"Who is she?" Vashti asked as they watched the woman being handed down by one of the cowboys from horseback.

"I don't know. We'll have to wait until we're told."

"Can we just send them off to Rendezvous?" Vashti asked, concerned.

"No ox train can make it up those hills from this side. Besides, we don't even know if that's where they wish to go."

"As you say, we will just have to wait and find out."

"Yes, and that won't be long now," Jonathan guessed. For striding toward them the tall man who had been guiding the oxen came. Jonathan continued to study his face. Seth Byrd? It could be, but Jonathan saw no family resemblance. Vashti seemed to.

"I think this is your kinsman, Jonathan."

At least he was the one taking the lead. Jonathan stepped down from the porch to await him. The sun was bright, clear, the air only slightly cool. Summer was quickly arriving.

"Jonathan Byrd?" the approaching man called out.

"Yes, that's who I am."

It was another minute before the stranger stopped in front of Jonathan and introduced himself, "I'm Seth Byrd, up out of Kansas."

The two men shook hands almost warily as they studied each other. "Nice to see you after all of these years," Jonathan said, although it really wasn't. Seth Byrd carried old, unhappy memories and new questions with him. "This is my wife, Vashti."

Seth's eyes narrowed in the sunlight as he glanced at Vashti and then examined her in a way that Jonathan didn't care for.

"I'm very pleased to meet you," Vashti said.

"This is my wife, Beryl," Seth said, fumbling with his words a little. He turned and summoned Beryl toward them with a wave of his hand. Angelica had returned to the porch to wrap her arm around her mother's leg and stare wide-eyed at the approaching woman and baby.

"That is your baby son?" Vashti asked.

"Nah, that's my daughter, Precious. My son is that kid over with the oxen. Name's Cason." Seth was still studying Vashti, although more circumspectly now. He had expected to find some well-rounded squaw who would run away shyly at the sight of so many strange white faces. This woman was very pretty, well spoken, and seemed nearly too young to be the mother of the little girl.

Beryl arrived, her face tight with uncertainty, disapproval, and trail-weariness. She flashed a meaningless smile and clung more tightly to Precious.

"May I see the baby?" Vashti asked, and Beryl seemed to tighten her grip still more.

"Sure!" Seth said speaking for her. He was happy to deflect attention from himself.

Angelica crowded closer as Beryl uncovered the baby's face and wriggling pink fingers.

Angelica, who had never seen a person smaller than herself, was entranced, delighted.

"You've had a long trip," Vashti said. "You and the baby must both be tired. Won't you come into the house and sit down. There is cool water, and Angelica's old cradle is still in the living room if you would like to lay the child down for a while."

"Sure! Why don't you do that, Beryl. It'll give you a chance to relax."

Hesitantly Beryl followed Vashti into the house, of which she was obviously proud. They could hear her talking to Beryl;

Beryl's answers were short and reflected discomfort with the situation.

"She'll loosen up after a few minutes," Seth assured Jonathan, whose expression was tense. "Then you won't be able to shut Beryl up. She is a talking woman!"

"Who are the others traveling with you?" Jonathan Byrd asked, hoping to get an idea of what exactly had brought Seth to Shywater without actually having to ask him. "I know that is your son, Cason, down at the creek."

"Yes, that's my lazy kid. I don't know why he hasn't brought himself along yet."

Jonathan nodded. If Cason Byrd was indeed lazy, he wasn't demonstrating it at this point as he unyoked the oxen and led them to water.

"And the others?"

"None of them is really with us," Seth said as his eyes wandered over the long valley and the woodlands above. "There's some Frenchman named L'Enfant . . ."

"I know L'Enfant," Jonathan said.

"Oh, that's right. He told us that. He agreed to show us the way up here so that he could stop by and see you. He said he owed you something from way back."

"Very little," Jonathan responded.

"Well, be that as it may . . ." Seth said uneasily. "He was our guide to your place. The other two are cowboys out of Texas, if you can believe it. They were on their way to Cheyenne, do you know it?"

"Only by name," Jonathan said. His cousin seemed very nervous, something Jonathan could not understand.

"Anyway, they decided to stop here with us because there was a source of water here and their ponies are pretty beat down, as you can imagine."

"I can. It's understandable if they've been ridden all the way from the Texas country." Looking downslope, Jonathan could see that the two cowboys had led their mounts to the stream.

"Hope they don't drink it dry," Seth said.

"They won't, so long as water continues to run downhill," Jonathan said, looking toward the Grand Tetons far away and high above them. "And I'm pretty sure that's always going to be the case. Seth, I've got a deer to see to if I'm going to feed you all tonight. I think I'll get to it. You could probably use the time to rest anyway. Go on in and join the women if you wish. We'll have plenty of time for talking tonight."

Seth apparently decided that he did not care for women's company just then, for he turned and started back toward his covered wagon. His nervousness was still obvious. Seth's gaze shifted from point to point, and his speech was slightly slurred. Jonathan wondered if his cousin had been ill.

Jonathan himself went to where the shade was deepest, beside the back wall of Angelica's room. He paused to look proudly at that section of the house. He had created it by building a new three-sided structure abutting the main cabin, then cutting a doorway through the wall logs. Vashti would never have complained about the lack of space, of course, but with Angelica then walking and getting underfoot, the girl needed some space of her own, especially in the winter. It was a hard job, but not particularly difficult with the experience Jonathan had gained from building the original cabin.

Across the saw rack in the back of the house a field-dressed four-point mule deer sagged. It had to be skinned and butchered, and now.

"Give you a hand?" Louis L'Enfant asked, seeing Jonathan's dilemma.

"I would accept help, yes." Jonathan replied. "I'm going to hang this deer in the woods and start peeling its hide off. Then I'll have to butcher it out for tonight's dinner party."

"I can help you with that," the Frenchman said. "I've become a fair woodsman since you saw me last. I had to," he said with a rueful chuckle. "Have you got a bucket or maybe a groundsheet to put the butchered meat on?"

"There's a fifty-gallon tub right inside that tool shed," Jonathan said. "If you'll get it, I'll shoulder the deer."

L'Enfant reached inside and removed the huge oaken tub, examining the woodshed as he did. It was not a thing of beauty, but it did the job, and Jonathan was pleased with it.

"This wasn't here before, was it?" L'Enfant asked.

"No," Jonathan grunted as he shouldered the mule deer. Even field-dressed, it was a load to carry. "The entire room wasn't here. I've built it since."

"Well, I was never outside the house much," L'Enfant said. "Just sitting inside by the fire trying to teach you a game you had no interest in."

"Any game of cards or dice leaves me disinterested," Jonathan said as they trudged up the slope into the deeper pines. "I guess I never have to worry about becoming a gambling man."

L'Enfant dropped the heavy bucket to the ground beneath the pines. Together he and Jonathan hoisted the buck, positioning it to hang by its antlers from a crotch in the branches. Jonathan already had his skinning knife out and was giving the slender blade a few last kisses of his whetstone. Louis removed his woolen jacket and borrowed Jonathan's stone to run along the sharp blade of his own knife. It was only then that Jonathan Byrd noticed the badge affixed to Louis L'Enfant's buckskin shirt.

"How'd you come by that?" he asked the Frenchman.

"How did I? That's a question, isn't it? I'll tell you," he said as the two men started stripping the hide from the deer carcass. "I believe I got it because I backed away from a fight."

"You care to go on with that tale?" Jonathan asked. "Or do

you just plan to leave me confused?"

Louis laughed. "It was like this. You know I had a hot-blooded need to find this Abel Robert Avery, the man who had cheated my father out of his property and possessions. Well I finally ran the man to ground—in Denver, Colorado. I'll skip a lot of this story here so it doesn't become a winter's tale, and just say that I braced the man in a saloon and called him out. I challenged him to a duel, that is. Well, Avery ran straight to the law and said I was looking to kill him.

"There was a territorial marshal named Oliver Coons down there, and he came to me to ask what sort of trouble I was stirring up. I told him a little about my grudge against Avery and that I had challenged the man to a duel.

" 'We don't view that as being legal in Colorado,' was what Coons told me, 'even under severe provocation.'

"I argued with him for a while, reminding him of the Alexander-Burr duel, and finishing with a rather pompous, 'I am both a Frenchman and a son of Louisiana.' I might have puffed up a little when I said this, but Coons just sat staring at me. 'The man has committed crimes, but he is far beyond the law here,' I added. 'Justice must be served.'

" 'Let the Lord handle that,' Coons said, and he went out."

"So you never fought your duel?" Jonathan asked, unrolling a section of skin as easy as rolling up a blanket.

"I was too fierce in my youth and indignation to let that be the end of it," L'Enfant said a little sheepishly. "By shaming him in front of his friends, I eventually goaded the man into meeting me on a hilltop one morning at dawn. Avery seemed willing to play it fair, but as I reached the dueling ground, I found that he had brought Coons with him.

"I discovered this after I had finished preparing my weapon. Coons appeared from out of the shadowed trees and said with a bare touch of sadness, 'Monsieur L'Enfant, if you go through with this I will be forced to charge you at least with attempted murder.' "

"What did you do?"

"What could I do? Putting my loaded dueling pistol behind my belt, I doffed my hat and walked away."

Jonathan, still listening, tugged a last section of hide free. Scraping and preparing the hide for tanning would have to wait for another day. There were a lot of people waiting for meat to eat on this day. It was growing later; there was an edge to the wind as it drifted through the pines. Once Jonathan thought he heard a distant shot echoing down the valley; he hoped he hadn't. Pausing to catch his breath, Jonathan rested on a huge fallen log, his bloody hands dangling between his legs, and waited for the Frenchman to continue with his story, for certainly that could not have been the end of his tale.

"All right, then," he said as L'Enfant sat beside him, "what happened next?"

"I walked all the way back into the city, pensive but still angry. As I passed in front of an alleyway I heard a small and metallic sound. I spun that way to see Avery, his face a mask of malicious glee, looking down the barrel of his pistol. I dove, rolled, and got to one knee as he fired. Drawing my dueling pistol I shot him dead. Then I sat down to wait for the marshal."

"Who was quick in coming."

"Was he not? Not satisfied that I was willing to give matters up so easily, he had been trailing me at a distance. Coons"—Louis shrugged—"was himself a witness to the murder attempt. He took me to his office and sat me down in a chair. What he said was not what I had expected. He told me that I had shown respect for the law in obeying his command to leave the dueling field, respect for his authority by remaining at the scene of the shooting and waiting for him to arrive, and a damned good shooting eye.

"We spoke a while longer, then, unbelievably, he offered me the job of deputy marshal, and since I found myself suddenly with nowhere else to go, no mad pursuit to continue, I accepted. When Coons was appointed federal marshal, three of us deputies became sanctioned deputy U.S. marshals. That's what I've been doing for close on to three years now."

Jonathan nodded and then returned to butcher the deer. There was little time for dawdling. The meat had to be bled, a fire built, and sharpened stakes produced for propping up the meat while it roasted. Fortunately, he thought, he still had some of those left from the last time they had conducted a roast.

"So what is it, exactly, that brings you to Shywater?" Jonathan wanted to know.

"It's just as I said. I wanted to visit you and see how things were going. I had to come this way on my way to Cheyenne anyway, so here I am."

"I see," Jonathan said. Whatever problems there were in distant Cheyenne held no interest for him. He supposed he had always been, and had a preference for remaining, a man cut off from the world and its troubles.

Together the two men dragged the heavy tub filled with meat and the folded deerskin down the slope toward the house, leaving the bare bones and unusable fragments of meat for the wild things.

"Is that the way you usually handle your leavings?" the Frenchman asked. "Feed for the animals?"

Cason Byrd had appeared out of nowhere, and now rose from his seat on a log stump to join the men as they reached the back yard.

"Often," Jonathan said, answering Louis. "The way I see it is that I've already taken a part of their rightful prey from them."

"Isn't that tempting them to come nearer?"

"I don't think so—at least it hasn't happened so far. The

coyotes, a wolf or two come to inspect my leavings, but they generally scatter at the sight of me."

"How about that mountain lion?" Cason Byrd asked. They still had not been properly introduced, but that seemed to matter little to Cason or to Jonathan, who knew who his nephew was.

"The mountain lion?" Jonathan said.

"Yes. I was walking in the hills and I came across him. I thought you maybe heard me take a shot at it."

Cason, Jonathan now noticed, had been busy reloading the revolver he carried, a fine, newly made pistol.

"I did hear that, but was hoping the shot wasn't taken on my property," Jonathan said. "If you see the cougar again, please don't shoot at it."

"What is he," Cason asked with a crooked little smile, "some sort of pet?"

"More of a totem, a mascot," Jonathan Byrd answered, unable to explain it even to himself. "The big cat has left us alone through lean summers and heavy winters. I do him the same service."

"Makes no sense to me," Cason said, tipping back his hat, "but it's your property, your puma. I'll do as you wish. Uncle Jonathan, do you mind if I look your horses over?"

"No, I don't mind. They're not much to look at, though."

"They're pretty old," Cason said. "I noticed that. Especially the gray. I can't see that he'd be of much use for anybody."

"Angelica likes to ride him," Jonathan said. "My little girl. The horse never gives her any trouble. His gait is easy."

"She rides at her age? Well, that's just fine, I think," Cason said. "Doesn't that worry her mother, though?"

"Vashti was riding at the same age," Jonathan said. Then he was tired of talking about inconsequentials. Later that night, they could talk for hours. Not that he found Cason rude or obnoxious. The young man was polite for the most part, his rough edges primarily due to his youth.

"You want to start building the fire, Louis? I'll be along as soon as I fine-cut some of this meat and see how Vashti has done searching for vegetables. That pile of firewood just behind the east wall can be used."

"All right," Louis answered. "I'll see what I can do."

"I'll be glad to help you," Cason offered, and Louis accepted his help with a nod.

Jonathan watched them go, thinking that Cason Byrd could be molded into a fine young man with the proper guidance. Which made him think of his cousin, Seth, whose opinion of the boy was low. Was there a reason behind that? There had to be, of course.

And where was Seth? Jonathan had not warmed to Seth immediately, but they could have spent this time talking, learning about each other. Jonathan had still not discovered what their little family was doing here, far from Kansas. Maybe Vashti had learned their purpose in her talk with Beryl.

There was really little time to think and conjecture at the moment. Jonathan began working to prepare for their feast. He did have the time to look up from his tasks now and then and wonder where Seth Byrd had got to.

Seth measured his whisky by its weight and figured the gallon jug he had purchased at Harris Fork was now nearly half empty. Sitting in the back of his Conestoga wagon, he took a deep drink of liquor.

*Well, this was it?* he was thinking. The end of the trail that had no righteous end.

He had been promising Beryl a new and better life since they had left their soddy in Kansas, maintained the fiction—or hope—through the winter in St. Jo when she had been forced to work in harsh weather, saving almost all of her meager wages, believing in Seth and his grand plan for freedom, a second start in life.

Wasn't that exactly what he had promised when he had taken her as a young woman onto the Kansas plains? And where had they got to since? Exactly nowhere—or rather, they seemed to lose ground with each mile they traveled.

Seth took another drink.

Anyone could see that Jonathan had a lot of land up in these mountains. Anyone could see it was virtually good for nothing—neither farming nor herd-raising. And he and Beryl had no house for the winter, which, when it came in the north country, could be merciless. How was he supposed to build even a rough cabin over the summer months and establish some way to feed his family? How was he to feed them even to the end of the week?

He had Cason to help him, of course . . .

His thought stopped short and darkened. Did he even have the boy to help with the work? Cason had grown sullen, and had separated himself from his family in favor of keeping company with those Texas men. It had become worse since he had somehow come by that red pony.

Had that older man, Tracy Camp, who seemed to be traveling with some money, purchased the horse for Case, trying his best to lure Seth's son to his side? And why would the Texan do that? To curry favor with . . . ?

Seth's thoughts again changed direction as he sipped another mouthful of whisky. Tracy Camp paid a lot of attention to his family. To Case, and especially to Beryl. Perhaps the Texan had his plan made: he would buy Cason that pony he had always wanted to display his kindness and to show Beryl that he had money enough to take care of her.

That could be it—the reason the cowboys were riding with

them. Following along to the end of the trail where Beryl could witness Seth's dream turn to ashes, then leave the choice up to Beryl as to what man she wished to throw her lot in with.

Tracy Camp was younger, was a well set-up man with a handsome face and gold in his saddlebags; Seth Byrd was a beggar, now shivering in the back of a worn covered wagon with only his whisky, not his family, to keep him company over the long nights to come.

No! Seth thought. He would not allow it to happen. As for the ungrateful kid, let him ride off wherever he wished. Seth would keep Precious and Beryl as a man had the right to do. He would keep them well. That very evening he would take Jonathan Byrd aside and explain that he wanted the use of a few acres on which to build a house. He had seen a small level patch of meadow among the pines as they approached Jonathan's house from the south. It was a good enough site for a cabin.

With all of the land Jonathan owned and all of the timber surrounding them, how could his own cousin refuse him? If only the past had not been as it was. Jonathan must have been too young to recall it. Seth could only hope so. Besides, was it his fault that his father, in a moment of rage, had killed Jonathan's mother, Angelica? Seth took another deep drink of whisky and tried to force his own memories of that evening away. He had erased the specifics of the moment from his mind many years earlier, but at times, in the dead of night, he could still see terrible bits and moments of that murderous evening.

Seth shook his head and placed the palm of his hand over one eye—the throbbing one.

It was growing dark outside the wagon. Seth could see a dull sheen of crimson laid over the yellow grass valley.

Shywater was a horrible place to come to die. Yet if Jonathan turned down his request, this was where they would plant his bones. He had not the strength to go on, to continue his meaningless quest. He had forgotten even what he was looking for. If he did not so much as have Beryl to stand by him, to believe in his foggy dreams, it would be the end of Seth Byrd, and he knew it.

If Beryl left him for that cowboy, where would he ever draw the strength to continue living, let alone hew a cabin out of the long forest? A man can outlive his usefulness; others simply outlasted their dreams.

# Chapter Nineteen

## Plans for the Future

The meat was roasting on angled stakes over an open cedarwood fire. Juice dripped down onto the low flames, scenting the smoky air around the camp with compelling primitive flavors.

They all had taken seats on sawn logs rolled over for that purpose by Cason and Jonathan Byrd. Once they had been urged to talk, the conversation was mostly between the two Texas cowboys and their doings down in that borderland. Cason was entranced by their tales of bad men and Mexican raiders, of life on the Texas plains, of Stephen Austin, Jim Bowie, Sam Houston, and other Texas notables, the cowboys at times correcting one another, and laughing as they did.

Beryl Byrd also seemed to find the tales fascinating, but more so when Tracy Camp was the speaker, Jonathan noticed. He and Vashti, for themselves, enjoyed the stories of a faraway land they would never see and had no wish to visit. Vashti had told Jonathan that, to her, they were good stories, but as far away from her world as those biblical tales she had heard at Reverend Blaylock's school. Jonathan felt pretty much the same way.

It was when Tracy Camp finally got around to relating why they were so far north, into Wyoming, that Jonathan listened more closely.

"Our boss, Ben Starr, is a far-ahead planning man," Camp told them. "The reason we rode up here is that Mr. Starr is planning a cattle drive north next year. There are a lot of mining camps opening up in Colorado, northern Arizona, and even Wyoming. Those people all have to be fed. Me and young Will here were assigned to look over trail conditions, water and grazing and gauge the mood of the Indians if we could."

"You surely can't mean to drive cattle through to Cheyenne," Jonathan Byrd said.

"Not next year, no, but as I have said, Mr. Starr is a long-planning man. There is a man named Tyler who is planning to bring the railroad to Cheyenne in the next few years. Now, tracklayers are also men who have to be fed. Mr. Starr wants to be the first one to approach Tyler about supplying beef to railroad workers. By then he intends to show that he has already driven herds through to Colorado and has the trail well marked. That will put him a step or two ahead of any other rancher who might come up with the idea."

"Seems a risky venture to me," Jonathan said, tossing a gnawed bone into the fire.

"Oh, it is!" Tracy Camp agreed. "But Mr. Starr has made a lifetime's work out of beating the odds. He plans ahead first, double checks what he is doing, and then acts decisively."

"Not like building a sawmill," Cason Byrd muttered, but only a few people heard him, and those who did had no idea of what he was talking about.

"We're going to meet with this man Tyler in Cheyenne and lay out the preliminary plans for him. Then I expect we'll be taking a flatboat south and back to Texas—that is, if Will here is as tired of sitting a pony as I am."

Will grinned, nodded, and carefully picked another piece of roasted venison from the fire stakes. He looked at Vashti and asked in a genuinely interested tone of voice, "Ma'am, what is this kind of yellowish plant here?"

"That is goldenrod," Vashti said.

"That so? I never knew you could eat it. What about this pink tea? What is that?"

"That's Vashti's sycamore bark tea," Jonathan told him. "Some like it a lot, but others find it kind of bland."

"I like it fine," Will said, sipping at his tea. "If we had the time, I'd like to learn a little more about wilderness foods. A man never knows when he might get stuck somewhere, does he?"

"I suppose we'll all be eating beef steaks in Cheyenne," Cason Byrd said. It was the first time he had ever used a plural concerning himself and his cowboy friends. Will only nodded, but Beryl's expression altered, her worst fears confirmed. Cason was planning to continue on with Camp and Will Hecht. Well, why wouldn't he? The two men were returning to a place they knew well, and the very place Cason had his heart set on traveling to. Beryl no longer had the strength to stand in Cason's way. But when . . .

The very voice she had been so wary of hearing now sounded loudly across the small yard where they had prepared their feast.

"Som'ne could've got me and tol' me it was time to eat!" Seth Byrd bellowed.

Jonathan looked up as his cousin stumbled toward the fire ring. It was obvious now what was wrong with Seth. Jonathan, inexperienced as he was, had seen this particular phenomenon among the mountain men at Rendezvous. It was frequently exhibited by Calvin Gunnert and his mates.

No one answered Seth as he moved nearer the tiny camp. The light from the fire carved his face into rough plains and gullies. His eyes were very bright. Behind him the darkening sky displayed a lurid crimson and violet sunset.

"I got me an appetite," Seth said, plopping himself down so roughly on the log where Cason, Tracy Camp, and Will Hecht perched that he must have bruised himself. He did not try to rise again, but called across the wavering golden fire to Beryl.

"Don't you serve your husband no more?"

"I'll get you something, Dad," Cason said, rising.

"Shut up! I'm talking to my wife."

Everyone around the campfire was silent, shifting uneasily. Beryl snapped to her feet, her face taut and defiant. "I've got to see to the baby," she said, then wheeled away from the company.

Jonathan and Vashti had been listening silently. Now Vashti rose as well. "Come along now, Angelica. It's time you were in bed." Angelica had been perched on a nearby stump, chewing on a small, sweet piece of an aspen's inner bark, watching the loud, funny man. She slipped down and followed her mother obediently toward the cabin.

"I would like to talk to you," Seth said to Jonathan, his voice oddly tight with feigned politeness. His face still appeared menacing in the firelight. Cason, who knew that expression, looked away deliberately.

"All right," Jonathan Byrd answered. "After a while, when you've had something to eat."

"Sure. That's the thing to do," Seth agreed, rising from his seat. His movements were awkward, almost uncontrolled, as he moved toward the fire bent over at the waist, staggering drunkenly. Tracy Camp's arm shot out and hooked Seth behind the knees, sending Seth Byrd sprawling against the ground.

"So that's your game, is it?" Seth hissed at Camp. "Finally ready to come out in the open, are you?" Seth rose, brushing away Cason's offered assistance. "I'll have to kill the bastard," he muttered to his son.

Jonathan helped his cousin to eat, trimming a good piece of venison haunch from the roast. Then he took Seth's elbow and guided him back to his seat on the log, where he planted himself roughly again. Seth continued to glower blearily at Tracy Camp, who seemed unperturbed by Seth's mood.

"Bastard knocked me down," Seth muttered in the direction of Jonathan, although it was quite clear to everyone around the fire ring that had it not been for the Texan's move, the staggering Seth Byrd would have ended up in the fire.

A deep silence settled over the men as the sky darkened and Seth whittled at his meal with a knife. He raised dark eyes and asked, "What's the matter with you all? Think I've got the pox?"

No, Jonathan thought, it was much worse than that. Seth Byrd had some private soul-rotting disease that would continue to manifest itself in violent eruptions caused by his deep frustration.

It would be better if he had contracted the pox.

Angelica was allowed to watch the baby be fed and changed before she was taken to her room and kissed into bed, giggling. Vashti leaned against the kitchen wall, arms folded, watching the agitated Beryl go about her tasks.

"The baby's a year old," Beryl said without turning toward Vashti.

"Precious is a fine, chubby girl," Vashti said. There was something disturbing about the tenor of Beryl's voice.

"I think I might go away," Beryl said, turning sharply. There were silent tears streaming down her cheeks. The thought of going away was so foreign to Vashti's way of life, she found she could not even answer.

"Away from Shywater?" she asked eventually.

"Away from Shywater, away from that man who calls himself my husband. I am at the end of my resources."

"Because he got himself drunk?" Vashti asked. "Many men do that."

"It's because of the reason he gets drunk," Beryl said. "He no longer loves me, his son, or his daughter. He no longer believes he is a man worthy of heading a family."

"He will get well with a woman to stand by him," Vashti said, either believing or pretending to believe what she said. "If you left, where would you go?"

"I don't know, probably to someplace with more problems." Beryl placed Precious back in her cradle. "But Vashti, don't you ever get tired of having the same man around you day and night, saying the same things?"

"No," Vashti said with all sincerity. In fact, she had never even thought of such a thing before. Beryl seated herself at the wooden table as Vashti prepared to light a fire in the hearth.

"Well, you must be very special, then," Beryl said. "You passed directly from your father's care to your husband's, so nothing was left to you. They controlled you completely."

"My father did not control me. Jonathan has never tried," Vashti said, the sparks from her flint and steel flying as she bent low to puff on the kindling bark. She sat back on her knees as the tiny fire wavered and began to catch. "My father fed me, housed me, protected me. Jonathan Byrd does the same—all that a man can do."

"We simply see things differently. The happiest time in my life was in St. Joseph when I did not have my husband around me."

"That," Vashti said, "is very sad."

"Worse, I cannot make Seth happy either. Not anymore. I must consider other plans. Can't you understand that, Vashti?"

"I believe I can understand many things. As for myself, I am Jonathan's wife. Our place is on the Shywater with our little girl and each other." She shrugged with one shoulder. "I cannot imagine any other life. I have everything I need or could dream of wanting right here. We are no longer two separate people, Jonathan and I. We are one."

★ ★ ★ ★ ★

Jonathan Byrd was returning the still-warm roasting stakes to his storage area behind the house when Seth appeared. Seth staggered once, squinted into the darkness, and made his uncertain way forward, seating himself on the sawhorse. There was a low half-moon just cresting the eastern mountains; it sketched a murky shadow across the yard and illuminated Seth's face, smoothing the wrinkles and sharp angles. He panted slightly as he spoke. He was bent over at the waist, his hat dangling between his knees.

"Jonathan? Can we speak for a few minutes? You said after supper would be the time."

"Certainly, if you wish," Jonathan replied. He dropped the smudged stakes he had been holding into a loose pile against the ground. He had actually meant to talk with Seth over supper, but Seth had not been especially communicative then. Jonathan squatted in front of Seth—a position completely comfortable to him.

"I'm sorry if I made a muddle of things," Seth said sincerely, wearily. "I am tired, Jonathan, tired to the pit of my soul. The trail was long, perhaps too long for a man like me."

"It's all right," Jonathan said, hoping to abbreviate what promised to be a long Jobic lament.

"The simple truth is that I'm beat down, Jonathan, and lost out here." He sighed and lifted his eyes briefly toward the moonlit pine slopes. "I was so anxious to leave where I was. My family was suffering and I could do nothing about it. I had failed at being a man." His eyes were downcast. Then he hiccuped once, breaking the mood.

"I told my family that we were leaving; I told them we were headed for a new land where everything would be better, more prosperous. I told them what I knew was a lie so often that I began to believe it myself. I told them that my rich cousin had a grand estate and he would let us stay there until we could construct our own fine home."

Jonathan listened in silent meditation. What golden pastures had led Seth's imagination; what illusions had he fortified with need and with liquor? What could be done now? Jonathan considered. He replied, "Whatever I had when I arrived on Shywater is still here: land and timber. It only has to be formed, arranged."

"That would take me forever!" Seth complained.

Being frank, Jonathan told his cousin, "You certainly can't stay in my house. You see how things are with us. And I certainly can't feed you all. You'll have to take all of that into your own hands, Seth. I know it can be done, because I did it. It was a damnably hard spring and summer, but when winter arrived, I was glad I had worked those months away instead of telling myself it was no use."

"Is that what you're telling me to do, Jonathan?"

"Yes, it is. Maybe you just need a second wind, as a runner gets. A fresh infusion of ambition. Everything you need is right in front of you. I did it alone. You have Beryl and Cason, at least."

"Cason won't be around to help. I know that now. When those cowboys go, he'll be riding with them."

"Then you won't have him," Jonathan said, standing, waving a hand sharply as if that could snap Seth out of his lethargy. He turned to look southward. Shywater Creek glittered dully in the silver moonlight. A hunting owl passed low overhead.

"You know about that small pocket valley a mile or so downriver, on the opposite side of the creek. There's room enough there for a house. The land would have to be leveled out some, of course. There's plenty of grass there, at least enough for your oxen. You could work all through this coming summer and be very close to finished before the snows come."

"I don't have any tools," Jonathan said with what might have been manufactured misery.

"I'll loan you what I have to spare," Jonathan said, "and I'll help you out with the work when I can. We can look at the land tomorrow. For now we can place some tools in the back of your wagon. I won't leave them out in the weather. I can't easily replace them. You can take team and wagon down there in the morning. For tonight, go on back to your wagon and get some sleep."

"If all this somehow gets done, I'll end up not much better off than I was before, and without even any neighbors or stores."

"You're welcome to travel on," Jonathan Byrd said with something less than charity. He seemed more eager than Seth himself to get the man started on his home. Any project, Jonathan thought, would be better than what sitting and moping and drinking all day was going to lead to.

"I'll fetch Beryl," Seth said, rising heavily.

"If you want to. Precious is probably asleep, though. You can let the both of them stay the night with us, if you want."

"That'll be kind of crowded won't it?"

"For one night, we can make do."

"All right. It's probably for the best. Precious will be asleep." Seth spoke as if he were excusing himself from another disagreeable task.

They walked slowly back to the front of the house. Seth only once slipped and banged his shoulder against the solid log wall.

Cason and the two cowboys were still seated around the glowing coals from the fire, talking. L'Enfant had probably retired to his bed among the pines.

Both Jonathan and Seth stopped as they heard a chorus of tiny pops, far remote from them, but identifiable as gunshots. Seth turned and squinted northward, toward the block of hills there. "What was that? No one would be out hunting this time of night."

"The boys are kicking up at Rendezvous," Jonathan told him. "Pay them no mind. They'll soon be gone back into the high mountains with their hangovers."

"They do a deal of drinking up there, do they?" Seth asked.

"More than their share. Outside of gambling, that's their chief pastime." Having said that, seeing the dull longing in Seth's eyes, Jonathan immediately regretted his words.

What, really, did he care if Seth traveled on those extra miles to Rendezvous? But there was no place farther along to go when Rendezvous was ended. Seth would be stranded. There was no point in considering that. Jonathan knew no ox team could follow the long road up to the big camp. It seemed to be only one last whisky dream in Seth's mind.

Morning dawned clear, bright, cloudless. Swinging the heavy plank door open to the day, Jonathan left Vashti to see to her overnight guests, and walked behind the house toward the Shywater Creek to bathe. There was no sign of activity near the covered wagon yet.

The vegetable garden, which was now referred to as "Vashti's Garden," despite the fact that Jonathan had begun it, was doing well. She had picked some of the more mature corn for last night's guests, and some of the young squash was missing. Jonathan had dug a narrow ditch from the creek, which watered the garden well enough. Along the watercourse, volunteer sulphur flowers, rock primrose, and blue columbine grew.

After bathing, Jonathan returned to the front yard and fed the horses. He watched them meditatively. He would have to mow more grass soon, a job he did not care for. But today was dedicated to helping Seth.

The Conestoga wagon had been drawn off down the slope

toward the building site, Jonathan saw. After considering, he led the big paint pony out of its paddock and started that way, the gray watching them go without interest. The old gentleman was retired and content to be so. After years of drawing a cart, his duties consisted now only of ferrying a thirty-pound girl up and down the valley.

The paint, on the other hand, always considered that they might be embarking on some great adventure and always seemed to grow a little sullen at Jonathan's lack of imaginings and narrow vistas. Jonathan rode little these days, just enough to keep the paint in shape, and the big Indian pony was still in fine fettle. The horse had so much to give; Jonathan sometimes thought that if Fire Sky had been three steps quicker, the paint would have had a life more to its liking.

The oxen, when Jonathan arrived at the tiny valley, were still yoked, dueling with each other for the nibbles of grass within reach. Jonathan inconsequentially thought that whatever else, his cousin would not lack for beef during the coming winter. Unfortunately, neither could the oxen, necessarily all neutered males, ever increase. Most of these stout animals ended up being eaten at the end of the trail by their pioneer owners after a few had been culled out for farm work.

Where was Seth now? Jonathan looked around, not seeing his cousin. He should at least have tended to the oxen by now. Slipping from the paint horse's back, he approached the rear of the covered wagon. Calling out twice, he opened the canvas flap.

Seth was caught with his gallon jug of liquor tilted to his lips. Shamefaced, he swallowed the whisky in his mouth and placed the jug aside as if that could conceal it.

"Just a swallow to wake me up," Seth said defensively. "It's going to be a long day's work."

"If we get at it. Drinking that won't help you get through it, Seth."

Seth's face grew sulky at the implied criticism. If anyone had seen his expression, they would have found it to be a near mirror image of Cason Byrd's own expression when he found his father's admonishments hurtful.

"Grab the other axe," Jonathan said, picking up his old double-bit from the wagon floorboard. "We'd better blaze some straight trees, and see if we can fell a few before your inspiration wears off. I've brought along twine and pegs to mark out a floor plan, which you should be thinking about while we work. We can discuss leveling the ground later. For now, let's start doing *something.*"

Vashti sat on the front porch, her shirt placed aside, drying her newly washed hair in the sunshine.

"How goes the house, Husband?" Vashti asked, running her comb through her thick dark hair. Jonathan was vaguely troubled by the fact that Vashti was without a top, although he never had considered it wrong before. These strangers brought many additional worries with them. With a sigh, Jonathan seated himself on the porch beside Vashti.

"I don't think it will ever be finished," he told her.

"But you've only just begun," she said with a questioning look.

"Yes, but Seth seems to have little interest in it."

"His own house! Isn't this the time his interest and energy should be at their highest?"

"You'd think so," Jonathan answered. "But sometime in the middle of the morning, I could no longer hear the ringing of Seth's axe. I went to make sure he had not had an accident. I found him in the wagon, drinking his liquor. From the angle at which the jug was tilted, I could tell that the whisky is nearly gone."

"What did you say to him, Husband?"

"Nothing. It could have only been rebuke, and Seth knows down inside that what he was doing is wrong."

"Did he return to work?"

"After a while I found him at the easier job of stretching out twine to mark his cabin's plan. The angles were all off. He staggered a little as he rose to talk to me."

"What will you do, Jonathan?"

"Fell and trim a few more trees. I gave my word. But I will not build his whole house for him. He seems to have given up before he's even begun."

"No," Vashti said after a moment's thoughtfulness, "it would not be right for you to continue working on the house for him. What is he thinking? What is supposed to happen?"

Vashti's gaze lifted involuntarily toward the distant Grand Tetons where the northern storms had their birth. "He has to protect his family in the winter. Store food and provide shelter. What is he waiting for?"

"Perhaps for tomorrow—the never-to-come tomorrow," Jonathan said in a frustrated voice. "Maybe for manna to fall from the heavens."

"What is manna?"

"You've read your Bible."

"I must have missed the manna part," she said.

"Sustenance from God," Seth replied sourly. "I wasn't speaking literally."

"Does Seth's god also build houses for men too lazy to do their own work? The Reverend Mr. Blaylock would be confounded by that. He more often said, 'God helps those who help themselves.' "

"I knew the old buzzard wasn't totally stupid," Seth said, transferring his frustration and anger to an innocent man.

"He tries to do good," Vashti said, still combing out her hair, which would have fallen to her knees were she standing.

"I suppose so," Jonathan said with a sigh. He rose to his feet, kissed Vashti's sun-warmed shoulder, and started away. The paint horse had not been put away yet.

"Husband," Vashti said. "Even if these people are your kinsmen, I will be happy when they are gone—every one of them."

Reaching the paddock, Jonathan found Louis L'Enfant and his pale horse there. The horse was fully packed.

"I was wondering where you were," Louis said. "I've been waiting to say goodbye and thanks again." The Frenchman offered his hand, which Jonathan took.

"I'm afraid our hospitality was a little thin," Jonathan said. "We weren't expecting company. Not so much of it anyway."

"I understand." Louis took off his hat and wiped his cuff over his perspiring brow. "Can I get some of that fresh creek water, Jonathan? It seems to have magical qualities."

"Does it? Well, it keeps us alive. But why didn't you go up to the house and get a drink if you were thirsty?"

"I couldn't do that, not with your wife *dishabille*. It would only reinforce the bad reputation of the French."

"I don't understand you, Louis. What bad reputation? The only ones I knew drank too much and generally raised hell."

"Those were Canucks, not Frenchmen." Louis looked northward toward the far peaks. "The French were the first to set eyes on those mountains, you know. And quite imaginatively named them the Grand Tetons. You know what that means, of course?"

"No," Jonathan said, genuinely perplexed. Louis's conversation had taken one too many bends for him to follow.

"It will come to you one night," Louis said. "You are a fine fellow, Jonathan Byrd."

"Thank you," Jonathan said uncertainly. "You are, too, Louis. Where are you headed now? Still to Cheyenne?"

"Definitely now," the Frenchman said. "I have an appointment to keep. I wasn't sure before, but now I am."

"A working appointment?"

"Just that. My boss, Oliver Coons, sent me up this way more on a hope than anything else. He thought my men might have attached themselves to the wagon train, believing it easier to blend in as two among many."

"You are speaking of . . . ?"

"Tracy Camp and Will Hecht, of course. A few months ago they murdered a big Texas rancher named Ben Starr, took all of the money in his strongbox, and lit out. Camp is known to have business associates in Cheyenne."

"I can hardly believe that of them."

"I know. Tracy Camp is a glib talker, a fine liar. The kid, Hecht—you might not want to believe this either—but he is the killer of the two of them. He's got more than a few posters out of Texas on him."

"But my nephew—Cason—is planning on riding with them to Cheyenne!"

"Maybe his father or his mother can talk him out of it. Jonathan, I have to ask you to promise me that you won't tell Cason why. I can't have it leaked to Camp or Hecht that they're the reason I'm on this trail. They might have seen my badge, though I was careful to conceal it once I found out for sure who they are. Cason might have told them. But if I leave now and get ahead of them, then they're liable to think it was their own imaginings, and that I've gone off to tend to other business that has nothing to do with them." Louis felt compelled to add, "I didn't want to try to take them here, not on a friend's property while sharing his hospitality." Louis turned, grabbed his reins, and put his boot toe into the stirrup. "I'll be meeting up again with those two real soon. Let them get to Cheyenne and get relaxed. Then the Cheyenne marshal, his men, and I can close the cell door on them."

"I won't say a word," Jonathan Byrd promised.

"I only spoke now so that you'll be watchful, knowing that you have killers among you." Then Louis started his pale horse forward through the timber, and Jonathan Byrd stood silently, watching him, knowing now that he had two killers as guests and a nephew whose greatest desire in the world was to join them.

# Chapter Twenty

**Leaving Shywater**

It was nearly sundown before the Texans decided to start their ride toward Cheyenne. It seemed to Cason that Tracy Camp had been waiting for a certain moment, but had no idea when that would be. No one else was around. The Frenchman had left; Jonathan was out mowing grass to use for his horses' fodder, Beryl was still in the cabin with Vashti; Cason had not seen his father all day, though earlier he had heard the ringing of axes.

Now he curried his red horse. Its coat shone like burnished copper in the late sunlight. The horse had gradually overcome its earlier apparent resentment of Cason and had now become a willing trail companion.

"Are you just about ready?" Will Hecht asked, wandering to where Cason stood.

"I've been ready all day. What's been holding us up?"

"Well, as you may or may not know, Camp has been keeping a daily trail log for Mr. Starr to look over. He let himself get behind a little and decided he'd better catch up on that before we leave for Cheyenne."

"But we're still leaving today?"

"Oh, yes. Tracy figures us for riding into Cheyenne town tomorrow." Hecht stopped and looked around at the empty land. "I'll bet on a winter night this place is as quiet as a mute's grave. Whyn't you give me another look at that Colt's pistol of yours, Case?" Hecht suggested. "What say we ride out into the woods and find us a spot for a shooting match?"

*Why not?* Cason thought. There was not another thing in the world to do at the moment. Besides, he was growing quite proud of his newfound proficiency with that pistol.

Swinging into leather, Case followed Will Hecht across Shywater Creek and up the other side into the tall pines. Moving softly through the big trees, they came upon a small clearing where they could try their guns. Cason knew his uncle was not in favor of guns being fired in his valley, but they were far enough off that he would not be riled. Or so he believed. If Jonathan Byrd did get mad about them shooting, what did that matter? They would never see the man again after today.

"You'll need to sharpen your shooting eye for Texas," Hecht said after they had swung down from their horses. The shadowed copse was cool; long pine shadows crossed the clearing. "Things are plenty rough down there. Let me see your pistol, will you?"

Cason handed his revolver with only a slight tinge of reluctance. Will Hecht turned it over in his hands. "Yes, this really is a fine weapon. I could use one like this myself." His eyes lifted, "Did you ever kill anyone with it, Case?"

"No," Cason said. Almost apologetically, he added, "I haven't had it that long."

"A virgin weapon," Will Hecht said, still holding the pistol. "Did you ever kill a man at all, Case?"

Not wanting to be branded an innocent among these Texas-hardened men, Cason Byrd told the story of Tom Pearl's drowning, making it more than the avoidable accident it had been. They had engaged in a fight, according to this rendition, and finally he had knocked Pearl into the break in the ice and held him down.

"His eyes were wide as saucers," Cason said. "Tom Pearl was

a big man, but I held him down, watching him flail until he drowned."

"That must have been something," Will Hecht said, nodding his head. "Did he have time to call out to you, to beg for his life?"

"He had the time, but he never called for mercy. He knew that once I had my mind set on it, he was a goner. No amount of pleading would have done him any good."

Will Hecht nodded. Then he drew back the hammer of the Colt's pistol, "Then you understand, don't you, Case? I'm going to shoot you dead where you stand."

Case thought it was a joke, but it wasn't. There was a coldness in the blue eyes of Will Hecht like none he had ever seen. Cason eventually managed to murmur, "Why?"

"I want your Colt and your pony, that's all there is to it. Besides, as Tracy Camp pointed out, you're contributing nothing to our pot, and we're going to have to carry you for a long time to come. It's easier just to get rid of you, Case, and I'll come out well ahead."

"You'll be caught," Case said, trying to convince the gunman.

"By who? Nobody saw us come up here. Your father's a drunk who probably won't even miss you. Your mother and Byrd will assume you rode away with us. That French lawman out of Denver is long gone. Oh, hell! I don't make a habit of discussing these things," Will Hecht muttered, and he shot Cason Byrd dead with his own prize pistol.

There was still a halo of color above the far peaks when Beryl Byrd walked out into the evening. She was tired of the confinement of the little cabin. Was she to spend the rest of her life penned up in such a place for six snowy months of the year? Of course, she had not even a cabin yet. If she had one, there would be no stove and no food to cook on it. Their first winter would likely be their last. They would be discovered starved to death or frozen by the time spring returned.

Drawing her shawl more tightly around her, she walked out into the empty yard, returning in memory to the warm, pleasant home of Mrs. Jasper. She had been a fool to leave St. Joseph, to adhere to Seth when he had shown that some vital part of him had been set aside and trampled by the passage of life.

"Odd hour to be out walking," a voice said from out of the near-darkness.

Beryl narrowed her eyes and squinted into the heavy shadows to recognize Tracy Camp, seated on a tree stump. He looked young, handsome, his smile bright, his eyes . . . surveying.

"You're out here," Beryl said with a laugh, knowing it was no accident that the Texas cowboy had come across her path.

"I wanted to say goodbye," Tracy Camp said, rising to his feet. Not far away, among the pines, his ground-hitched horse waited, its eyes evilly bright with starlight.

"Goodbye?" Beryl said foolishly.

"Yes. You knew we were riding off toward Cheyenne. By this time tomorrow I mean to find myself in a fine hotel fed on beef steak and apple pie."

"Sounds quite luxurious, compared to . . ." Beryl gestured with her arm, indicating all of the Shywater valley.

"Do you want to go with us?" Tracy Camp asked abruptly. "You could always catch a riverboat south to Missouri if you found Cheyenne was not to your liking." Beryl could barely meet his gaze now. His eyes were calm, confident. She was at a loss for words. The whole idea was absurd, too rushed, leaving her entire world behind—her entire, quite dismal, world.

Beryl was not so naïve that she did not understand Tracy Camp's invitation might have been nothing but a hungry man's urge, that the day after tomorrow might find her in an even worse situation.

"I have my husband to consider, and my children," Beryl said, unable to explain to herself the regret she felt at not simply answering Camp positively as he wanted her to.

"When we miss opportunities," Tracy Camp said, looking down at her, "we eventually find that they never return."

He put his arms around her and held her for several long minutes. Then he kissed her forehead and said, "I'll be thinking about you in Cheyenne."

He walked to his horse and swung into the saddle. A tall, lean figure in the night, promising much, soon to forever be out of her life.

Beryl turned and started back toward the cabin. The sun's memory had utterly vanished from the high peaks; the slowly rising moon had arrived to claim the land of the night beasts.

Beryl heard a horse approaching, and she turned her head to look up at the rider. Beryl did not make even a pretense of a struggle as Tracy Camp's strong arm reached out and swept her up onto his horse.

It was time to go, Seth Byrd still believed. He had rolled out of his blankets and clambered down from the wagon after a brief hour's sleep and now stood staring up at the dark sky. The stars seemed a little hazy now. It could be that smoke from some distant fires were smudging the sky. For the men were still up there; he had seen the sparkle-glimmer of their faraway campfires earlier.

Seth stretched his back, shivered, and reached for his buffalo coat in the bed of the wagon. These mountains had little respect for a calendar spring, it seemed. Seth also snatched up his whisky jug, finished off the little remaining liquor, and tossed the jug away.

The hardest part was the first step, but Seth had planned for it carefully. The paint pony was an alert horse, given to raising the alarm at every unfamiliar sight, scent, or sound. Seth had made it a point to visit the horse frequently, carrying a handful of grass to offer it. As a result of his planning, the horse made not a sound as Seth entered the paddock and saddled the Indian pony. The gray made no response except to shuffle its feet as Seth led the younger horse out into the valley. Looking at Jonathan's cabin, where smoke rose from the stone chimney, Seth swung swiftly aboard the horse. To hesitate was to lose all chance at success. The paint's hoofs sounded loud splashing across the Shywater Creek, but no one came out of the cabin to call to him, and then they were up onto open grassland, riding toward the skirts of the dark forest. And to think that Seth had worried about this phase of his plan! When something is to be dared, it must be done with confidence.

He did not know the trail, but knew its general trending. He had marked the campfires earlier, and now as they climbed the pine-studded hill in the darkness, Seth remained alert for any sight, sound, or distant smoke indicative of human activity.

At one point, a mile or so along the twisting trail, the paint pony came alert, and perhaps out of some nearly forgotten memory, hastened its pace a little. Seth convinced himself that the horse remembered the way. If not, it was of little importance; he would find the Rendezvous site. The place could not be missed. It would be fire-bright and rowdy with carousing.

Seth relaxed in the saddle as the horse made its way through the dense, dark, fragrant forest.

The silver moon was at his back, fortune ahead.

Seth had money in his pockets, and there was whisky to be had ahead on the trail. Not that that was all he was determined to obtain, he told himself. He would purchase some basic supplies so that Beryl would quit complaining about their condition, which was bordering on dire.

According to Jonathan, there were also a plethora of gambling opportunities. Seth had blurred visions of himself earning enough at the tables to ease their way. He was like every other gambling man, consciously oblivious of the possibility of losing. Returning home with empty pockets seemed to lie beyond the ken of every dedicated gambler.

The horse lifted its head sharply and its ears twitched. Something ahead had caught its attention.

It was another two miles on before Seth could scent woodsmoke in the air, hear the monotonous yet stimulating sounds of drums beating, see the low glow of distant fires.

He snapped the reins and rode on as eagerly as a hound on the hunt—all that was good lay ahead of him, and it was long overdue.

He began to pass a few men who had been out walking on their own. Most of them wore fur caps, a few long fur coats in deference to the cold night air. He rode by a couple of Indians—of what tribe, he could not tell—then he was into the main camp, an orgy of jubilation celebrating nothing but life and drunkenness.

So this was Rendezvous? Seth sat the horse for a while, trying to take it all in, but it seemed only a mad confusion of men whirling, dancing, fighting, and chanting, with a handful of uncertain women watching them; a few playful older children ran seemingly amok in the camp; a dozen or so dogs ran everywhere, often biting at people. Rendezvous was exuberant; it was a barbarous bacchanal.

Seth had found his home.

He started slowly out of the heavy shadows at the verge of the pine forest and rode cautiously toward a campfire, hoping to have some questions answered. Already one had been resolved. Not a man Seth saw did not have a jug of whisky, or sat waiting for one to be passed to him. Seth only needed to find the source, for his few hours away from liquor had already turned him into an uncertain, trembling wretch. Seth knew that, knew the cause, but it seemed far better on this bonfire-lit, frolicking, tumbling night to find an immediate cure.

"Mister," a man said to Seth as he approached the fire. "You might find you've got yourself some trouble. That's a known horse you're riding."

"What do you mean?" Seth demanded defensively. The man who had challenged him, a burly older man with a graying beard, had taken hold of the bridle to the painted horse. Several other men had appeared from the wavering shadows to approach them.

"What is it, Calvin?" one of them asked the bearded man.

"What? Tell me you don't recognize this horse, Stinky."

"Do I not!" the younger man with the handlebar mustache and neat blue suit answered. "Damn me if that's not Jonathan Byrd's prize horse."

"Look, men," said Seth, who had never been averse to a fight, but now was clearly outnumbered among a rough crowd. He tried to placate them. "It is Jonathan Byrd's horse. He knows I have it."

"Seeing you astride that horse would offend the Crow Indians," the man called Stinky said. "They're kind of notional that way. Fire Sky, for one, would be mad as hell seeing you on that horse."

"I don't see why this Fire Sky should care," Seth said, "and I don't see what business it is of any of you. I told you I knew it was Jonathan Byrd's horse, didn't I?"

The man with the beard, the one they called Calvin, looked up with glassy eyes and told Seth, "I was Jonathan's partner in the high mountains for a long while. The name's Calvin Gunnert. You see, stranger, this horse and Jonathan Byrd have become a sort of myth among the Mountain Crow."

"Mostly perpetuated by Fire Sky, who never liked admitting that a mortal *Baashciile* could better him," Stinky said.

"I don't know what you people are talking about or what it has to do with me," Seth growled. He was growing progressively more ill-tempered.

"It's like this," Calvin Gunnert said. "There's a Crow Indian legend that a mighty *Baashciile* descended from the highest peaks of the Rocky Mountains, defeated the greatest of the Crow runners in a long and arduous foot race, winning a noble horse. Then he defeated the great marksman and chief of the Crow, Shaw-at-Duan, in a shooting contest, winning the chief's beautiful daughter, Vashti. Then Jonathan Byrd, having found everything he had come for, departed the mountain lands and returned to the high-cloud country, Vashti riding the big painted horse. This horse."

"What a lot of nonsense," Seth said, sputtering.

"No one said it wasn't, but it does us no harm to have the Crow thinking about our mighty hero, Jonathan Byrd. Besides, in most respects it is true. I know. I was there."

"So was I," the man they called Stinky said.

"Well, I wasn't," Seth said. "What am I supposed to do? I seem to have collided with a fable. Look, men . . . Sure, this is Jonathan Byrd's horse. He loaned it to me. I'm his cousin."

"You don't look much like him," someone said. "I think something's happened to Jonathan, and this gentleman knows . . ."

"Hold on there, men," said someone from beyond the close ring. "I can identify this man. It's Seth Byrd, and he is Jonathan's cousin. Get yourselves a drink and cool down."

The speaker was the short, stout man with overgrown side whiskers Seth had met at the American Fur Company warehouse in St. Joseph, Robert Pyle.

"I'm sure happy to see you," Seth said, sparing a scathing

look for the men who had surrounded him.

"I'm glad to see you as well. How's Jonathan?"

"Fine when I last saw him—this afternoon," Seth said apparently for the benefit of the few listeners who had not wandered away from the scene, which now showed no promise of offering more entertainment. Seth swung down from the tall paint's back.

"What are you doing up here?" Pyle asked as the two shook hands. Calvin Gunnert, plainly mistrustful still, held back a little, as did the man in the blue town suit and handlebar mustache they called Stinky.

"Well, it turned out I couldn't find any suitable work in St. Joseph, so I came up to visit Jonathan while I was weighing my prospects."

"You showed up at our warehouse just a month or so before our busy time of the year. This is going to be our first full shipment of the season. It's too bad you couldn't have waited to apply . . ."

"Will you take me on now? Right now?" Seth asked.

"Are you serious?" Robert Pyle asked, his eyes narrowing

"I am. I'm ready to report to work in the morning."

"I suppose I could hire you on my own say-so," Pyle said, frowning thoughtfully. "You do realize, of course, that after we have a full load of furs on board we're going to sail off immediately downriver. Can't let the competition gain an hour on us."

"I'm willing," Seth said, answering quickly, as if he were afraid the offer would be withdrawn.

"It's just that sometimes a man needs more notice to get his affairs in order."

"Mr. Pyle, I'm as ready as I will ever be. I'd be more than happy to buy some whisky to drink a toast to you and seal the deal, if you'll show me where they sell it."

"You're not forgetting the horse, are you?" Stinky asked, and Jonathan halted momentarily, his arm still around the shoulders of his newfound benefactor, Robert Pyle.

"Perhaps we can find somebody . . ."

"I'll take the paint home," Calvin Gunnert announced. "I know where Shywater is." There seemed to be doubt in the big man's tone, so Seth merely nodded and led his new friend away so they could lose themselves in the confused jumble of campfire shadows. Pyle lifted an arm and pointed in the direction of the whisky tent.

"You didn't really want to take that horse back to Jonathan, did you?" Stinky asked as they walked toward Calvin Gunnert's small campsite.

"I wanted to make sure it got back," Calvin said. "Besides, I figure I owe Jonathan that much, the years we worked together."

"I'd go myself except I have to get back to my inventory, and I don't know where Jonathan is," Stinky added with a rueful smile. "Tell him 'hello' for me, and let him know that my life has changed for the better since last he saw me."

"I will, Stink—" Calvin caught himself using Mr. Reginald Foote's former nickname and grinned an apology. "I will, Mr. Foote."

As the hour grew late, Calvin Gunnert busied himself saddling his own sorrel horse and shaking out a length of rope to be used for a tether on the paint.

He hesitated only a few seconds before snatching up his whisky jug for company. Hell, the night was cold and a man hates to travel alone. Besides, Jonathan Byrd had seen him drunk before.

# Chapter Twenty-One

**Shywater Grows Smaller . . . and Larger**

"Who was that man who was all duded up in the blue suit back there?" Seth Byrd was asking Robert Pyle. The two men were sitting at the base of a massive pine tree, sharing a jug of good flatland whisky. The flatland distillation was definitely smoother than the sort of corn liquor Seth was used to. Whether it had the same sort of kick remained to be seen, but already Seth felt warmer, more relaxed, a prince in a small way again. He was a man with a belly full of whisky and a promising job.

"That was—" here the fur trader hiccuped—"Mr. Reginald Foote, now a prominent citizen of Cheyenne, though in his younger days . . ."

"He was a hell-raiser, was he?"

"No, nothing like that, but look—" here another hiccup escaped Robert Pyle—"that's all passed. Did I tell you what happened to Mr. Foote?"

"No, sir. That's kind of what I was wondering about," Seth Byrd replied. He tilted the jug and flooded his organs with another huge supply of liquor. He offered the jug to Pyle, who waved a hand in refusal.

"I believe (hiccup) I've had my share for the night, Mr. Byrd."

"You were talking about Mr. Reginald Foote," Seth prodded. He again put the jug to his lips and swallowed deeply, just managing to suppress the reflex that would have sent the whisky back to its origin from his overindulged stomach.

"Yes—our Mr. Foote. He was raised among the Crow Indians, you see, and he knew no other life but the mountain way. He was a fair trapper—as good as most of us, you'd have to say, but he had one problem. That was, he was unfit for normal human companionship on account of the remarkable odors his body emitted."

"They would have had to be remarkably strong among such company—in the open air."

"I don't think there's a word for how he smelled, like the breath of an open sewer. Funny thing, remarkable thing, is that last year Jean-Luc Colbert's daughter showed up here with a message for her father. From her mother, it was. The letter only said, as I recall, *You'd better get your great, bearded body back here.* I guess the woman figured old Luke had had enough time to make his fortune in the west and actually missed the brute."

Robert Pyle refused another drink while Seth helped himself to one more. His hiccups now having subsided, Pyle continued with his story.

"Well, the girl—I think her name was Yvette—was just as pretty as a peach, perky and good-natured. At some function or the other Yvette met Reginald Foote. Her words to him were, 'You stink like a rotted hog wallow.' I saw Reginald Foote the next day, bathed, his hair brushed, and he said kind of sadly, 'All of you my friends—and not a one of you could be bothered to tell me I smelled that bad.' I told him all of his friends had told him, but he chose just to ignore us.

"I suppose Yvette had a different way of telling him, of making him pay attention. I never saw Reginald after that when he was not clean and spruced up. When I next came upriver from St. Jo, here was Reginald on the docks with a small fleet of his own rafts in wait. He was wearing a town suit and a flourishing handlebar mustache.

"Reginald had decided, he said, that fur trapping was not a

fitting trade. He and Yvette had built a couple of stores in Cheyenne, and he stocked them cleverly. When the downriver fur traders were ready to float home, having concluded their business here, Reginald Foote would wander the riverfront, offering to buy all of their unsold trade goods. Well, of course he was quite successful. Of what use were those goods to the traders who were headed back to St. Jo or St. Louis, where such trade items were cheap and plentiful? The fur traders were happy to unload all of their unsold items, and as a result Reginald Foote became a wealthy man, peddling them in his Cheyenne stores at slightly higher, still bargain, prices."

"An interesting story . . ." Seth Byrd muttered. "Though not sure if there's a moral to be had . . ." Then he fell asleep at the base of the giant pine with his jug in his hand.

Robert Pyle threw Seth's blanket over him and then wandered his unsteady way home to his riverboat bunk. His face, as he glanced back at Seth Byrd, clouded a little with concern. Morning came early, and he needed a sober crew to finish loading the year's furs. Pyle himself had overindulged, he knew, but what had bothered him slightly about Seth Byrd and the whisky jug was that the liquor seemed to have no real effect on him. That, and the man did not know when to quit.

Pyle mentally shrugged off Seth's drinking. The man had between here and St. Joseph to either prove up or demonstrate he was not a man John Astor would want on his crew. It was all up to Seth. Being Jonathan Byrd's cousin only carried so much weight.

Calvin Gunnert had viewed the valley in bright sunlight before, the forest and the stream, but now in the middle of the night with the silver moon making pixies of every fascicle of pine needles, with the high trees standing straight in the haunted woods, he disliked this aspect of Shywater.

When he finally emerged from the forest, it was with relief. Truthfully, Calvin was not sure he had remembered the trail from years earlier, and he had been wondering if he had been wandering into Blackfoot territory. Now the moon-daubed clouds floated across the dark sky, a silver glow edging each of them.

He had never seen Jonathan's cabin, but he had never doubted that his old partner would get the job done. Now the sturdy log building stood on the protected bench, smoke rising lazily from its chimney, much as Jonathan Byrd had projected it in his mind's eyes. There was a small garden at the rear, cord upon cord of stacked firewood, a neat little paddock, which the tall paint pony Calvin was leading, immediately recognized as home.

"Almost there, big boy. Don't get yourself so worked up. I'm taking you home."

It was not until after supper that Jonathan noticed the flour on the floor. He crouched down and touched his finger to the powder on the floor. Tasting it with the tip of his tongue, his smile turned into a frown.

He rose to speak with Vashti, who was sitting by the fire, quietly but intently studying her books. She already spoke better than Jonathan himself did by far, but she seemed determined to be perfect.

In the back bedroom Angelica could be heard as she tried to teach Precious the ageless game of counting piggies. She did not understand that Precious would not be able to speak for quite a while to come.

"Who was in our house, Vashti?" Jonathan asked. She turned a puzzled gaze toward him.

"What a question. You know everyone who has been here: Cason, Seth, Beryl, and Louis at different times."

"You never let Tracy Camp or Hecht in?"

"No. Why would I, Husband?" Her dark eyes, like liquid obsidian, followed him as he briefly paced in front of the fire. Jonathan ran his hand across his head. He was obviously disturbed.

"Are you going to tell me what you're thinking?" Vashti asked.

"I was just hoping it was some stranger and not . . . come here and see what I have found." He beckoned to Vashti, who rose and followed him toward the kitchen area. Jonathan squatted down and pointed at the white splash on the floor. Other dust had been sprinkled lightly about. Reaching into the lower cupboard, he withdrew the five-gallon flour can that was seldom used. Vashti had tried cooking with white flour only once or twice, and found that she had no real use for it in her traditional recipes.

There was a small smudge on the can's lid, Jonathan noted. He removed the lid, looked inside, and gestured for Vashti to crouch beside him. She looked at him quizzically again.

"What am I looking at?" she asked.

"At nothing, because that is what's left of the four gold forty-franc Napoleons Louis L'Enfant once gave me."

"Our emergency money," Vashti said. "I had forgotten you even had it." She smiled, "We have been lucky enough to have had no emergency over the years."

Jonathan made no answer. He closed the canister and slammed it back into its place on the pantry shelf, then walked across the room to the bed, where he sat and stared at the flickering red and gold of the fire. Vashti waited a minute, then seated herself beside him, taking his hand.

"You are upset because you think one of your kinsman has stolen from you?"

"If they needed it, I would have given it to them—any of them."

"I know. Without a purpose, gold is just shiny metal. But which one do you think thought he needed it so badly, Jonathan? One thinks first of Cason, of course, young people being impulsive."

"And he's gone now, off to Cheyenne with those two cowboys."

"You don't think it was Cason, do you?"

"Seth was the desperate one among them. He was worried about providing for his family over the winter. And beyond."

"Working on his house would have been a help."

"Yes," Jonathan agreed. "I think he absolutely feared working the entire summer as a sober man."

"How could that be?" Vashti asked.

"I don't know. I suppose I'm lucky I never caught that particular disease."

"Where could he get whisky around here? Oh." Vashti recalled that they had seen the campfires. Rendezvous had returned this year to Granger. "He would have to walk there—ten miles? What would he tell Beryl?"

"Where is Beryl?" Jonathan asked. "She should be home, shouldn't she?"

"Yes, although earlier she was complaining that she was cold and wished she were somewhere warmer. She was always talking about the home of a nice older lady in St. Joseph where she had been happy."

"Well, she can't have gone there, could she? I mean, Precious is still here," Jonathan said. He could still hear Angelica's chirpy voice in the back room. She was talking to the baby still.

"Could she have walked down to see Seth at their home site? That's quite a walk."

"Unless she took a horse," Jonathan said.

"Beryl cannot ride," Vashti said. "She told me that."

Not ride? The idea seemed preposterous to Jonathan. He had

never met a man, woman, or child above the age of three who could not ride. "I don't suppose the cougar . . . no, that's unlikely. It has never shown anything but fear of the scent of humans."

But there were still "bad" Indians around, by which to Jonathan and Vashti meant Blackfoot people, but they had no idea of where the Blackfoot were camping this year. Besides, the Blackfoot had never troubled them during their years at Shywater.

"I think I had better have a look around," Jonathan said, reaching for his leather coat and his Hawken rifle.

"All right." Vashti would stay with the children. That was what Jonathan would have asked her to do anyway. "Beryl may have taken a walk and got lost in the woods," she suggested hopefully.

"A child could find the cabin again with our fire burning."

"Find her, Jonathan," Vashti said, glancing toward the bedroom. "A child needs its mother; sometimes that is all a child has in this world."

Deciding he would not take a lantern with the moon riding high as it was, Jonathan went out into the dew-heavy yard. A light breeze was blowing, gently swaying the tops of the sentinel pines. His rifle felt cold, comforting in his hand. Crossing toward the paddock, he saw a shadow to his right and heard the clopping of hoofbeats. A somehow familiar voice bellowed out, "Looking for something, Jonathan?"

Turning, Jonathan saw the big, bearded man riding into his yard, leading his tall paint pony. Standing, hands on hips, Jonathan watched as the man approached, a smile gradually forming on his lips.

"Calvin Gunnert! I'll be damned."

"Me, more likely," Calvin said, swinging down from his sorrel.

"What's kept you from visiting before?"

"I guess I was thinking that I needed an excuse," Calvin said, removing his round fur cap to wipe at his brow. "I've brought one with me this time, as you can see." He nodded in the direction of the paint.

"And I'm assuming you brought a story with it, as well. Let's water the horses and put them away. Then you come up to the house and we'll have a talk."

"All right if I bring this along?" Calvin asked, showing Jonathan the jug he had with him.

"Sure, I wouldn't want you to get thirsty. Vashti won't mind, if that's what you're thinking. She believes it is the man who commits the sins and not the liquor."

"Vashti?" Calvin said as they led the horses to water. "We never even knew her name when last I saw her, if you'll remember."

"I remember," Jonathan nodded. "And all these years later, I can now admit that her father was the wiser man."

"It's been that good, has it?"

"It's been fine, Calvin, just fine. You'll have to meet our little girl. I hope she's awake."

"It's all right if she isn't," Calvin said. "I could just peek at her."

"You say that almost as if you're afraid of little children," Jonathan said.

"It's not exactly that," Calvin said, leading his sorrel back to the paddock. "It's just that the conversation always kind of lags. That and they always have questions I can't answer."

"You always did all right with me," Jonathan said, remembering as far back as he could.

"You were almost four years old," Calvin said as they started to walk to the house, "and you were a boy child."

"Didn't I ask questions you couldn't answer?" Jonathan asked.

"At first, then only rarely as time went by. Which was just as well. How do you tell a kid that his mother's been murdered and won't be coming back?"

"However you did it, it seems to have been the right way, Calvin."

"Well, I always tried to do what was best. Anyway, you've grown into a fine man. I wouldn't like to think I had nothing to do with it."

"It could be the water," Jonathan said as they approached the porch.

"What's that?" Calvin asked, pausing to let Jonathan precede him into the cabin.

"Nothing. A friend of mine told me earlier today that he thought Shywater Creek water had magical qualities."

"Anybody that I know?"

"No, you would never have met him."

Calvin shook his head. "Well, there could be magic in that water, or . . ." The door swung open to reveal Vashti standing there in her fringed, beaded elkskin dress, the firelight behind her highlighting her long black hair. "There's all kinds of magic, I guess," Calvin said, and they walked in from the chill.

"What are you two grinning about?" Vashti asked, showing them in to be seated.

"Nothing," Calvin answered. "Just something Jonathan's friend told him."

"Oh?" she looked at each of them expectantly. They weren't going to tell her, she saw. "What friend was this, Husband?" she asked, settling beside him.

"Just something whimsical that Louis said once."

"Do you know Louis L'Enfant, too?" Vashti asked Calvin.

"No, I don't. But I was talking to a few of your old friends who wanted me to remember them to you," Calvin said. "Robert Pyle was at the camp, and Stin—Reginald Foote."

"Stinky! How is he?"

"I'll tell you after a while. I would guess you're more interested in how I happened to come by your prize horse." Calvin had removed his furs and settled his jug between his legs. Vashti exhibited no censure.

"You had our paint horse?" Vashti asked with astonishment. "How did . . . ?"

"Someone stole him, I suppose. Unless you gave your permission to take it to Rendezvous."

"No, of course not," Jonathan answered. "It's just that I wonder anyone could sneak that horse away, as wary as he is."

"It had to be someone it knew," Vashti said. Both of them looked to Calvin for enlightenment. After one sip at the jug, Calvin nodded. "It was your cousin, Jonathan. He gave his name as Seth. Robert Pyle corroborated that. It seems he met Seth not long ago down in St. Joseph."

"But why would Seth take your horse and sneak off to Rendezvous?" Vashti wondered.

"His whisky supply was awfully low," Jonathan said bitterly.

"He had no money," Vashti said. Then she remembered the flour canister. "Oh, but he knew he would have to come back. His wife and baby are here!"

"No, I think Beryl is gone as well," Jonathan told her. "At least I couldn't find a trace of her."

"Wasn't there a woman with Seth?" Vashti asked Calvin.

"No, she would have been noticed right off in a place like that. Seth was alone."

Vashti turned to Jonathan, "Where, then? Could she have gone off to Cheyenne to be with her son?"

"Cason was going all the way to Texas. I suppose if she wanted to take a riverboat with him, she could get off anywhere along the way—in St. Joseph, for example."

"Maybe she would," Vashti said, looking down at the floor,

her eyes troubled. "She liked St. Joseph better than the far places. But if Seth took the money, then neither Cason nor Beryl could have any for riverboat fare."

"Maybe they split the money up," Calvin Gunnert chipped in.

"No," Vashti said. "Beryl would not have gone, not without her baby."

"All women are not so good as you are, Vashti," Jonathan Byrd said, and she turned up fire-bright eyes to meet his gaze. "Children have been abandoned before." But parents had to have a motive for desertion, and there were few of those. Jonathan had been thinking that Beryl could be on her way to Cheyenne, all right, but it would not be to be with Cason, who did not intend to stay long in that town. She might have gone off with Tracy Camp, however, seeking to regain her youth, perhaps, or to escape from a wearying marriage with no obvious future.

"Tracy Camp," he said out loud.

"You don't mean it!" Vashti said, looking around the room as if the cowboy was there in person.

"Am I missing something?" Calvin asked.

"There was a cowboy staying here—two of them, in fact—and they were on their way to Cheyenne. I always thought Tracy Camp had a kind of longing look in his eye when he studied Beryl."

"Such things have been known to happen," Calvin said. "I wouldn't know how this Beryl thinks, but isn't there one other possibility? If she was going to Cheyenne, isn't it possible she and Seth plan to meet up there and travel downriver together?"

"Do you think that's where Seth is going?" Jonathan asked.

"I know he is. He talked Robert Pyle into hiring him on with the fur company. Come morning, he'll likely be on his way to St. Jo himself."

"Beryl wouldn't be allowed on a fur transport," Jonathan said more for the sake of argument than anything else. Beryl and Seth could certainly make their independent ways back to Missouri.

If both were willing to abandon Precious.

Maybe Seth was unaware of Beryl's plan, had no idea that she was rushing to catch up with him. That seemed unlikely unless Beryl knew that Seth was going—and the two of them had not had any private conversations for days.

"The lady sure picked a bad departure point for herself," Calvin said, breaking the moody silence. "Unless that was why she decided to leave the baby behind, maybe out of some sort of blind panic. I've heard of things like that happening too."

"We're not following you, Calvin," Jonathan said, glancing at Vashti. "What do you mean a 'bad departure point'?"

"Just this. Everyone knows the railroad is coming to Cheyenne before long."

"That's not the way Tracy Camp told it," Jonathan said.

"Well, it's so. They're throwing up saloons, hotels, and stores as rapidly as they can, anticipating it. Men are thronging to Cheyenne, hoping to find jobs. Women are flooding there, knowing that as soon as a dance hall is built, there'll be employment for them. The cattlemen will be coming and as the railroad creeps closer, so will the tracklayers. I don't know if those boys dance much, but they'll soon be trying to learn."

"You sure know a lot about it for a high mountain creature," Jonathan said.

"I got this all from Stinky, who lives and works there. He's getting slowly wealthy and is bound to grow wealthier soon."

"Stinky!"

"Yes, Reginald Foote is apparently making his way well in the world. I'll tell you what I know of his affairs after you've finished with your topic."

Jonathan looked again at Vashti, who shook her head slightly. What was there left to discuss? Seth had stolen money and their prize horse and left them without so much as a word. It seemed Beryl had gone as well, maybe with her cowboy. Cason was gone. By now Louis L'Enfant was convening with the marshal in Cheyenne, figuring out how they wanted to go about capturing the two Texas killers.

And where would that leave Beryl? Alone, abandoned in Cheyenne, probably eventually resorting to the only source of employment in town.

"Well, aren't you a pretty little thing?" Calvin Gunnert exclaimed, and Jonathan and Vashti lifted their eyes to see a sleep-tousled Angelica standing at the bedroom door. Her face was overly concerned for one so young.

"Mother," she said, "I think Precious is getting quite hungry. Isn't it time for her to eat?"

"All right, dear," Vashti said rising. "I'll see to that. Don't you worry."

Jonathan gawked at his wife, and she smiled and lightly tapped his shoulder.

"Not that, you foolish man. Precious is a year old now. We'll just have to wean her. I'll make up something she can eat, but she won't care for it. It's not the right way to wean a baby. Prepare for a little extra crying at night."

Calvin corked his jug and rose. "I'd better be making my way back while there's still a moon," he told Jonathan. Outside he added, as Vashti bustled about in the larder, "That baby won't have a thing to worry about so long as she is on Shywater."

"Not if I can help it," Jonathan said, knowing too well how abandoned children can hurt.

"She's likely young enough that she'll never remember ever having another home," Calvin said. He placed a hand on Jonathan's shoulder. "Good luck to you, Jonathan—although it looks like you already have that." As he swung aboard his sorrel horse, he added, "I'll maybe drop back this way some day, if I'm invited."

"You're always welcome on Shywater, Calvin. Maybe next time we'll roast an ox for you. I'm suddenly beef-rich, it seems."

"Rich in many ways," Calvin Gunnert said, and he turned his horse toward the creek and the forest beyond.

# Chapter Twenty-Two

## The Day the Visitors Came

Jonathan Byrd was at the rear of the house on that day, splitting wood, mindful of the fact that one could never have too much firewood during the long Wyoming winters. He heard the horses arriving, and what sounded like a wagon wheel hub that needed grease, squealing. His head came up, and he put on his deerskin shirt and picked up his Hawken rifle. The voices from the porch area were audible before he reached the front of the house. One of the voices was a woman's, totally unfamiliar to Jonathan. The other was a voice with which he was completely familiar.

"As we were told . . ." the woman in a long black dress was saying.

Vashti knew the scolding tone of Olive Blaylock. Although it had been a long time since she had seen or heard Olive, certain memories become permanently etched in one's mind. "And it's Veronica at the center of it!"

"My name is not Veronica," Vashti said. She was not angry, but there was an uncharacteristically stern tone in her voice. Perhaps she had a foreboding about why these people had come.

There were three of them. Olive and an old white-bearded man, barely recognizable as the Reverend Blaylock of her youth, sitting in a covered buggy, and the same very thin acolyte minister who had approached Shywater asking for directions and a meal not so long ago.

"Just take a look. It's as we were told!" Olive Blaylock said with triumph.

Angelica had emerged from the house, drawn by curiosity. She was holding the hand of the little eighteen-month-old toddler with wispy, coppery hair. Both were clad in elkskin dresses with fringes, manufactured by Vashti's skilled hands.

"They will make a savage of the girl," Mrs. Blaylock said to her husband, who as yet had not spoken.

"What is this?" Vashti demanded. "Of what business is my family to you?"

"The older girl may be your family, but the little one obviously is not," said the younger man, speaking up from horseback.

"This is my sister, Precious," Angelina said with a touch of pride.

"No, little girl," said Olive. "I am afraid you are mistaken; she is not your sister, but a poor waif fallen among savages."

Reverend Blaylock now spoke up. His voice was kind as he met Vashti's hot gaze. "I'm sorry, Vashti—for you see, I do remember you—but a white orphan cannot be allowed to remain here. Her presence here was reported to us, and we have come to take her to the orphans' home where she will be safe and nourished physically and mentally."

"Does the girl look undernourished?" Vashti asked. "And as for being nourished mentally and emotionally, she has love and care here. You wish to take my child out of the fresh air and the light and place her in a dark, cold dungeon. I forbid it. I am well-acquainted with your orphans' home, Mr. Blaylock. I must admit that you have tried your best to help some of those poor abandoned children, but Precious is not in need of your kind of help. She is content here, and here she will stay."

Angelica was now clinging to her mother, still holding Precious's hand, while with the other the toddler sucked her thumb.

"It's not so simple," said the young reverend, who had apparently come west to replace the aging Blaylock among the savages. He had a piping voice that reminded Vashti of an uncertain lecturer. "We have been advised that a white girl was being raised among the savages, and here we find her. It is incumbent upon us to . . ."

"It is incumbent upon you to get yourselves immediately off my land," Jonathan Byrd said, appearing from around the corner of the cabin. Speaking to Blaylock he said, "I know you have done a lot of good out here, sir, but even you must see that taking Precious away from us is wrong. Whoever sent you here was wrong. This is my family. All here are kept safe and warm."

The young minister interrupted. "That aside, Mr. Byrd, there are legal considerations."

Jonathan Byrd flared up. "Mister—whoever you are—this is my niece, Precious Byrd. Her parents are both gone away. I am her nearest blood relative. Here she stays."

Jonathan held his Hawken rifle loosely in his hand, but not so loosely that the others weren't aware of it. He addressed his words to the white-haired Reverend Blaylock again.

"I am of these mountains, sir. After all this time among us, I'm sure you understand a little about mountain men. I mean to offer you a proposition. As you might or might not know, I own the land in all directions for a mile or so. I have a very good rifle here, which can easily shoot that far. I don't know how accurately, but if I see any of you still on my land in twenty minutes, I shall test out my shooting skills with you as my targets." In a softer voice with which Vashti was more familiar, Jonathan added, "And don't think of pausing to steal one of my oxes."

There was enough menace in his words that the Reverend Mr. Blaylock immediately backed his two-horse team away as the younger man, his narrow face now ashen, followed suit.

Jonathan stood on the porch with Vashti, his arm around her, watching as the small party disappeared from sight along the forest fringe. Angelica had apparently already lost all interest in the visit. She led Precious back into the house and soon the two were busy at some game without rules.

"Who could have told them about Precious?" Vashti asked, looking up at Jonathan.

"I don't know," he said shaking his head. "Beryl, of course, or Seth—but I can't see what the point in that would be. They both seemed to be happy to leave Precious here, believing perhaps they had done their best for her under the circumstances."

"Not many people knew she was here, and I cannot see a reason any of them would have reported it."

"Not unless Cason, for some reason, wanted his sister back, and that makes no sense at all. What would he do with the baby?"

"There was Tracy Camp—I dismiss the idea that it could have been Will Hecht—he might have done it to curry favor with Beryl, I suppose. But then, I don't think babies figure in his plans at all."

"I imagine all of Camp's dreams, whatever they were, are either locked behind bars or lying facedown in the streets of Cheyenne by now. Do not underestimate the determination of Louis L'Enfant. He spent years tracking his last man."

"I know," Vashti said with a sigh, leaning her head against Jonathan's shoulder. She was emotionally exhausted. "Maybe Calvin Gunnert," she suggested, "said something that someone else misunderstood."

"That could be. Maybe he related his visit here to Stinky or to Robert Pyle, and they thought they heard something he was not saying. I doubt it though. Any of those speculations are improbable."

"I haven't got any more thoughts," Vashti said, yawning. "I'd better get inside and fix some dinner for you and the girls. Precious has developed a huge appetite for strained squash, though she doesn't like her green beans much."

"No, and one of these years our apple trees will start to bear, and the girls will gorge themselves on them for the first few weeks."

"Until they start getting stomachaches."

"Yes. Well, then we'll find something new to satisfy their finicky palates. I think I'll bring a couple of the oxen up nearer the house tomorrow."

"To eat?" Vashti teased.

"Just to have them around. I may try to train at least one of them to pull a plow. I think I can make a wooden plow. I know Shywater is not fit for cultivation as people think of it, but maybe we should expand our garden just a little."

"Those people are gone now," said Vashti, whose eyes had never strayed from the point at which the Blaylocks and the young reverend had disappeared.

"Yes. They won't be coming back. Vashti, you certainly gave them an earful."

"Not half of what I could have, but your speech was more convincing than mine."

"That was because of my silent partner," Jonathan said, lifting his Hawken rifle by the barrel.

"Would you have shot them, Jonathan?"

"I doubt it . . . but to protect my family, yes. Maybe I would have."

"That rifle has lasted you well and done right by you," Vashti said as they turned for the open door.

"Has it not," Jonathan said reflecting. "This old rifle has given me my entire world, a world I could never have dreamed of previously."

Vashti stopped, put her arms around Jonathan's waist, and

asked with a bright smile, "Does any of this have to do with me?"

"All of it, my lovely, Encircling Heart, all of it."

"You do not find the cabin a little small for us these days?"

"Well, I was thinking about various things I could do with the wood from Seth's wagon before it rots out in the weather, but that's hardly urgent. The girls can play outside, and they have all the room they need to sleep."

"True, Jonathan. But we must think about the baby as well."

"Precious? But . . ." Jonathan was briefly confused.

"Not Precious," Vashti said, placing her finger across his lips. Her eyes were unusually bright and playful. "The next baby Byrd, I mean."

"I don't . . ."

She placed his hand on her softly rounded belly. He could feel nothing. "It is a boy," she said confidently.

"How in the world can you know?"

"Because it is, because it must be, so that the land will always be owned by a Byrd! Our daughters are so beautiful, one day some strong young men will come and take them away. That is as it should be. They will change their names as is your custom. Our son, however, wherever he chooses to roam, will carry his name with him, and so there will always be Byrds of Shywater."

A child cried with frustration, and they entered the cabin to solve one more small problem on the great, magical land.

# AFTERWORD

As I was completing the last few pages of this novel, I realized there were some readers who might feel cheated in not knowing the fates of all of the characters: Beryl and Seth, Tracy Camp and Will Hecht, Louis L'Enfant and Calvin Gunnert for example. All of their ends can be surmised from the information provided.

These characters, of interest or not to the reader, must necessarily continue their lives beyond the boundaries of Shywater where we may not follow. This is a tale of Shywater and concerns itself with other matters only so much as they are essential to our story.

I, myself, would like to further follow the lives of Vashti, Jonathan, Angelica, and Precious as time goes by and the girls mature, but I have reluctantly chosen not to at this time. I feel almost as if it would be an intrusion on their well-ordered lives, where even with the best of intentions, a chronicler might become tiresome.

I do have a not-so-secret desire to return unannounced someday, so perhaps we shall all meet again on Shywater.

# ABOUT THE AUTHOR

**Paul Lederer** is a native of San Diego, California, and attended San Diego State University before serving four years in an Air Force Intelligence arm. He has traveled widely in the United States and in Europe, Asia, and the Middle East.

He is the author of *Tecumseh, Manitou's Daughters, Shawnee Dawn, Seminole Skies, Cheyenne Dreams, The Way of the Wind, The Far Dreamer,* and *North Star.* His most recent novel is the contemporary, *The Moon Around Sarah,* published by Robert Hale, London (2013).

Now living in La Mesa, California, Lederer is an amateur musician and enjoys spending time with his two grown sons and his daughter.